Are You Sure You Want to Know?

A Novel

ALAINE M. NEILSON

Published in Australia by Sid Harta Publishers Pty Ltd,
ABN: 34 632 585 203
17 Coleman Parade, GLEN WAVERLEY VIC 3150 Australia
Telephone: +61 3 9560 9920, Facsimile: +61 3 9545 1742
E-mail: author@sidharta.com.au

First published in Australia 2020
This edition published 2020
Copyright © Alaine M. Neilson 2020

Cover design, typesetting: WorkingType (www.workingtype.com.au)

Alaine M. Neilson
Are You Sure You Want to Know?
ISBN: 978-1-925707-19-9
pp350

for Anthony

Chapter 1

'I didn't see Anton's car go out this morning,' Leeann said.
'No, he stayed over at Steve's last night. I did think of calling you up, but I got sucked into watching a movie,' Morgan said. 'So how are you settling in?'

'Oh, it's great. Thanks so much for letting me rent your gorgeous unit downstairs. I'm loving the air conditioning — what a lifesaver. And I love the smell of everything when it's new. He's a good builder, isn't he?'

'Yeah, he's always pretty busy.'

Leeann gazed around Morgan's house, noticing everything. Her eyes latched onto the photograph of Anton taken after he had won a go-kart race. He was grinning at the camera, displaying his perfect teeth.

With one arm he held his helmet, with the other he held Morgan, squashing her to him. His dark hair fell over one eye, and his olive skin glistened with the afterglow of adrenalin. Morgan's mousey brown hair straggled to her shoulders; her eyes were watery and squinty from the wind. It wasn't the best picture of her, but Anton liked it so he had it framed. Leeann stood up to have a better look.

'Are you older than Anton?'

'Thanks, Leeann. No, he's thirty, only a few months older than me.'

'Oh sorry! I didn't mean you look old …'

'Never mind, it happens a lot. People often think he's younger than I am. He's got good skin.'

Leeann pushed her blonde hair behind one ear. She picked up the photo and peered at it. 'Looks like a conquering hero,' she said, 'and you're his trophy. Is he Greek?'

'No, but his mother is Italian. His father's English. He's really Robert — Robert Anton Shelford, but he uses his middle name instead. He thinks it sounds more exotic. Don't tell him I told you.'

'And you're English, too aren't you?' Leeann asked. 'You have a slight Pommy accent. Or is it Kiwi?'

'Scottish, actually. I was born there but I've lived here all my life.'

'Oh, really? I wouldn't have thought that. Sounds Pommy to me.'

✦   ✦   ✦   ✦

Morgan had spent the afternoon cooking coq au vin with a lot more vin than the recipe specified. She had chosen the dish because it could be made in one pot, and it was hard to ruin. She was pleased with the rich taste and the delicious aroma of the sauce. Just as she was about to serve it, she heard a sharp click and instantly, the lights cut out, casting the house into sudden darkness.

She felt for candles and matches in the pantry while her eyes adjusted. Anton headed outside with a torch to see if the neighbours had lost power. They had; all the streetlights were off and every house was blacked out.

She set the candles on the table and dished out the meal. 'At least it didn't go off before dinner was ready.'

'Yeah, just as well. I'm starving.'

They ate the meal by candlelight, sharing the rest of the Burgundy, just the two of them. This was actually pleasant; they could have a conversation. She smiled at him.

'Was work busy?'

He looked up, frowning. 'Hm? Work? I don't want to talk about work.'

'Oh, sure, I get it. Do you like the dinner?'

'Yeah, pretty good. Better than usual. A bit winey. Do we have any beer?'

'Of course,' she said, taking a candle from the table. She opened and closed the fridge quickly, to conserve the cold air. There was no telling how long a power outage might last.

'This is romantic isn't it?' she said, putting the beer in front of him. 'We should sit out on the verandah and look at the stars. And watch the lightning.'

'And get eaten alive by mozzies? No thanks.'

She blinked at him, waiting to see if he would offer a suggestion. His phone pinged with a new message. She reached to pick it up, but he snatched it out of her hand. 'Don't touch my phone.'

She immediately withdrew her hand. 'Sorry. I didn't think.'

He read the message and deleted it. 'I'll probably be late home tomorrow so I won't need dinner.'

'Okay.'

'Yeah, Steve wants me to look at the hydraulics on his go-kart so I'll eat there.'

'Okay, sure. I have a website I need to work on anyway.'

'By the way, remember we're going to the kart club Christmas party this Saturday night,' he said. 'So, can you make an effort to look nice?'

'I'll do my best.'

'That would be good. Because you always look the same. Same hair, same clothes. Maybe you could just try to look more feminine. Jazz it up a bit.'

Suddenly the lights flickered and blazed on, dazzling them, stinging her eyes.

'Oh, at last,' he said, picking up the newspaper. 'What's on TV?'

He embedded himself on the couch in front of the television while she cleared away the dinner dishes. Happily, there was enough chicken left to freeze for another night. She would never serve him the same meal two nights in a row. But now she needn't worry about what to cook tomorrow because he wouldn't be home anyway.

Across the street, as if in protest against the last twenty minutes of imposed silence, the young guys living in the rental house played AC/DC's *High Voltage* with the volume turned up to eleven. She started the dishwasher and sighed.

Chapter 2

Saturday morning. Morgan glanced at the clock and smiled: eleven minutes past eleven. Uncanny how often she noticed the time was eleven-eleven, either am or pm. Possibly because she was born on November eleventh, or maybe just because she liked the symmetry of it.

She slid the Anzac biscuits she had baked out of the oven. The aroma of fresh, hot, oaty biscuits filled the kitchen. Her cooking skills had not progressed much past year ten home economics, but Anzacs were easy. She transferred each biscuit onto a wire cooling rack. An image of Leeann flashed into her mind. At the same time she heard a knock on the door.

'Hi, Leeann, come in. I've just made the best Anzac biscuits ever. Would you like tea or coffee? You'll have a bickie, won't you?'

Leeann smoothed her hands over her slim hips. 'Maybe just tea please. Do you have green tea?'

'Certainly do. Are you sure you won't have an Anzac?'

Morgan and Leeann sat out on the back verandah drinking

tea. 'I have an assignment to write,' Leeann said. 'So I had this overwhelming urge to come up and chat to you,' she giggled.

'And, you know what else is funny?' Morgan said. 'I pictured a clear vision of you moments before you knocked.'

'Yeah, that's always weird isn't it?'

Suddenly, an ear-splitting screech made them both jump.

'Shit. I didn't know you had a parrot,' Leeann said, glancing around.

'Not ours — he's Anton's mother's pet cockatoo, Wilbur. We're bird-sitting while they're away on a cruise.'

'Scrawny, isn't he? Do you think he'd like an Anzac?' Leeann broke off a tiny piece of biscuit and poked it into the cage. Wilbur just looked at it. 'So why did you make these?'

'Same reason as you, I guess. Procrastination. We're going to a Christmas party with Anton's kart club tonight and I'm under strict instructions to look great. So I baked. And now I've eaten five of them, so I'm going to feel like a fat pig.'

'Gee, that's a bit rough. You'll look gorgeous. Do you have something nice to wear?'

She looked at Leeann, who really was gorgeous — tall with short, straight platinum blonde hair, a trim figure and a pretty face. She reminded Morgan of Naomi Watts. Had it been such a good idea to have let her rent their downstairs unit?

'Probably just my usual black jeans. And I was going to wear my pink floaty top but I can't find it. But it doesn't matter what I wear, Anton will probably hate it.'

'Really? How long have you guys been married?'

'Five years now.'

'And no plans for kids?'

'No, Anton doesn't want any. I think he's too much of a kid himself. I mean, who races go-karts at thirty?'

'He's pretty hot though, Morgan. I mean, he's like an Adonis or something. I can understand he wants to show you off in front of his mates. You know, I've got a lovely long chiffon top that would look fabulous on you. Would you like to borrow it? I think it'll fit. It's actually a bit big on me.'

'Thanks Leeann, that's kind of you to offer. Yes, I would, if you really don't mind. I can't seem to be bothered to go out and buy myself new clothes these days.'

'Going to a party with the kart guys might be just what you need. Don't worry about what Anton thinks, enjoy yourself and have a good time. Talk to someone you've never spoken to before, dance, and let your hair down a little.'

Morgan smiled at her. Leeann was being genuinely kind. But she didn't know Anton at all.

That night, Morgan wore Leeann's soft, blue shimmery top over her black jeans. It enhanced the blue of her eyes and she was pleased with the effect. She was slightly overweight, but not much, and the long top covered her hips well. She took the time to wash and blow-dry her hair, and carefully applied more makeup than usual. She had misplaced her favourite pale pink lipstick so instead she applied a deeper cherry shade. It added the colour she needed, a vibrance.

She wished her appearance didn't always matter so much to Anton. She could remember only one occasion when he had complimented her looks. It was in a photograph where she was staring, eyes half-closed, into the distance towards the low afternoon sun. He had admired the photo because he said it didn't look like her at all.

Sometimes she wondered what he even saw in her, although when they first met, she had felt a real spark, an instant mutual attraction. Wouldn't it be liberating if other people never judged you on your physical appearance? If they somehow could see and appreciate your essence without you having to resort to all this dressing up, this artifice. She was dreading a night with the go-kart group.

Anton shouted from the other bathroom, breaking into her thoughts. 'What's the time?'

'It's … no, it can't be. This clock has stopped. Hang on!'

She found her watch and grabbed her handbag. 'It's six-thirty, time we were going.'

'Are you going like that?' he said.

'Yes, why? Do you like it?'

'Yep, it's fine, let's go.'

He stopped to study himself in the hall mirror near the front door and smoothed his hair.

'Does this look okay? Or do you think I should wear my other shirt? The tighter one?' He held his arms up in a body builder pose to check his muscles were visible.

'It's great. Very smart. I like the one you're wearing. It emphasises your shoulders.'

'Okay, well, it will have to do. Come on.'

The Christmas party was being held in a large steel shed on an acreage property belonging to Gary, one of the karters. The music grew louder as they walked up the path. Bamboo Bali lamps lit the way, and a bonfire made a feeble attempt to keep mosquitoes away. The air reeked of beer, cigarette smoke and burnt sausages. Most of the go-kart group were already there. She had met many of Anton's mates before, but still she felt the eyes scrutinise her as they entered through the roller door.

'Sorry we're a bit late,' Anton said. 'All that titivating in front of the mirror takes time.'

Jodi, a skinny new girl she hadn't met before, and who could have been no older than eighteen, looked her up and down. 'You look lovely, Morgan.'

'Yes, she does. You stop that Anton. I bet you're the one who does the most *titivating*,' said another woman, smirking, holding a beer can.

Empty tinnies, stubbies and wine bottles cluttered every bench top. The drinking had evidently started early.

'Here you go, mate.' Gary handed Morgan a chilled glass of Champagne which she held up to her cheek.

She tried to speak to Steve above the deafening music. 'Did you get your hydraulics fixed okay?'

'Eh?'

'On your kart ... Anton was helping you ...'

'Oh, yeah, yes,' Steve said, nodding. 'Thanks, all good now.'

Anton overheard and spun around. 'Since when have you been interested in hydraulics?' Then, to the group surrounding him: 'She wouldn't know what a hydraulic was if it slapped her on the arse.' Muffled giggling.

The evening deteriorated to raucous karaoke and drunken dancing. Morgan sweated, feeling overdressed. Most people were wearing shorts with casual t-shirts or sleeveless tops. And now some of the men had changed into women's wigs and frocks padded with enormous boobs which they thrust out as they minced around, puckering their lips, trying to slobber on everybody they could catch. She slipped outside for some fresh air and to escape the screaming. Douglas, another new member, stood outside in the shadows smoking a cigarette. Except it didn't exactly smell like tobacco.

He slurred his words, 'Will ye have a wee dance with me, Morrrgan?'

She spilled some of the wine from her glass. 'I'm sorry, thanks, but no. Anton would … Anton doesn't like me dancing.'

'Och, tell him te away an' bile his heid.'

She laughed. 'Yeah, right. That'd put him in a real good mood if I told him to go away and boil his head. So what part of Scotland are you from?'

'I've lived all over, but I grew up in wee place outside Aberdeen, on the banks of the bonnie River Dee.'

'Really? My maiden name was Dee.'

'Aye? Well, how about that.' He took her wine glass and plonked it on an oil drum. Then he grabbed her waist and swung her round on the grass in a clumsy waltz, making her shriek with laughter.

'What's going on!' Anton appeared, glowering. He gripped her arm roughly, wrenching her away from Douglas.

'Ow! Nothing's going on.'

'We're leaving. Now.'

'Are we? Okay, I'll just say goodbye to —'

'*Now!*' He dug his fingers deep into her arm giving it a painful hard squeeze.

Douglas leant on the oil drum looking bewildered.

'My bag …' She hastily retrieved her handbag from inside the roller door, avoiding eye contact with anyone.

Anton seized her by the arm and dragged her, tripping, down the path to the car park. In the car, her eyes stung with tears. 'There was no need to drag me away. That was really embarrassing.'

'What were you playing at, dancing out there in the dark with Douglas McTwat? Flirting and leading him on.'

'I was not. I'm sorry, I know you don't like me dancing. I was standing there on my own, getting some air, and he came over. We weren't doing any harm. He was just a bit drunk, or something … it wasn't my fault.'

'Well, you made me look stupid,' he said.

'What? That's rubbish. No one probably even saw us. They were all too busy laughing at the blokes in drag routine. And you hurt my arm.'

She tasted salt; a familiar tight knot formed in her stomach. Her eyes overflowed involuntarily. Hydraulic eyes. Liquid under pressure.

Chapter 3

It was well after midnight. Something woke her, a noise outside, banging. She reached over to Anton's side of the bed and he stirred in his sleep. 'Anton,' she whispered. 'I can hear noises. Somebody's out there.'

He jolted awake and sprang out of bed, naked, as he always slept. He grabbed a towel from the en suite. The front door opened and closed. She lay still, straining to hear. She listened for a while but fell asleep. She dreamt of a small boy calling to her, smiling and waving. It was always the same dream — he seemed to know her but she didn't recognise him. He was trying to tell her something, to give her a message, but she couldn't understand what he was saying.

She awoke sometime later when Anton's cool body slid into bed beside her.

'What was it? What was making the noise?' she asked.

'It was a burglar prowling around, but I scared him away. I've had a good look all over and he's gone now.'

'Did you go outside with nothing on?'

'Yeah, I got the shit bitten out of me by mozzies. I'm okay. Go to sleep.'

A prowler — shouldn't they be worried? Shouldn't they call the police? But he didn't seem bothered so she snuggled up to him and eventually fell asleep again.

◆　◆　◆　◆

She awoke with the disturbing memory of another familiar dream. She was small, watching a woman in a red cape running down a long passage. She could smell a distinctive soapy scent she could never quite identify. Why the dream disturbed her she couldn't say; its significance always eluded her. She wiped the tears from her eyes.

Anton had already gone out. She had no idea where — the gym, probably. But he had brought in the Sunday newspaper. She picked it up and turned to the horoscope section at the back to read hers. She did this every day.

Scorpio. Change is the name of the game for you, Scorpio. Now that the Mercury retrograde is complete you should start to see an improvement in your life. The Sun in Sagittarius, however, means that things might not go quite as smoothly as you would like. Mars enters your sign this month, blessing you with powerful energy. If you can harness this energy anything could be possible for you right now.

That all sounded fine and dandy. If only it were true. She

turned on the television to watch a re-run of Oprah. Today's show discussed 'The Narcissism Epidemic'. *Narcissists are a pleasure to be around. They're wonderful and entertaining and the life of the party but God help you if you cross them.*

It accurately described Anton, except he wasn't wonderful to her, only to other people. Had he changed, or had she just never noticed before? She had been so thrilled someone had actually wanted to marry her she had overlooked his narcissism.

At the end of the show an advertisement appeared for a clairvoyant, with a website address and a phone number. She scribbled down the web address. Then she watched a recorded program about walking through the highlands in Scotland. The country looked so beautiful bathed in muted colours, atmospheric and ancient, she felt a physical longing to be there. She imagined herself wearing leather boots, a soft woolly jumper and a tartan scarf. She would stroll along winding country lanes with a dog, come across a little village, stop for a cup of tea in a charming tea shop.

Leeann knocked, rousing her out of her fantasy. She knew it was Leeann — she never used the doorbell.

'How did your party with the karters go last night?'

Morgan tugged down the long sleeves of the shirt she was wearing to cover the bruises on her arm.

'Yeah, it was good, thanks. Come in. The top worked really well — thank you so much for lending it. I'll get it dry cleaned before I give it back to you.'

'No need, it's washable. I'll just chuck it in when I do a load. So … how was it?' Leeann wasn't letting go.

'Oh, you know, the usual — loud karaoke, dirty jokes, swearing and hard drinking. And that's just the girls. They're all keen racers but it's not really my scene. I did try racing once — I crashed my kart into someone else who had also crashed and my helmet flew off and bounced over the track. I never got in another one.'

'Sounds dangerous,' Leeann said. 'You're not hot wearing long sleeves?'

'No, I'm quite comfortable. I'm glad you're here. I was going to come down and see you today, anyway. Did you hear the prowler last night?'

'Shit, really? A prowler? That's a worry. No I didn't hear a sound.'

'Anton went out in the middle of the night with nothing on and scared him away. Strange for a prowler to make so much noise; it sounded to me like someone banging at the door. It was probably just kids but still, you'd better be careful with locking up.'

'Yeah, thanks, that's creepy isn't it. Makes you wonder if someone is watching the house. It's weird though ... why would they go up the stairs to your door instead of trying to get in through the windows downstairs? Then I definitely would have heard something.'

'Yes, you're right. I thought there was something odd. I might get Anton to install security cameras. That should frighten them off.'

'Anton out?' Leeann asked, looking around.

'Yep, don't know where. I've just been spending a pleasantly indulgent couch-potato morning in front of the TV.'

'How delicious. Anything interesting?'

'Yes, well, there was one thing — an advertisement for a clairvoyant. I thought I might try her.'

'Oh my God, why would you want to do that? Blind Freddie can see you've got a great life. I reckon those so-called mediums are really just clever psychologists. They read your body language and tell you what you want to hear. Don't waste your money, I reckon.'

'You're probably right, but I can't help feeling like crying for no reason, even when I tell myself I should be grateful for what I have. And I have these persistent dreams that seem too real, not like dreams — more like memories. They drive me nuts.'

'It sounds like you're stuck in a rut. And it's up to you, of course, but retail therapy always cheers me up — why don't you go out and treat yourself to some nice things?'

Morgan smiled. 'Not such a bad idea. I'm still interested in calling this psychic though, maybe just for guidance. I can't shake off this nagging gut feeling I'm missing something, and you never know, it might give me some kind of insight, some kind of direction.'

'Okay, well, if she turns out to be accurate … maybe I'll visit her too and she can tell me when I'm going to meet my own gorgeous Greek god.'

Chapter 4

Morgan lounged on the back verandah of the house Anton had built for them, enjoying the cooling afternoon summer sea breeze faintly tinged with eucalyptus. She looked down at the garden edged with lilly-pillies, banksias and golden wattle, the seed pods of which were just beginning to open. Then her eyes travelled to the disfigured carcass of a gum tree. She slapped a mosquito that had landed on her forearm, smearing her skin with blood.

A strong gust blew straight into the house, catching newspapers off the dining table, strewing them around the room. As she collected the papers, she noticed the *Escape* travel magazine from yesterday's *Sunday Mail*. Flipping it over she saw the flight specials. Brisbane to Edinburgh. The shrill front doorbell jolted her. Her godfather, Don Erskine, stood holding a bottle of mature Margaret River Cabernet.

'Hey Don! Lovely to see you, come in. And you've brought wine!'

He was agile for his ninety years, and he still drove a car. He smiled at her with his deep brown eyes which Morgan always felt could see right into her. He glanced at the newspaper in her hand.

'Everything all right, love?'

She swallowed. 'Fine, Don, thank you, yes … great. And you?'

'I'm pretty good for an old fella,' he said. 'Have I caught you at a bad time?'

'No, not at all. Would you like to sit out on the verandah, or would you rather stay inside? I can turn on the air conditioning.'

'Verandah sounds good. I prefer the fresh air.'

She brought out two wine glasses, cheese, crackers, and the last of the Anzac biscuits.

'What happened to the tree?' Don asked.

'Anton was doing a bit of pruning. He was going to trim only a few small branches but he got carried away with the chainsaw. I hope it'll recover.'

They stared at the stump of the gum tree; its hacked branches lying dead on the ground.

'What a shame. Whenever I see a mutilated tree, it takes me right back to the war. I've seen forests of trees completely blackened, just miles and miles of stumps, no leaves. It's a terrible sight — you never forget it.'

Wilbur screeched, startling Don.

'Oh, sorry, that seems to be Wilbur's favourite party trick.'

They turned to look at the cockatoo on its perch. Dark pink bald spots remained where it had plucked out its own feathers. It tilted its head to the side and stared back at them with one round eye.

'Poor thing,' Don said. 'Well, I came over because I wanted to see how you were, of course, and also to lend you this book. It talks about how we are all ultimately connected through infinite and universal, but unknown energy. Fascinating stuff.'

Morgan smiled at his shining eyes. He was remarkable; ninety years old and still reading physics books. He had been a science teacher and he was passionate when it came to his favourite subject.

'Thanks, Don, I'd love to read it. Sounds like something I could happily lose myself in at the moment.'

'And so, how are you really, love?'

'You're amazing — you just seem to know things about me, don't you?'

'Lou and I know you so well, pet. We care about you. We know when things are not as good as they could be. I remember the terrifying nightmares you used to have after you lost your parents. You were so small and fragile, we often wondered if you were even going to survive. All through your childhood we knew you were different. Then we watched you grow into a beautiful young woman.'

'Oh, Don, I'm nowhere near beautiful. Sometimes I think I'm so ordinary people don't notice me at all. And what do you mean by *different?*'

'Well … you know … "fey". Do you remember how you often knew when something was about to happen, especially when you were very young? Friends used to say about you, *oh, she's been here before*, meaning the baby looks like they've lived previously — they're already worldly-wise.'

'Yes, I remember hearing that before. Occasionally I'll think of something just before it happens, but I'm probably no more psychic than most people. More likely it would have been caused by the trauma of losing my mother and father and then growing up in a strange country.'

'Mm. Maybe,' he said. 'But don't forget your mother was clairvoyant. She was such a lovely girl … only eighteen when Lou and I moved to Australia. She was a gifted healer even then; she helped so many people. And she'd help them connect with their loved ones. I wouldn't be surprised if you had a gift too if you'd nurture it.

'It's often inherited, you know,' he said. 'Your grandfather also had that same prescient ability. He actually saved my life in the war. He was a major when I was just a cadet. He yelled out to me and another young fellow to move away immediately from the fallen log we were hiding behind, and seconds later that log was obliterated by an explosion.

'Just a matter of seconds, a wrong decision, one mistake, can mean the difference between life and death. It was spooky. It was his sixth sense that saved us, no doubt about it. There was no way he could have known otherwise.

'We shared a bond after that war incident. He took me under his wing. Maybe also because we were both Scottish. Anyway, our paths crossed again years later and he asked if I would be his daughter's godfather. That was your mother, of course. I think he was afraid he may not be around to look after her — he was getting on in years.'

'Do you have any photographs of him at all?' Morgan asked.

'No, I've not kept any photographs of that time. I try not to dwell on memories. Usually, anyway. I try to live in the moment. Some would say he was an imposing, intimidating man. He was always good to me though.'

'Do you ever miss Scotland?' she asked.

'Well, I lived there for fifty-one years, so I sometimes can't help thinking about it. I don't miss scraping the ice off the windscreen, that sort of thing. It's the people you miss more. I had some good friends there.

'We went back for a few days for your mother's wedding, and then for another few days to collect you eight years later. But both times we were pleased to come home. We're happy here. There is much to like about Australia. It was Lou's choice to come back here to live, even though half her family is in New Zealand. She prefers the warm climate.'

Don poured them both more wine. He cleared his throat and said, 'We care about you deeply, you know, love. And I've been … concerned about you lately. You're so talented; you have so much to live for. Remember, you can make choices. You can … do whatever you want with your life. As a wise man once said, you should always follow your bliss.'

'Are you talking about Anton?'

'Yes, I'm afraid so, love. I'm not sure if he's making you happy. I don't see that you're *blossoming*.'

Don looked flustered. He must have felt it was important to come over and tell her his concern. She loved this old man, this kind man with his loving wife who generously took her into their home when, at four years old, her world had just fallen apart. After her mother died, Don and Lou became Morgan's legal guardians. She was well aware he had been disappointed in her choice to marry Anton.

'You're right, Don. You're always right. Things are a bit strained between us right now. But you know what? I don't know why. I don't know what I've done wrong. He has this ability to make me feel inadequate, and I don't know how I can change to please him. He can be loving, then he can turn really mean.' She looked at the bottle of Cabernet. It was nearly empty.

'Would you like some more wine?' she asked.

'No, thanks pet,' he said. 'I'd better get going. Don't forget we're always there for you, any time you want to talk, or … to come home for a wee while. Here's this book … I hope you like it.'

She took the book inside and turned it over to read the back cover. *New studies in quantum theory confirm that consciousness exists outside of the human body.* She put the book on the sideboard. It was getting late to start dinner.

Anton arrived home shortly after. He kissed her on the cheek and sniffed. 'You pissed?'

'No, not at all.' Don came over and he brought some lovely Caber—'

'What's for dinner?'

'I'm just about to put something on now.' Her heartbeat quickened; she rapidly peeled and washed potatoes.

'Shit, haven't you even started yet? Too busy gasbagging with that weird old codger.'

'That's my father you're talking about.'

'I know, sorry. But he's not your real one. What's this crap?' He picked up Don's book, grunted, and threw it down again.

'Call me when it's ready. I'll be in the garage polishing the kart.' He grabbed a beer from the fridge and she cooked the meal as fast as she could.

During dinner she said, 'Don reminded me today my mother was clairvoyant.'

'So?'

'Well, nothing, I guess. I just wondered if it was hereditary. You know how sometimes I have a premonition just before something happens?'

He looked up sharply and stared at her. 'Really?'

'Yes, well occasionally. Remember the time I told you I was going to win the Easter chocolate raffle, and I did.'

'It would be great if you could win something worthwhile.'

'Yes, wouldn't it. I don't think it works that way. It's not anything you can influence — you just get this flash of an image that something's about to happen. Maybe I should take more notice next time.'

Chapter 5

Morgan was wearing no makeup. Since she had woken late and was hungry, she decided to have breakfast first, before showering and putting on makeup. She stretched her arms up in her bathrobe. One of the perks of working from home.

She had just settled down with her muesli, coffee and Don's book when the doorbell rang. *You've got to be kidding.* She looked at the clock — nine-thirty. Served her right for having a lazy morning. She assumed it would be some kind of delivery. She would sign for it quickly, and too bad about the bathrobe and slippers.

The young fellow standing on the porch was immaculately dressed in a salmon coloured shirt and designer jeans. His hair was stylishly streaked and swept to one side. He was only about five centimetres taller than Morgan and extremely thin. He shifted from foot to foot; his eyes flitted everywhere.

'Hello, yes? Can I help you?'

'Hi, umm … Morgan is it?'

'Yes that's right.'

'Um, I'm Shannon … could I come in and talk to you please? About Anton?'

She regretted her decision not to dress before breakfast. About Anton. What did that mean? What had he done?

'Yes, I suppose so. Sorry, I'm not dressed yet.' She tried to comb her hair with her fingers.

The guy wafted past her and she caught the whiff of a spicy aftershave — expensive, smelled familiar.

'Sorry, please sit down, I'm just having a late breakfast. I'll put this away. Would you like a cup of tea or coffee?'

'No thank you.' Shannon squirmed in the seat and looked around. 'I need to talk to you about —'

'About Anton, yes I got that. What is it?'

'Well, I've been seeing him, and I needed to find out, you know, if he really was married or not. Are you married actually?'

The blood pounded in Morgan's ears. The table seemed to be a long way off as if her arms had suddenly grown in length, and she was watching from a distance. She blinked, then stared at him.

'Sorry … what? Seeing Anton? Yes, we're married — I'm his wife. What do mean *seeing* him?'

'Well, we're a couple, we're lovers, and Anton said he wasn't married anymore. But I see you are still married, and this is … awkward.' Shannon flushed pink and looked up at the ceiling.

'You're yanking my chain! *A couple!* You're having an affair with my husband? Are you sure you've got the right Anton? Anton Shelford?'

Shannon nodded.

Then she twigged. 'Is this a joke? Did one of the kart guys send you?'

'Kart guys? No. It's not a joke. Anton and I are together.'

'And how long has this … affair … been going on?'

'Six months … but it's not just an affair. He said he had been married but it was over. I suspected he was lying and I had to come and find out if he was telling the truth or not. I had to see for myself.' Shannon's eyes filled with tears. 'It was hard for me to come over here but I just needed to know …'

'I bet it was hard. Six months!' She fought to keep her head together. Her heart thumped so violently she thought it must be visible. She took a deep breath. There was nothing to be gained by being angry with this guy so she willed herself to keep calm, stay in control.

'I'm sorry, Shannon, please excuse me, I'll be back in a minute.'

She rushed into the en suite and vomited. Then she grabbed up the bedroom phone and punched in Anton's mobile number. When he answered she said, in as cool a voice as she could manage, 'Guess what? Your *boyfriend* is here and we're having a lovely chat about you.' She slammed down the phone without waiting for a reply, breathing rapidly.

Back in the dining room, she sat down and faced Shannon calmly. She deserved an Oscar for this performance. 'So he must have been staying with you all the times he said he was with Steve. Obviously. And what else has he been saying to you?'

'Well … he told me your name … and he said you were

separated and he lived on his own, and, mmm …' Shannon's eyes scanned the verandah, kitchen and dining room until they locked onto the photos displayed on the sideboard.

Her soul had been sucked out. She stared at the boy with a mixture of horror and curiosity. But also, instantly, everything made sense. There had been a reason for all the nastiness and sneaky behaviour. And lack of sex. But in hindsight that might have been a blessing.

'So did you come around the other night after midnight, when Anton said he chased away a burglar — was that you?' she said.

'Yes, I felt so desperate. Anton told me we would be together and I thought so why can't I stay with him tonight if he lives on his own? I really badly wanted to see him. And he sent me away, saying it wasn't the right time but it would be soon.'

Her blood ran cold. Was he planning on getting rid of her? What a prick!

'Well, obviously he's been spinning you bullshit stories as well as me,' she said. 'And yes, we've been married for five years, but I don't know how long we're going stay married. I guess you'll be the first to know. Clearly our marriage is over now. Where did you meet him, anyway?'

Shannon wiped the tears from his eyes, half-smiled and preened his hair back. 'Well, I'm a dancer at a nightclub and Anton and some work mates came in one night …'

A dancer, is that what they call it now?

'A bunch of blokes were giving me a hard time, calling me names, and Anton got rid of them. He was so generous and kind to me …'

Well, she had news for you, kiddo.

'He sort of singled me out, and we just immediately clicked, like we were soulmates or something.'

Morgan gulped a mouthful of cold coffee, doing her best to show no emotion, and trying to resist the urge to vomit again. The guy was clearly besotted. So Anton was the handsome rescuer, the good old knight on a white horse. That was so like him, such a narcissist.

But with a *boy*? How could she not have known? Was that why her clothes and makeup had been disappearing? She had no idea Anton was bisexual. Why had he never said anything before? The realisation dawned on her that everything she had ever known about him was wrong.

Her head told her to give him up, let go of him willingly, and good riddance, but then somewhere within her lodged a resistance. Why should she make it easy for someone else to waltz in and take the best of him? And, God knows, there was a best of him. It was the same charming, exciting, flamboyant and slightly dangerous Anton she herself had fallen in love with years earlier. Where had that man gone?

Shakily, she stood up from the table and said, 'Look, I'm going to make some more coffee, this is cold. Would you like one?'

'No thanks, it gives you bad breath.'

'Oh, right, okay.' God, how young was this guy? He was obviously still at the self-obsessed age.

She sat down again with a fresh coffee just as Anton's car squealed into the driveway.

'Well, Shannon,' she said, 'here comes Anton so now we'll

hear what he has to say. But you know what? I've just decided my marriage is worth fighting for after all, so you can just fuck off.'

Shannon's large doe-eyes widened and filled with tears again, wetting his long eyelashes. 'But you said your marriage was over!'

'So I've changed my mind.'

Anton burst in looking like he'd run a marathon. 'What are you doing here? You can't be here.'

'You called him!' Shannon wailed.

Anton grabbed Shannon by the arm and pulled him, quivering and sniffling, to the door. 'Come on, what were you thinking? You need to go.'

She followed them to the front door and watched Anton almost push Shannon into his car parked on the road. Then he returned to his own car and said, 'Babe, I'll sort this … I'll call you later.'

Babe? He'd never called her babe in his life. Anton backed out of the driveway and followed closely behind Shannon's car as they drove away. She shut the door and shuffled back to the dining room in her bathrobe and slippers. She couldn't have felt like less of a babe if she'd tried.

'Fark,' Wilbur squawked.

Well said, Wilbur.

Chapter 6

She was assuredly not psychic in any way, if she didn't see that one coming. It had probably been perfectly obvious to everyone else. If Anton had always been bisexual then her whole marriage had been a sham. When he married her, he had either made a genuine choice of one sex over the other, or it was a smokescreen, an attempt to appear straight. If he had only recently realised he was bisexual, that was even worse. Did that mean he found her so unattractive that sleeping with a man was preferable?

She searched in her memory for any clue. Apart from her clothes and makeup disappearing, which had happened only recently, she couldn't think of any other evidence. He'd always been a bloke, a man's man. He was a builder, he liked cars, go-karts, speed racing. He could fix anything. And yet an anger, maybe it was frustration, had always bubbled under the surface.

He constantly sought reassurance and compliments on his appearance; something she grew tired of giving. Is that why he had looked elsewhere? Or had the urge just become too overpowering? Was there anything she should have done? Or was nothing she could do ever going to make any difference? Her head throbbed.

Despite having told Shannon she was not giving up on her marriage, that had been an instinctive reaction, a desire to punish him, make him suffer. Could she realistically stay in this marriage, knowing what Anton was, what he'd done?

She thought back to the kart group Christmas party. Maybe the guys dressing up in women's clothing had triggered his anger that night, and not her dancing at all. She wondered if the kart group knew, and if they had been deliberately teasing him.

Did his mother know? Oh, God, his mother. She couldn't have. She would never have been able to keep that to herself. But then, a mother would definitely know, surely? The thought of facing his mother was too much.

She cried for two hours until she gave herself a headache. She swallowed three Panadol, climbed into bed, and slept all afternoon. When she awoke it was after six pm. The house was in darkness and she hadn't prepared anything for dinner.

She looked in the mirror and her reflection shocked her. With matted hair and puffy eyes she was almost unrecognisable. She painted on layers of dark eyeshadow, added thick eyeliner, blush, and red lipstick. She scrunched her hair with hairspray. She resembled the *Bride of Chucky*, but she was pleased she had made an effort to make herself presentable for Anton when he came home. If he came home.

He did. She heard the car pull up a few minutes later. He

opened and closed the front door quietly and called, 'Morgan? Are you home?'

She didn't answer. She took a deep breath and forced herself to take deliberate steps out to the main room to meet him. The nerves in her arms and hands tingled.

'Oh, there you are,' he said. 'No lights.' He switched on the light and caught sight of her. 'Jesus! What have you done?' Then he stopped. 'How are you?'

'*How am I?* How do you think I am? I'm shit. How am I supposed to deal with this? You've been seeing some male "dancer" for six months and treating me like crap.' She started crying again despite having been determined not to.

'I'm sorry, babe, I really am.'

'*Babe?* Stop calling me *babe*. Is that what you call *him*? It's revolting.'

'I'm sorry, Morgan, but it's all over now, really. It's been over for a while; I just haven't been able to get him to believe it.'

'Would that be because you're a total liar? That's just such a crock. You told him you would be together soon. Why did you say that if it was over?'

'Yeah, I know, but I had to tell him something. He was so clingy. He kept coming round work — he wouldn't leave me alone.'

'And he came round here that night, didn't he? That was no burglar. Now he's hanging around our house. That's bad, Anton, that's really bad. And I suppose all your mates from the kart club know. Makes me look like an idiot.'

'No, it doesn't. Well some of them might know, I don't know, it doesn't matter ...'

'It *does* matter! It matters to me they're thinking I'm too stupid to know what's going on, that you're screwing around with someone else — a *bloke*. They're all looking at me with pity, and *knowing* — Steve, Gary, all the others, even that kid Jodi — they all *know!* It's humiliating. And embarrassing. And no one told me. Some pals.' Her sore eyes overflowed again.

'Look, honestly, I've told Shannon it's off, well and truly, and he's not to make any more contact. He just has to accept it's over. Trust me on this, please Morgan, he's gone.'

'Trust you? I don't know if I can trust anything you say ever again. I just need to think and be alone. I can't deal with this. And since when did you become bisexual? I'll have to go and get tests done. How could you do that to me?'

'Come here and have a hug,' Anton said, pulling her close to him.

She let herself be drawn in. A hug, yes well, that would fix everything, wouldn't it? Did he really think she was so naive she could just forget about it, forgive him, and get on with life as if nothing has happened? His strong arms clasped her close to his body, enveloping her. She felt no emotion at all.

'Does your mother know?'

'Of course. She's my *mother.*'

He tried to stroke her badly scrunched hair. 'I'll go and get Thai takeaway for dinner. How about that?'

'You can if you like — I'm not hungry.' But then she realised that, in fact, she was hungry. Very hungry. 'Well, okay, if you're going out anyway, I'll have Pad Thai chicken. No — seafood.'

They ate in silence. Anton read the TV guide. Although she was hungry, she could actually eat hardly anything. Questions arose in her mind she couldn't bear to think about, let alone ask. She didn't trust herself to speak in case she set off another waterfall.

Also, strangely, even though she had slept all afternoon, she had trouble keeping her eyes open, and her head was still on fire.

'I'm exhausted, I'm going to bed. I can't sleep with you tonight — can you sleep in the spare room?'

Then she did something she had never done before. She stood up from the table leaving her plate where it was, and left Anton to deal with the cleaning up.

He started to call out, 'What do you want me to do with …' but she was already out of the room.

She showered and prepared for bed, going through her routine mechanically; she was incapable of any more thought. She swallowed three more pain relief tablets and crept into bed alone.

✦ ✦ ✦ ✦

Water swirled around her, surrounding her, pressing down on her. She gasped for air but breathed in water. Drawn deeper into wet blackness, she was being crushed under the weight of a vast volume of water. She struggled and scrabbled but walls, as soft as marshmallow, confined her. Pinned down, her limbs became too heavy to lift. She awoke in darkness, coughing, her heart racing, her pillow soaking wet.

Chapter 7

She had discarded her sodden pillow sometime in the night. Now early morning sun filtered through the blinds and raucous, incessant screeching shredded the air. Pulling on her robe she walked, half-asleep, out to the verandah. Wilbur, his yellow comb erect, agitated up and down on his perch. The squawking was deafening.

'What's all the racket, Wilbur?' She peered into the cage. 'Oh, sorry, mate … no water.' She filled the dish and gave him fresh sunflower seeds, his favourite. He moved to the back of the cage and watched her, his head to one side. Then he scooped up gulps of water with his beak and drank by throwing his head back. His skin was exposed where there should have been white feathers. Poor bloody thing. 'You look like a battered pluck, Wilbur.' Whatever that meant, something she must have heard Don say.

She caught sight of herself in the hall mirror. Talk about a battered pluck. She had learnt her lesson about eating in her bathrobe so she showered and dressed before breakfast. She applied makeup with difficulty, the puffy skin of her swollen eyes still soft and delicate to touch.

After cleaning the kitchen properly, necessary due to Anton's unsuccessful effort to clean up last night's Thai, she sat at her computer to update the website she was working on. But she couldn't concentrate. A marketing email advertising travel in Scotland distracted her so instead she spent the next fascinating hour exploring cottages to rent on the internet.

A familiar yearning twisted at her heart. She was born there and she belonged there. Australia was casual, bright, and modern, but somehow it didn't feel like home anymore. She should be in Scotland. Was her birthplace really calling her back, or was it just a profound desire to be far away from this house, this marriage and this sweltering heat?

She needed advice. She should talk to someone. But who? Leeann was studying. Don and Lou? Yes, but not yet.

She found the 'Peace Channelling' web address she had scribbled in her diary. A photo of the clairvoyant appeared on the web front page. She looked like a regular woman you'd see anywhere, no unearthly makeup, headscarf or oversize earrings.

Morgan read the web pages, as well as she could over the lurid background decorated with stars and angels, and with the terrible typography. Could do with a new website. The clairvoyant sounded genuine — she didn't use tarot cards, astrological charts, a crystal ball or any other props. Interesting. Just a pure psychic reading. Before she had time to change her mind, she began dialling the clairvoyant's number.

A woman answered in an unexpectedly high-pitched voice, but she sounded friendly.

'Hello, Amantha speaking. May I help you?'

'Hi, Amantha.' Was that even a real name? 'My name is Morgan and I'm interested in booking a reading with you please.'

'Most certainly. I can do readings for you over the phone, by Skype, email or text if you prefer.'

'Really? You don't need to see someone face-to-face?'

'Oh, no. That's not necessary at all, I pick up and tune into your energy and the result is exactly the same. When would you like to book in for a reading?'

'Okay, yes please, any time really — today or tomorrow? And I think by phone would probably be the best way.'

'All right … how about this afternoon, say four o'clock? Now, Morgan, could you just email me three photos of people you'd like me to concentrate on. There can be other people in the photo, that doesn't matter.'

She wrote down Amantha's email address and agreed to pay the hundred dollars for a half-hour phone session by PayPal before the reading. Then she emailed photos of herself and Anton, plus a scan of a tiny photo she kept in a locket: the only photo she had of her mother.

Promptly at four pm her mobile rang.

'Hi Morgan, are you ready for your reading?'

'Yes, thanks Amantha. Is it okay if I record the session?'

'By all means. In fact I recommend it. Things may turn up which make no sense now but will in the future.'

After a pause, Amantha started to speak slowly. 'I'm

sensing some tension here, Morgan, a dilemma of some kind. It's like "should I stay or should I go". This might not mean anything to you right now but it's coming through strongly.'

'No, that does make sense.'

'Okay, now I'm seeing, your husband, is it, in the photo? He's … is he an angry personality? No need to answer — I will just relay the pictures I'm getting in my mind. So, I'm getting troubled feelings here. He can be dominating, and, he's … I'm sorry to say, he's not truthful. He may not be what he seems. I'm sensing he's causing you some anxiety. Your husband's soul has some issues to work through, I think. It could cause imbalance.'

Amantha was silent again for a few moments. Then she said, 'Morgan, I'm getting some strong messages here. I'm seeing a tragedy which happened in the past … an accident, something to do with water. I'm getting your mother clearly. It's your mother in the small photo isn't it? She's coming through as a powerful spirit. Oh … she's passed over … but she's there for you. And, okay, I'm getting … she's a healer, spiritual healer. And … Morgan, I'm getting this message "work out", or "find out".

'Your mother is encouraging you, urging you to do something. I don't know exactly what she's trying to tell you but it seems to be important that you go somewhere. It could even be somewhere overseas, not close.'

After a pause, 'Now I'm seeing a very young boy.' Morgan heard the blood pounding in her head. 'He's smiling at you … no it's faded away.

'And now there is another strong image coming through.

He's an elderly man. He's significant to you, but you might not realise it. There's a lot of activity, you know, in the spirit world and I'm getting an intense reading around you. You may not think you are actually psychic yourself, but you do have some powerful psychic connections.'

Amantha paused again. Then she said, 'Morgan do you have any questions?'

'I have many. But I guess what I'm mainly looking for is guidance. I'm unsettled and confused about what to do, and I'm having conflicting thoughts about my marriage.'

'Okay …' Amantha was silent again. 'Look, Morgan, I'm going to suggest you have a past life regression therapy session. Have you ever heard of that? I'm sensing there are issues arising, unresolved issues, and you might benefit from exploring a past life. I'm also receiving messages from your spirit guides telling you to follow your heart. But you will have to decide what that means for yourself.'

Chapter 8

She went out onto the verandah to replay the recording. Wilbur immediately raised his yellow comb to greet her and bobbed his Wilbur-dance. The afternoon sun, low behind the house, bathed the trees in an eerie green light. She shivered slightly despite the heat of the day.

Exploring a past life sounded intriguing but she didn't see how it could be therapy. Was there any proof we have lived past lives anyway? She doubted it. It would be an illusion, your own imagination or some trick of hypnotic suggestion — ideas implanted by the hypnotist, or else false memories filtering up from something you've seen on television.

But parts of the clairvoyant reading were spookily accurate. She would call Don and ask him what he thought. She was going to have to tell him about Anton sooner or later.

'Hello, my darling. How are you getting on?' he asked.

'Oh, Don, not good. I discovered Anton has been having an affair with a … bloke. A *man*. For six months.' Her eyes stung with tears.

'*Eh?* A man, you say? Good lord.'

'Apparently he's bisexual. I never knew; I never even guessed. This fellow came round to find out if he really was married, and then it all came out … all those nights Anton didn't come home, he was with him.' She took deep breaths.

'Oh, love, that's so upsetting. I can hardly believe it. You poor wee thing, that's just awful. No wonder he was being so unpleasant to you. You deserve better respect than that, pet. A *man*. Goodness gracious.'

'And, Don, I had a clairvoyant reading today. She said my mother is sending me messages, encouraging me to go somewhere. So, you know how I've been feeling a strong urge to travel to Scotland, I thought maybe I should go and explore where I was born, escape from here for a while.'

'Oh, yes, a holiday might do you good. Scotland's a long way away, mind.'

'And she said other stuff about me, like you did. She said I have strong psychic connections, and I might benefit from past life regression therapy. Have you heard about that?'

Don was silent for a moment. 'Past life regression … reincarnation in other words. Well, it might be interesting. Only you can decide what is best for you, pet. We'll support you, whatever you decide.'

'But do you believe in it?'

'I'm a physicist, dear. I believe anything is possible, until proven otherwise. Like we were talking about the other day, with all the unknown energy in the universe, it would be limiting, and ridiculous, to believe only what we can see. So my advice would be to listen to your instinct, darling. It sounds like you're being guided. Perhaps just go with the flow, and all will be as it is meant to be.'

After a moment, he said, 'But if you are going to, I mean, if you do want to go to Scotland …' he faltered and stopped.

'Yes?'

'Well, never mind. You have a cousin there, you know. She'd be a few years younger than you. Her father was your uncle Malcolm. His first wife died and he remarried. Then he died too. His second wife married again. I can't remember the new husband's name right now but it will come to me. I think they still live in Ayr, lovely place. I'll find their number for you. And don't forget, if you want to get away for a while, you're always welcome to come back and stay with us. Anytime … I mean it. Lou and I would love to have you.'

She sat in the dark, hot tears trickling down her cheeks. She tried willing herself to stand up to begin making dinner, but her body felt heavy; it was too much effort to move. She heard the distinctive throb of Anton's Mazda sports car as it pulled into the driveway. Her stomach constricted.

Anton banged the front door behind him and swore in the dark. 'Shit, Morgan, no lights again.' He flicked on the switch and saw her sitting on the sofa crying, no dinner ready.

He appeared dishevelled. Had he been drinking? She eased herself up from the sofa and caught a whiff of spicy aftershave as she walked past him into the kitchen. The knot in her stomach tightened.

'No dinner again?' he said. 'For Christ's sake. What are you crying for this time? Jesus, Morgan, I can't take this, you're too bloody needy. Forget about dinner. I'm going out. Don't worry about it, I'll get something out. Just get yourself together, for fuck's sake.'

She smelt the alcohol on his breath strongly now. He turned away and slammed the door. She didn't have the energy to suggest he shouldn't be driving. She really didn't care. Seeing him had justified, without doubt, what she had decided to do.

She heated a frozen pie in the microwave and poured herself a glass of Cabernet. Then she Googled houses to rent in Scotland on her phone. Ayr. That was where Don had mentioned her aunt and cousin live.

A cute detached cottage was available for rent at £495 a month, but it was unfurnished. She also found units to rent, which were cheaper and furnished. But how would she cope with living in a unit? She was used to living in a house; she wasn't sure if she liked the idea of living so close to strangers.

Probably the first thing should be to contact her cousin and family. Funny, Don had barely mentioned them all the time she was growing up. Of course, apart from the cousin, they were not actually blood relations. Still, maybe she could stay with them just for a few days and then find somewhere to live nearby.

How much was £495 anyway? Another quick phone search estimated it at $210 a week. Affordable. She had a modest income from her parents' estate set up as an annuity — enough to live on if she was careful. Plus she could always boost it with freelance web design if necessary.

The familiar longing returned. Imagining travelling to Scotland helped take her mind off Anton and the mockery that was her marriage. It seemed right, inevitable. She would explore the place she was born and investigate her birth family. She would find out about her mother and father, and how they had died.

Over the following days, she spent most of her time reading about the country and its complex history. She wrote a detailed list of everything she could fit into one suitcase and compared prices of flights. She visited Don and Lou to tell them she had made up her mind and, although they were both a little tearful, they understood her determination.

Don remembered her cousin's name was Kirsty. Uncle Malcolm Murray and his first wife, Jane, had no children, but Kirsty was his daughter with his second wife, Ali. After a bit of searching, Don found a phone number. 'Ah, yes, Iain. That is Ali's new husband's name. I remember now. Iain Ogilvy.'

During these days Anton came and went as usual. They hardly spoke, and on the nights he spent at home he slept in the spare room. Eventually she summoned enough courage to tell him her plan to travel to Scotland.

'So what am I supposed to do while you're away on this soul-searching junket?' he said. 'And how much is it going to cost?'

'It's not going to cost you anything. I can manage, and I can stay with my relatives for a while. But, to be honest, I don't know how long I'm going for. I mean, I won't be coming back here, to you, Anton. It's not something I can deal with. I can't live with you anymore. I'm leaving. For good.' She sighed deeply. She had finally said it.

Anton stared at her for a long time without blinking.

'Well fuck you then. Fuck off, I don't care.' He stomped out, slamming the door behind him. He revved his Mazda loudly and sped up the road, squealing the tyres.

So that was it. No remorse, no emotion, no discussion, no trying to talk her out of it. She felt a curious mixture of emptiness and relief, along with a touch of sadness.

Chapter 9

Anton didn't return that night. By now she was getting used to sleeping alone. She assumed he was still seeing Shannon and staying over there, wherever he lived. So much for the affair being over — what a prize liar. She couldn't believe anything he said. But she wouldn't dwell on it. She had exciting planning and thinking to do.

But really, why had he not confided in her, been honest, told her he was conflicted, and shared his feelings? He hadn't even given her a choice. He had instead shut her out, hidden his true nature, and then punished her for expecting him to be something he wasn't. What had happened to the loving marriage promises they made to each other and plans for their life together? He had just used her.

The lack of trust was at least as hurtful as the affair, which, with a girl would have been bad enough. But a male was not even something she knew how to compete with. They would obviously have to get divorced. The whole thing was too depressing to think about. She started sorting through jumpers and warm tops.

On the other hand, was she giving up too much? Giving up too easily? What if she stayed? Could she possibly overlook his bisexuality? There must be plenty of examples where a couple had remained together, married, but in a platonic relationship, with other sexual partners. She could think of some advantages: stability, friendship, financial security, no upheaval to their lifestyle, no stress of divorce, no rigmarole of changing legal documents.

The idea had its attraction, but it would be a lie. Even if she could accept his sexuality, she would also have to accept the knowledge she couldn't trust him, even as a friend. And he wasn't exactly friendly to her anyway. She would be just as lonely in that kind of marriage as if she really was alone.

✦ ✦ ✦ ✦

Early in the morning she had another of her recurring dreams. She and a boy were hiding in a grove of trees on a hill, spying on a parade of soldiers assembled inside an old-fashioned timber fort. Some of the soldiers wore metal armour, some of them wore leather tunics. This dream was always accompanied by a sense of foreboding. It was one of several lucid dreams which had haunted her throughout her life. More vivid and realistic than regular dreams, they would play on her mind the next day and affect her mood.

She pushed the dream aside to concentrate on packing, the fun of planning and selection. What a pity she had to do it on her own, with no one to share the adventure. Her other personal belongings she packed into a dozen cardboard boxes: summer clothes, shoes, thongs — she couldn't imagine needing those in Scotland — books, childhood teddy bears, a few ornaments. There wasn't really much to show for a lifetime.

One by one she carried the boxes down to the garage. On her last trip back she called in to see Leeann to tell her everything that had happened, over two bottles of Sauvignon blanc and a delivered supremo pizza.

'Oh my God, Morgan, I thought something was happening. Are you really doing this? You're just leaving the door wide open for the boyfriend to move straight in.'

'I don't think I care. Honestly, I can't wait to get away and not be a housewife anymore, to be free to make my own decisions about where I go and who with. To be myself, whoever that is.

'But you can do that here, if you're serious about leaving Anton. You don't need to go to the other end of the earth. How are you going to cope with the wet weather and the cold? Everything will be different. But anyway, if you do go, it doesn't need to be forever, does it? I will miss you. You will be coming back home, won't you?'

She shrugged. 'I have no idea. And you're right — it might look like I'm trying to run away, but that's not the only reason I want to go. Maybe it's just curiosity about the place I was born, but it feels so much stronger than that. I have this irresistible urge to be there and experience it for myself.'

'Crazy. But good on you, anyway. I have to admire that you've made a decision to get away from a destructive marriage.

Couldn't have been easy.' Leeann shook her head. 'Who would have ever guessed about Anton? I still can't believe it. He's like the opposite of gay. What a shame. It all looked so perfect.'

Morgan booked her flight for the next week — an open return to Glasgow. She chose a return ticket only because it was not much more expensive than one-way. Don and Lou had insisted on buying her a business class fare, even though they themselves had never flown anything but economy.

'It's our special gift to you, love,' Don had said. 'You can lie down and sleep properly. It takes more than a whole day and night on a plane, you know, and it's all part of the excitement. We'll be so much happier knowing you're comfortable and enjoying yourself.'

Finally the day came for her to leave. She was up early, packed and eager to go. She hugged Leeann goodbye and promised to email her. On his way out, Anton kissed her goodbye, after having spent a rare night at home. It was strange; he looked almost dejected, and for a moment she wondered if she was doing the right thing.

'Well, see you then,' he said. 'I suppose we'll talk some time about what you want to do. Like if you change your mind or anything. Skype me when you get there so I know you're okay.'

A twinge of regret twisted at her heart. 'Yes, I will. I'll tell you all about it.'

They hugged stiffly and he left for work. She followed him to the door and watched as he reversed out of the driveway. His phone was already clamped to his ear. He was smiling and nodding. Then he threw his head back and laughed. Her feeling of remorse disintegrated.

Don and Lou had offered to drive her to the airport and she was ready at the door when they arrived. She loaded her suitcase into the rear of the station wagon and slid into the back seat.

'Thank you for driving me,' she said.

'It's a pleasure, darling. We want to see you off safely.' Lou turned around from the front passenger seat. Her kind, wrinkly face was smiling but Morgan could see sadness in her eyes. This was the woman who had been the only mother she could remember. Morgan smiled and reached out to gently squeeze her arm.

She could feel the bone under Lou's loose skin. She was so old. They both were. She had always been aware her foster parents were elderly. People would assume they were her grandparents. In their compassion and selflessness they had welcomed her into their home when they should have been enjoying their retirement.

Lou had told her though, because she had never been blessed with children of her own, Morgan was the child she had longed for. When Don and Lou had applied to adopt her, they were told they were past the legal age, but they were allowed to remain her legal guardians. Was it selfish of her to be leaving them? It was too late to change her mind now.

Just as they were coming to the end of the driveway she suddenly said, 'Oh Don, I'm so sorry. There's something I forgot to do. Could you stop for a moment please? I need to go back inside quickly.'

She unlocked the front door and ran through the house to the back verandah. She reached up and unlatched the door of Wilbur's cage. She put her hand in and pulled out the wriggling, flapping bird. He was warm and scrawny; he weighed practically nothing. She stood him on the railing and watched to see if he would catch the breeze and fly.

'Go Wilbur. Be free. Live long and prosper.' He just sat there. She gently poked the bird until he flexed his wings. The condition of the poor thing was shocking, with his pink scaly skin and missing feathers. Finally, after flapping on the railing for several minutes, he took off and soared up to a high branch of a gum tree.

Chapter 10

The business class ticket had other benefits — the business class lounge, featuring a glorious smorgasbord of food and alcohol. Seeing Don and Lou had paid for this expensive flight it would have been ungrateful not to partake. By the time her flight boarded she was tipsy on French Champagne and enjoying every moment.

As promised the seats were spacious and comfortable. She settled into her wide seat and stretched out her legs. The seat beside her was vacant. Bliss. More Veuve Clicquot arrived. Bless you, Don and Lou. She had nothing to do other than revel in the happiness of being warm, cosy and sleepy. Comfortably numb.

Sometime in the night, this feeling wore off. She had slept soundly in her little pod, but now she was wide awake, persistent thoughts invading her contentment. She had been so proud to have been married to Anton, at first. Did he change or did she? Or were they both really somebody else the whole time, and eventually their true natures had leached through?

It occurred to her it was an enormous undertaking to travel to a distant country on her own. She regretted she and Anton were not travelling on this overseas voyage together. They would never travel together again. Now she was alone; she would be doing everything in the future by herself, and she would have to get used to it. She wiped a tear away from the corner of her eye.

She tried to concentrate on the thrill of travelling to Scotland, the land she had yearned for. She had wanted this, and now she was doing it. She wondered what her aunt Ali and her uncle Iain were like. Ali had certainly sounded friendly enough on the phone. Technically they were not really her aunt and uncle, not blood relatives at all.

After more than twenty-four hours in the air, with a short stopover in Dubai, she finally disembarked at Glasgow airport, at lunchtime. Iain had insisted on collecting her, even though it meant nearly a two-hour round trip from their home in Ayr.

She couldn't resist a display of woollen tartan scarves in one of the airport shops. She chose one she liked, and which she thought would suit her — dark blue and green with stripes of black, yellow and red, priced at fifteen pounds. Probably a rip-off, but she bought it anyway. She was relieved her travel Visa card was accepted.

Once she had endured the security procedures and retrieved her suitcase, she filed through to the arrivals area, where she heard Kirsty before she saw her.

'Morrrgan! Helloo! Over here!' Kirsty ran over and gave her a warm embrace. 'My long-lost cousin from Australia,' she yelled. Morgan felt, rather than saw, the heads turn their way.

She immediately took a liking to Kirsty. She was petite and cute with dark brown eyes and hair cut in a short dark bob. Her wide jaw, with an equally wide smile, displayed an amazing array of even white teeth, like a dolphin's. She wore light blue jeans and a crisp white shirt which unfortunately accentuated how rumpled Morgan looked in her slept-in tracksuit.

Iain, who was the opposite of petite, squashed her in a hug with his massive arms. He was about sixty-eight, portly, balding except for a few wisps of grey hair, and had a florid face mostly covered with a short grey beard. She could imagine him tossing a caber, no problem.

He spoke with a booming voice, and such a broad Scottish accent she had to concentrate to follow him. 'Helloo, Morrrgan, it's grand to meet you. Welcome to bonnie Scotland. Did you have a good flight over?'

'Yes, thank you. It was long, but I really enjoyed it, very relaxing. It's so kind of you to pick me up. Will you let me buy you some lunch?'

'Well, now, I wouldn't say no to a spot of lunch. It's something of a treat for us to come to *Glesga*, ye ken.'

She found an ATM and withdrew three hundred pounds. The notes looked formal and ornate, different from the bright, colourful Australian money she was used to, but they had the same plastic feel. She wasn't all that hungry, having been well fed on the plane, so she ordered a small quiche and coffee. She had asked for a flat white but, after receiving a puzzled look from the attendant, changed it to a cappuccino.

Iain managed to scoff a double Angus beef burger with a mountain of chips, a sticky date toffee pudding, and a double whisky. She was surprised at his choice of drink but felt it would be impolite to question it. After paying over fifty pounds for the lunch, she wondered if she should have withdrawn much more cash.

During lunch Iain and Kirsty bombarded her with questions about Australia: have you ever seen any deadly snakes? Have you seen any deadly spiders? What about crocodiles? What about dingoes? Do many people get bitten by sharks? Is it dangerous to go backpacking? She wished she had thought to bring more photos of where she lived. It hadn't occurred to her Australia would be so exotic to them, or that they would have the impression it was one giant death trap.

A row of tantalising shops taunted her with more tartan and woollen clothes, but she thought it might appear rude if she abandoned her hosts to go off shopping. Plenty of time for that later.

'Are you allowed to keep a kangaroo as a pet? Do you have koalas in your garden? What about wombats?' Kirsty was lovely but she did have a loud voice. 'Have you seen the Sydney Opera House? What's the Great Barrier Reef like?'

Morgan was aware other people in the restaurant were stealing looks at her and listening to what she was saying. She tried to speak quietly and wished Kirsty and Iain would do the same. She was not used to being the centre of attention.

The long flight had made her weary, but with almost an hour's drive ahead of them, she had to somehow find the stamina to answer all their questions.

Outside the airport Iain loaded her large suitcase into the back of his Land Cruiser. Although it wasn't raining, heavy clouds hung low. She breathed deeply. The atmosphere had a different quality — cool and damp, bracing on her face, with a freshness she found invigorating.

Once they had navigated their way out of the airport and onto the M77 her energy returned along with a sense of rising excitement. She could not help smiling. This was Scotland. At last. She belonged here — her home country.

She tried to take in all the scenery. The road was good, and wide, but had a rougher surface than she was used to. The bushes, trees and open fields were a spectacular vivid green, a colour she had seen in Australia only rarely, after a deluge. She was surprised just how much of it was rural.

'Well, Morgan, what would be your plans now then?' Iain asked, breaking into her rapture. 'You're welcome to stay with us for as long as you want, mind.'

'Thank you, Iain, that's kind of you. I'm hoping to be able to rent a place nearby pretty quickly, so if I could stay with you for a couple of days that would be really great.'

'We'd love to have you stay. I know Kirsty would like the company, wouldn't you, pet?'

'Aye, I would! I've been looking forward to you coming. I want to hear all about Australia. We've made the spare room nice and comfy for you.'

'Thank you, Kirsty, I am looking forward to sleeping in a bed again — it sure is a long trip from Oz. Oh, and Iain, would you know if there is a car hire place nearby? I'd like to rent a little car so I can travel around exploring.'

'Absolutely. I can take you out when you're ready, once you've rested up a bit. Well, here we are,' Iain said. 'This is us.'

Chapter 11

The trip hadn't taken as long as she had expected. They pulled up to a reddish-brown brick house with white framed windows and two turrets. On second look she saw it was actually two properties on one block, a duplex.

'What a lovely house. But this is not Ayr, is it?'

'Not quite, this is a wee town called Prestwick,' Iain said. 'Although it's not all that wee, you ken, we do have an airport. *International* airport. And it's a good town if you like the golf; we've five golf clubs nearby, and there's Troon, of course. Not only that, about half an hour's drive south is a world-class golf course and hotel owned by the United States' President, would you believe.'

'Wow, it punches above its weight, you might say.'

'Aye, and we're a bit lucky here, too. We have off-street parking, so if you do get a wee hire car you can park it in the driveway.'

Ali appeared at the front door. 'Hello, Morgan! How lovely to meet you. Come away in and have a cup of tea.'

Inside, the house was warm and welcoming, and filled with the aroma of baking. Ali looked to be a good ten years younger than Iain. She was plump with a lot of soft, dark curls. She had the same dark brown eyes and wide smile as her daughter.

'Iain will put your case in the spare room upstairs for you,' Ali shouted. Morgan realised where Kirsty's strident voice came from. She wondered if the neighbours on the other side of the wall would be able to hear the three of them having a conversation. Iain seized the large suitcase like it was a briefcase and disappeared with it up the carpeted stairs.

Ali, Kirsty and Morgan sat at the dining table for tea and fresh-baked scones with jam and cream. 'So you're Isla's daughter, now, all the way from Australia,' Ali said. This was the first time anyone had mentioned her mother. 'You've had a long trip — you'll be looking forward to a good kip the night.'

Morgan liked Ali straight away. She was always nervous before meeting new people, but Ali's relaxed, motherly nature put her at ease immediately.

'I'm really grateful to you for letting me stay here, Ali. I promise I'll get out of your hair as soon as possible. I should be able to find somewhere to live pretty quickly, so it'll only be for a couple of days.'

'Och, never you mind that, you are welcome to stay as long as you like. Dinner won't be too long so why don't you unpack your things and have a wee relax. Kirsty will show you your room.'

Kirsty led her up the narrow staircase to a tiny room at the back of the house. 'I'm sorry it's so wee. I usually use this room as my study, but I'll use my own room while you're here. It's the one on the other side of the stairs. Ma and Iain's room is across the passage. They have an en suite so the bathroom next to your room is just for you and me. And we do have an extra loo downstairs too. Ma calls it the powder room when she's trying to be posh.'

Morgan's room had a steep ceiling like an attic, a small timber desk and chair, a single bed covered with a soft-looking doona, and thick woollen tartan drapes. Iain had put her suitcase in a corner. If she squinted through the low western sun, she could glimpse the sea in the distance. 'This is beautiful, Kirsty. Thank you, I'm really going to sleep well tonight.'

'I'll leave you to unpack or whatever, just come down when you're ready.'

Left on her own, she yawned deeply. All she wanted to do was to flop onto the comfortable bed and sleep, but she knew if she slept now, she would not wake up. She still had dinner to get through before she could indulge in that luxury.

Luckily, she had dragged herself away from the Brisbane airport smorgasbord long enough to collect some Australiana souvenirs which she handed out at dinner. She gave Ali a tea towel printed with Australian slang expressions. Ali read: '*Fair suck of the sav* — means someone is not being fair. *You little ripper!* — means something is really great. *Root rat* — means someone constantly looking for sex.'

Ali laughed. 'Thank you, dear. I'm sure that will be useful. The tea towel I mean.'

She gave Iain a stubby cooler with an Aboriginal design,

and Kirsty a kangaroo-shaped car key ring, and a flat toad purse.

'This is a what? A *toad?* Seriously?' Kirsty held it up between her thumb and forefinger.

Morgan had to explain what a stubby cooler was — Iain only drank whisky. Kirsty didn't actually own a car, and yes, it was made of real cane toad skin. She was glad she hadn't opted for the kangaroo scrotum purse. 'It's a Queensland thing,' she said. She sincerely regretted her choice of souvenirs.

She knew they were bursting to ask her questions.

'So Morgan, dear, what made you decide to come to Scotland all by yourself?' Ali initiated the onslaught over dinner.

'Well, it's hard to say, really. Not just one thing. I felt a strong urge to see where I was born, and hopefully find out about my real mother and father. Plus I felt like I needed to get away and be on my own ...'

Ali's eyes travelled down to Morgan's wedding ring. She should have taken it off, a mistake. She hadn't wanted to mention her marriage, but now it was inevitable.

She wiggled her ring finger. 'And, yes, I am married, but that has pretty much turned out to be a disaster. So I guess, I'm just looking forward to seeing Scotland, exploring new places, and getting to know you guys.' She was aware her explanation sounded lame, but it was impossible to adequately express the heartache which had led to her conflicted decision.

Iain, who had been quiet until now, cleared this throat and said, 'Ah, and how are your parents now? They would be your foster parents, is that right?'

She took a breath and smiled at him. 'Yes, they're great, really well. It was sad leaving them but they're wonderful people and they gave me their blessing. I couldn't wish for better godparents.'

'Don and Lou,' Ali said. 'Yes, I heard about them, but I never met them. They had already taken you to Australia when I met your uncle Mal in the hospital where I was looking after your dear aunt Jane at the end of her life. Very sad. It was the cancer, you know. She was so young. A terrible pity.'

'You were a nurse then, Ali? Are you retired now?'

'Aye, yes, I was a palliative care nurse in the Ayrshire hospice. And Mal would come to visit her. I'm mostly retired, Iain and I both are, but sometimes I still help out if I'm needed.' Ali poked at her meal with her fork and blinked a few times. Iain gently laid his hand on her arm.

Morgan realised how powerful a memory is, even after twenty years. The hurt, the sorrow, never really leaves you. You absorb it and it becomes part of who you are, always present just under the surface. She hoped, in time, her pain would fade and she, like Ali, could get on with her life.

'I'll look out some photos for you later, if you like,' Kirsty said.

'Yes, please, I absolutely would like. I'd be fascinated to see them. Ali, that meal was delicious — that chicken in tomato sauce was divine, and the best mashed potato I think I've ever tasted.'

'Aye, that will be all the cream in it. And the chicken dish was my own special recipe.' Ali beamed her wide smile at Morgan.

'Let me help with —'

'No, no, no. Definitely not. You just relax and chat to Kirsty.'

'Come on through here.' Kirsty stood up from the table. 'We'll have a wee drink.'

Morgan followed Kirsty through to the cosy living room. Full length gold brocade curtains, plush carpet and subdued golden lighting gave her the impression she was entering Aladdin's cave. She sank into a large yellow sofa filled with feathers, and Kirsty handed her a glass of red wine. If she had closed her eyes, she would have had difficulty opening them again.

'We bought this specially because we knew you were coming — it's called *Jacob's Creek*. Do you like it?'

She was touched by her effort and gave Kirsty a warm smile. 'It's lovely Kirsty, thank you.'

When Kirsty was also settled on the luxurious sofa, Morgan asked, 'So, Kirsty, you're living here with your mum and Iain? Are you working?'

'Well, not at the moment. I studied graphic design at the Uni and then, after working in a design studio for four years in Edinburgh, I felt I'd had enough. I found it quite stressful, the constant pressure to be creative can be exhausting. So I decided I'd like to try my hand at teaching. I think I'm confident enough to be a design teacher.'

'Wow, what a coincidence. I'm a web designer so we're actually in the same industry. How about that? And I think you'd make a fantastic teacher. You have …' She was about to say, 'a great voice for it' but changed her mind and said, 'Well, I think you would be really good with the students.'

'I hope so. I've been accepted to the course, a Professional Graduate Diploma, in Ayr, but it doesn't start until August so I've a few months up my sleeve. I moved back in with Ma and Iain to save a bit of money while I'm studying for the year. I also do a bit of freelance here and there. Anyway, it means I can spend some time with you, showing you round if you like.'

'That sounds great, Kirsty, I would love that. I need to get a car and find a unit. So much to do.'

'A unit? Oh, you mean a flat, don't you? Of course. Yes I can help you with that … we'll have loads of fun.'

Iain came into the lounge room carrying an armful of photograph albums which he deposited onto the coffee table. 'Here you are, girls, plenty of history here to keep you out of mischief.'

'Thanks Iain. We might need your help to go through them — many of these are people I don't know,' Kirsty said.

'Aye, well, I don't think I'll be much help. The old pictures are all before my time, ye ken. Your ma might be better able to point out who's who.' He noticed Morgan's half-closed eyes. 'But I'm thinking that might be something to leave until tomorrow.'

Morgan nodded. She was keen to start on the photos but the wine was having an effect, and she was losing the battle with her heavy eyelids. After saying goodnight she found her way to her room and collapsed into the bed. She was asleep almost before her head hit the pillow.

Chapter 12

Lying snuggled under the doona in the heavenly warm bed, Morgan breathed the chilly morning air. She rolled on her side to check the bedside clock. Holy crap! It was eleven-thirty. How could she have slept so long? She hurriedly threw on jeans and a sweatshirt and went downstairs. Ali had hot porridge with sultanas waiting for her.

'Ali, you're a darling. I had no idea it was so late.'

Ali smiled. 'There's plenty of cream in the jug to put on your porridge.'

More cream — delicious. At this rate she would soon need to buy looser clothes.

After breakfast, which was really lunch, she went through to the lounge where Ali sat reading a newspaper, and Kirsty was already engrossed in the photo albums.

'Look, Morgan, these photos are you, I think. You're just tiny.'

She saw a small, dark-haired child about one year old, staring fixedly at something over the photographer's shoulder.

'That's me is it?' she asked Ali.

'Aye, I believe that will be you, right enough', Ali said as she studied the photo. 'I remember Mal mentioning they used to say you'd been here before.'

'Yes, I've heard Don say the same thing to me.'

It was odd to see herself as a baby for the first time. The earliest photos she had seen were those taken by Don when she was four, and she had lighter hair. The child in the photo looked strangely serious. She was not smiling; her dark eyes concentrated on something in the distance. It was possible she'd just been crying. She understood why people used to say she'd been here before. She didn't look like any usual happy-go-lucky little kid. It was hard to detect any resemblance to herself now.

She saw a faded photo of a tall bearded man about thirty, his brown hair in long dreadlocks. He held a tattooed arm around a young, slim woman with unkempt blonde hair, wearing a tie-dyed t-shirt. Something flashed suddenly in her mind: momentary recognition, a fleeting memory, but then it was gone. At the same time, just for a split second, she smelled a distinctive odour. Like something fermented.

'And, Ali, would this be Jane with Uncle Mal?'

'Aye, that's Mal, and Janie in her twenties, bless her.'

'Uncle Mal. Wow. I wasn't expecting the dreadlocks.'

'His father hated them,' Ali said. 'So I think he wore his hair like that deliberately. You've probably heard it said: the more authoritarian the parent, the more rebellious the child. He told me he cut them all off the same year his father died.'

They looked at page after page of photos: the house where Mal and Ali used to live in Ayr, Kirsty as a young schoolgirl, and many taken on family holidays around Scotland. She could see Kirsty was moved by the old photos of her father.

'Your dad looks like a bit of a character,' Morgan said. She politely avoided saying *stoner*. 'You would have been young when he died.'

'Yes, I was only four. He died of leukaemia. He was forty-four, wasn't he Ma? I wish I could remember more about him. I only remember he didn't have dreadlocks, or a beard.'

'Aye.' Ali sighed. 'He was a lovely man, our Mal. Gentle.'

'I know he was kind to me,' Morgan said. 'I wish I could remember him better too. I'm so sorry he's gone.'

'Thanks,' Kirsty said. 'Thinking about him makes me sad, but Iain has been such a good father to me. I don't call him Pa though. And my name's still Murray, not Ogilvy.'

It struck her that she and Kirsty shared another similarity — they had both lost parents at a young age.

She found two colour photographs tucked behind a flap in one of the albums, showing a couple in their twenties. She recognised the woman as her mother. In one of the photos they were standing in front of a new BMW. The man, whom she assumed to be her father, was holding up keys, and both were smiling proudly. The second photo showed the same couple, taken on the same day, this time the woman was holding a baby. With a shock she saw the woman's face had been crossed out with a thick black marking pen. Shaking, she handed the photos to Kirsty who turned the photos over and read, 'Isla and Jack'.

Ali's hand also trembled as she took the photos. 'I'm so sorry, Morgan. I didn't know we had any of these.'

Morgan had difficulty holding back tears. 'You don't have any more photos of my mother … Mal's sister?'

'No, as I said, I didn't even know we had those. I didn't think they'd been kept.' Ali rose from the recliner and walked stiffly into the kitchen with her coffee mug. Morgan looked at Kirsty.

Kirsty's eyes were wide. 'Can I see those again? I've never seen photos of your parents before. This one where your mother is holding you and her face is crossed out — what an awful thing. I'm so sorry. That's really upsetting.'

'Would you mind if I hung onto these for a while? I do want to find out about my parents — that was one of the reasons I was so keen to come to Scotland.'

'Of course, you should. There must be more photos somewhere. I can't believe Pa would have discarded photos of his own sister.'

Morgan and Kirsty searched through all the albums, packets and loose pictures. They found photos of Morgan at about age two with her aunt Jane, Mal's first wife, but no further photos of her mother and father. Not been kept — what did that mean?

Hours had passed and it was already close to dinner time. Morgan yawned. 'It's weird, this jet lag, if that's what I have. I can't believe I feel like sleeping again.'

◆　◆　◆　◆

'How are you getting on with the photos, Morgan?' Ali asked at the dinner table. 'Did you find them interesting?'

'Yes, extremely, thanks Ali. It's extraordinary to see photos of people I'd only ever heard about. But you were right, there weren't any more of my mother and father. I know it was a long time ago but I wonder why they weren't kept.'

'I don't remember ever seeing any photos at all of your parents,' Ali said. 'I was surprised to see those. Mal was never one for hoarding. And then of course a lot of things were thrown out when I sold the house and moved in here with Iain.'

'Yes, I see. Well I'm thankful you've even got the ones you have. You know, they are the first photos I've ever seen of myself as a baby.'

'You are welcome to keep any photos of yourself you want,' Ali said. 'They're probably better off with you.'

She understood Ali had no reason to keep old photos that had no meaning for her. Morgan was not related to her at all. 'Thank you, Ali, I would really love them. There's a nice one of Aunt Jane and me I would like to have.'

'Do you have any plans for tomorrow, Morgan?' Iain asked.

'Yes, tomorrow I'm hoping to start searching for somewhere to live, and also to make enquiries about hiring a car.'

'How long would you be looking at keeping the car for?' he asked.

'Well, I don't actually have a definite time frame in mind. I bought a return flight because, weirdly, it was almost the same price as a one-way ticket. Isn't that ridiculous? I have no plans to go back, so it's open-ended really.'

'Only, I was thinking,' Iain said, 'if you're going to be here for a while, a few months say, it would cheaper for you to buy a wee motor and sell it later. And some hire places have a time limit, you ken. I'm sure we'd be able to pick up something suitable for you under two thousand pounds.'

'Great idea, Iain. I'll start looking online tomorrow.'

'I can help you with that,' Kirsty said. 'I'll research rental properties nearby for you. It'll be fun!'

After the meal Morgan insisted on helping Ali with the cleaning up, despite her protests. She was hoping to talk to her alone.

'Ali, why do you think Mal would have thrown out photos of Isla? She was his sister.'

'I wish I could be more help, dear. It is strange, I agree. Maybe the memories of her were just too painful. I really don't know. But I can tell you when I moved to this new house I didn't throw out any of his photos. Not knowingly, anyway.'

'Do you have any idea why someone would cross out my mother's face like that?'

'I'm sorry, dear, I couldn't say. Really. It was all before my time.'

That night, although dog-tired, she slept fitfully. There had been something in Ali's reaction to the photos; something had definitely unnerved her. She had so few photos of her mother, the idea someone would deliberately cross out her face was distressing. She thought back to her conversation with Ali. What had she meant? *What* was all before her time? Did she believe Ali? She couldn't help feeling she didn't.

Chapter 13

It was a glorious, sunny spring morning, but to Morgan it could have been Brisbane in mid-winter. She checked the weather app on her phone — ten degrees. She felt a bit silly wearing thermals and Ugg boots when everybody else was dressed so lightly. She reminded herself the chill was a welcome contrast to the oppressive, humid summer she had just endured.

By the time she came downstairs, Kirsty had already found a few properties to look at online and was bursting to show her. She was so enthusiastic, Morgan didn't have the heart to tell her she had been looking forward to researching properties for herself.

'Look at this one, Morgan! It's furnished nicely and it's only about a mile away, just a few minutes down the road.'

She looked at the flat Kirsty was showing her on her laptop. It certainly had everything she needed. It was in a quiet location, it looked clean and neat, it was fully furnished, and it had off-street parking. A quick search of her currency conversion app calculated the £450 a month rent to be $207 per week. That seemed affordable — cheap even. They looked at seven other properties on offer, varying widely in price, depending if they offered a golf course or sea view. She had to admit the flat did suit her needs well.

'It looks great, Kirsty. I see it's available now. Do you think we could go and look at it today?'

Kirsty called the number on the website and made an appointment for three o'clock, at which time the whole family piled into Iain's Land Cruiser. Ali had insisted on coming to ensure it was up to her standard.

They drove past a golf course through a pleasant tree-lined area of neat, detached bungalows. But the flat seemed to be at the poorer end, and the exterior could have done with a coat of paint. Andrew, the estate agent, met them at the entrance of the building to show them around.

'It's a bit far from the shops but I think there's a small Spar at the end of that walkway,' Ali said.

'It will not matter, then, Morgan will have a wee motor to get to the shops,' Iain said.

Andrew explained the total cost of living was actually £612 a month including council tax and energy. The new total worked out at $281 a week; still reasonable considering it included electricity and gas.

The building consisted of four flats over two levels with only one ground floor flat currently occupied. They climbed the stairs to the top floor flat. It had a compact, modern timber kitchen and a cosy lounge room with a built-in gas fire. It was nothing like she was used to, but she could picture herself being happy here.

'It's clean enough. I hope you get nice neighbours,' Ali said.

'It looks better inside than it does outside,' Kirsty said.

'Aye, and it's not too wee either. It's got everything you need.' Iain opened a drawer. 'Even cutlery.'

As it met with everybody's approval, she decided to take it on the spot. There were a few formalities, a deposit to pay and forms to fill in at the agent's office. Andrew seemed apologetic when he said, 'And I must take your photo if that's all right. Sorry, it's just a requirement of this landlord — for record purposes.'

He said it should take only a couple of days, then he'd ring to confirm she had been accepted, and when to collect the keys.

'Good work, Kirsty, finding that flat,' Morgan said on the way home. 'Isn't it perfect! I can hardly wait. And, to celebrate, I would like to treat you all out for dinner tonight. Is there a good place nearby?'

'Aye, that would be grand,' Iain said. 'Let's do that. The Red Lion's always good. But there's no need for the treat, mind.'

'Oh, I insist,' she said. 'I really appreciate you letting me stay with you, and taxiing me around.'

'Och, it's no bother at all,' Iain said. 'We've enjoyed having the company. And by the way, I've had a wee word with a pal o' mine about a motor for you. He has a few good cars to choose from, but there's a little minter in his yard right now and he'll do a good price for you. £1500 for a Volkswagen Polo, 2005 model, 105,000 miles on the clock. He worked with me for years at the airport and I know fine he's a straight bloke.'

She had really wanted to find her own car, but Iain was clearly knowledgeable about vehicles so she decided to go with the flow, seeing everyone was so eager to help her. 'Sounds perfect, Iain. I'd love to see it.'

After a hearty meal and several rounds of drinks, during which the four of them contributed significantly to the noise level in a boisterous pub, Kirsty suggested she and Morgan walk home along the promenade. 'It's only about a mile, and it's a lovely evening.'

Not being used to miles, Morgan did a quick calculation — a little over one and a half kilometres. Ali adjusted the seat of the big Toyota so she could drive home, as by this time Iain was staggering, having consumed an alarming quantity of whisky. Kirsty and Morgan set off along Monkton Road and then turned down to the esplanade.

'This is a delightful town,' Morgan said. 'I'm loving all these old stone and brick buildings. You can see history everywhere you look. Where I live in Brisbane, the houses are large, new and modern, completely different.'

Kirsty sighed. 'I would just love to see Australia.'

They walked beside the golf links and onto the promenade. Kirsty showed Morgan where the old swimming pavilion and lake had once been. It was Morgan's turn to sigh. 'It would have been magnificent in its day.'

'You can see the old photos in the Ayr library, they have quite a collection. They're not all on the internet.'

'Ah, good. And you've given me an idea. I could also search in the library newspaper archives for anything about my mother and father. I've been told they died in a car accident hereabouts but I know practically nothing about them.'

Suddenly, a deafening roar overhead made Morgan jump. 'Jesus!' She clutched Kirsty as a plane flew low over their heads.

Kirsty laughed. 'The airport is just over there. And helicopters come and go at all hours. You get used to it.'

They strolled along the promenade beside the stunning Firth of Clyde, shielding their eyes against the setting sun. Kirsty pointed out the island of Arran. The evening was so clear they could even see the distant round island of Ailsa Craig.

Morgan found the northerly wind chilly so they stepped up their pace. She was glad of the tartan scarf she'd bought in Glasgow airport; it was fast becoming her favourite item of clothing.

They turned left into Grangemuir Road towards home. 'So, you haven't told me much about yourself yet,' Morgan said. 'Do you have a boyfriend?'

'I do actually — Callum. I met him in Edinburgh. He's in his final year of a medical degree. It's a demanding course so I'm staying down here to give him time to concentrate. He'll finish his degree at the end of the year, and I'll be halfway through my teaching diploma so we'll get together again then. He's lovely and I miss him. I hope you will be able to meet him.'

'I hope so too.'

'And, Morgan, are you not married anymore?'

'Technically I am because you have to be separated and living apart for twelve months before you can apply for a divorce. After that you can submit the application online, which makes it easier. So that's what I'll do, but I've got nearly a year to wait yet.'

'Was he a horrible husband? I can't imagine anyone wanting to be horrible to you.'

'Yes, pretty horrible. He had an affair with a man.'

Kirsty laughed. Suddenly, she grabbed Morgan's arm and looked at her with wide eyes. 'Oh, my God, Morgan. You're serious! I'm so sorry.'

'That's okay, Kirsty. I'm still trying to get my head around it myself. He turned out to be not the man I thought I married. Luckily, we didn't have any children — he didn't want any. So at least the divorce should be straightforward.'

'Hell's bells. So he's bisexual? And you didn't know?'

'No idea at all.'

'Wow. It must have tormented him, trying to hide his secret life from you all that time.'

'I suppose so. I've never thought about it like that before.'

'No wonder you wanted to get as far away as possible. But now you're here — you can make a new start and find out about your family. That will keep you busy. And when you get your wee car you can travel around and see the sites of Scotland. There's a lot to see. *And,* when you're settled into your flat and everything, I think we should go into the big town — Ayr that is — and we'll have some fun. We might find something or *someone* to take your mind off your husband being a plonker.'

Chapter 14

By the time Morgan came down in the morning, Iain, who showed no evidence of any aftereffects from the previous night's heavy drinking, had already organised for them to inspect the car at his friend's car yard.

After breakfast, Iain, Kirsty and Morgan climbed into the Land Cruiser. Ali had declined to join them this time, not being interested in cars. A few minutes later they arrived at the yard in an industrial estate. His friend, Jimmy, specialised in Volkswagens; apparently it was either a VW or nothing. Morgan willingly let Iain take charge as he was evidently enjoying himself. Jimmy had presented the light blue Polo on the forecourt, ready for inspection.

After running through the features with them, Jimmy handed her the keys. 'Well, now, Morgan, have a wee drive in the car yourself and see what you think.'

'I'll come with you,' Kirsty said, hopping into the passenger seat. Iain stayed behind to catch up with Jimmy. She was relieved Kirsty was coming and not Iain; he would have taken up too much room in the tiny Polo and made her nervous.

Because a busy two-lane road ran in front of the car yard, she drove, tentatively, onto a quieter dead-end side road. The car had surprisingly good acceleration. She practised turning and reversing. She was familiar with driving on the left side of the road, but she would have to get used to the left-hand indicator switch. And the speedometer displaying in miles was strange too. She must try to stop converting to kilometres and think in miles.

Back at the car yard, Iain and Jimmy were engaged in a loud, laughing conversation. 'Well, how did you go? What do you think, Morgan?' Iain asked.

'It's great. Goes like a rocket. I was planning to see other cars as well, but I do really like this one.'

'Aye, it's everything you need,' Jimmy said. Automatic, air con, electric windows, and not a mark on it. Very good little motor. I've done an extra special price for my pal here, so you will no' find a better bargain.'

She accepted that the decision had already been made for her, so she nodded. 'Okay, little blue Polo it is then. I'm trusting your judgement here, Iain.'

'Good call, Morgan. Jimmy will take you through the paperwork and get you all set up. I've a golf game the noo so I'll be off. Kirsty will be able to navigate you back home when you're done.'

With the forms signed and formalities taken care of, she found herself the proud new owner of a Polo.

'It's so cute!' Kirsty said. 'I love it.'

Before they left the showroom, Morgan's phone rang. It was Andrew, the estate agent. 'Helloo Morgan, good news. The flat is all ready for you today. You can collect the keys any time now from the office.'

'That was quick. I thought it was going to take a few days for the approval.'

Kirsty squealed. 'How exciting — a car and a flat in one day.'

Morgan drove cautiously to Andrew's real estate office while Kirsty navigated.

'Congratulations, Morgan,' he said, 'you've been approved for a six-month lease. After that you can negotiate the flat on a month-by-month basis. The landlord was a little hesitant at first, mind, because you've no references but I reassured him you have family nearby, so it's all fine.'

She signed the final agreement and confirmation of handover, and Andrew gave her the set of keys. He said she could have a ten per cent discount if she paid six months' rent in advance. It sounded unusual, and it would eat into her dwindling funds, but ten per cent worked out to be a reasonable saving.

On the way back to the car she said, 'This is all new to me — contracts and references, forms to fill in for everything. It's like I've never had to do anything for myself before. I'm really glad you're here.'

'Och, that's no bother. I'm enjoying it. Will we go round to your flat now?'

'Bloody oath. I've never had my own place before. I can't wait.'

With Kirsty navigating it took less than ten minutes to drive to the flat. One key opened the front door and another opened the door of the flat at the top of the stairs. It was thrilling entering the front door of her own space for the first time. It had a pleasant freshly-cleaned floral fragrance.

'Oh, look, Morgan, someone has left you a vase of fresh flowers, and a note: *Welcome to your new home.*'

'How considerate, that's really nice. I would like to move in straight away.'

'Ma will have dinner organised,' Kirsty said. 'You'll be wanting to have dinner first won't you? Why don't we pick up some champers on the way home and we'll celebrate?'

They had celebrated last night, but Morgan sensed Kirsty was keen to have her stay one more night. She was so sweet. 'Okay, sounds like a plan — let's do that. I'll need to find out where the nearest shops are anyway.'

Kirsty took her to a large supermarket where they bought two bottles of sparkling wine. Morgan was impressed with how cheap the food and groceries were until she remembered the prices were pounds, not dollars.

The mouth-watering aroma from Ali's delicious shepherd's pie confirmed she had made the right decision to stay for dinner. They made short work of the two bottles of wine, then Iain started on the whisky. He offered some to the girls; Kirsty declined but Morgan thought, *when in Rome.* It was like drinking pure alcohol; no wonder they call it firewater. After a couple of these, she was driving nowhere, so she staggered up the stairs to her familiar little bedroom for one final night.

She awoke with a sense of excitement, despite her rough head. She would be giving the whisky a miss in future. Today was the real first day of her life as a single person. The Ogilvys were up bright and early as usual, Iain again showing no sign of having drunk until he passed out the night before.

'Well, Morgan, let us know how you get on,' Ali said, clearing away the breakfast dishes. 'Come around any time, or stay any time you like, if you get lonely. We're always here for you.'

'Bloody oath,' Kirsty said.

Morgan laughed; that sounded so funny in a Scottish accent. As she drove away in her little blue Polo the three of them stood outside and waved her goodbye, like she was embarking on a big adventure, although it was only five minutes down the road.

She stopped again at the Sainsbury supermarket for supplies. She bought all the things she thought she might need, plus a small espresso coffee machine and pods as a treat. She had to remind herself she was buying groceries for only one, not two, and something flickered through her heart.

As soon as she opened the front door to her own flat her elation returned. This was *hers*. She could do whatever she wanted, whenever she wanted. Luxury. She lugged her suitcase up the stairs and unpacked her groceries. Somebody had thoughtfully switched the fridge on already.

Instead of a laundry, a combination washing machine and dryer sat under the kitchen sink — a bit odd, but it probably saved space. She drank a glass of water from the kitchen tap. It was ice cold and didn't taste of chlorine, or any chemicals at all.

She looked around in all the rooms, opened cupboards and drawers. The flat was well appointed, with all the crockery, appliances and towels she needed. There were even sheets on the bed.

She made her first cup of coffee and sat on the long vinyl couch to enjoy it. Despite it being the middle of the day, she turned on the gas heater, a mock wood-burning fireplace, wondering if she would ever get used to the chill.

Her finances had taken a hammering, but she wanted to delay transferring any funds out of her annuity for as long as possible. She set up her laptop on the small round dining table and connected to the internet to check her bank balance.

Then she switched on the television and stared at it, mesmerised by the programs and even the advertisements. It was such a delight to see local news and hear Scottish announcers. This is what she'd been longing for.

She spread out the photos she had taken from Ali's albums: two baby photos, one with her and Aunt Jane, and the two photos of her parents. She gazed at them for a long time. These were the first photos she'd ever had of her parents, apart from the tiny photo of her mother she kept in the locket.

Her mother was holding her as a baby, wrapped in a yellow blanket. She shook her head. Why would someone have crossed out her face like that? She held the photo sideways in the light, trying to see her features better. Luckily, she was also in the other photo with the car. Morgan could see she was attractive, beautiful even, with sapphire-blue eyes and burgundy hair, not a natural colour. She wore a long-sleeved dark purple dress, a lot of jewellery and large hoop earrings. She had a bohemian, almost gypsy, appearance.

Her father, dressed casually in jeans and a *Nirvana* sweatshirt, stood beside her mother. Tall and good looking, with a moustache and touches of grey at the sides of his dark brown hair, his deep brown eyes were visible even though his face was creased into a grin as he held up the car keys. They were both standing in front of their new car, a white BMW. It must have been the car they were killed in. The thought was chilling.

Something about the photo puzzled her but she couldn't quite put her finger on it. Where was it taken? She looked more closely. In the background to the left of both photos was a white bungalow she assumed was their home. She wondered if it would be possible to find that house. Tears pricked her eyes as she gazed at her parents, so young and full of hope. What happened to you?

A rattling at the window disturbed her. It had started to rain, but this wasn't a normal shower, it was forceful, horizontal rain, and it was becoming heavier. Funny, she hadn't noticed any warning; it had suddenly just begun pelting down. She jumped up to check the window was tightly shut and closed the thick wool curtains. She pulled on her Ugg boots and then her dressing gown over the top of her clothes. She was still cold. She turned the heater up to the maximum. She'd hate to think what winter would be like.

She looked at her weather app — seven degrees. Ali and Iain must have had central heating. She dragged all the blankets she could find out of the linen cupboard. Then she turned back the bed quilt to switch on the electric blanket. Oh my God, no electric blanket! She'd freeze. In a cupboard under the sink she found a hot water bottle. She couldn't remember the last time she had used one of these.

After a while she became aware of the unmistakable pungent aroma of cooking curry wafting up from the flat downstairs. She had heard no noise from the people in the flat below but, clearly, the building was not that well sealed.

The smell of curry was making her hungry. She opened a bottle of Spanish red wine and a tin of baked beans and unpeeled a packet of microwave lasagne. This she ate while curled up on the couch, wrapped in a blanket, watching television: *East Enders*, a bizarre game show called *The Button*, a sitcom *Into Thin Air*, a soap opera completely in Gaelic, and *Reporting Scotland*, until she was too tired to avoid going to bed any longer. She filled the hot water bottle with boiling water, put on her thermals and woolly socks and threw an extra blanket on the bed.

Chapter 15

At nine o'clock the next morning, Morgan Skyped Don and Lou without the video.

'Happy Anzac Day.'

'Hello, darling!' Don said. 'We're so glad to hear from you. Yes, we got up very early this morning to attend the dawn service, as we always do. I'm grateful I'm still fit enough to join in the march as well. We're tired now though.'

'He looked splendid in his uniform and his medals,' Lou said. 'I was very proud. And how are you getting on, dear? Tell us all about it.'

She told them about her comfortable and indulgent flight, staying with Iain, Ali and Kirsty, buying a car, and setting herself up in a flat.

'My goodness, all that in a week! You have been busy. But, dear, that must have been awfully expensive. Do you need some more money? We can deposit some for you tomorrow ...'

'Oh, no Don, that's kind, but I'm okay thank you, honestly. Iain worked out it was cheaper to buy a little car than to hire one, and the flat is affordable. I don't have many expenses. But I really appreciate the offer, and I promise to call you if I get stuck.'

She gave Don and Lou her address and her new mobile phone number. She told them her plans to visit the Carnegie library and to explore Scotland as much as she could. But she didn't elaborate on what she intended to look for in the library, and she didn't mention the two photos she'd found of her parents. Don and Lou had been so good to her, she didn't want to hurt them by telling them her hankering to know about her real parents.

'Oh, Morgan, before I forget,' Don said, 'Anton called me wondering what to do with your things. I told him he could store them in our shed for as long as you want.'

'Thank you, Don, that would be great. I suppose I should have thought about that before, but I didn't know he'd be in such a hurry to move my stuff out. It's kind of you to store it for me.'

Her stomach churned, the way it did every time Anton was mentioned. It was true though; she hadn't given her belongings much thought. But there was plenty of room under the house; a few boxes were hardly going to be in his way. She slightly resented that he had evidently moved on so quickly.

She looked at her laptop screen. She had promised to Skype him to let him know how she was getting on. She closed the lid. Fuck him.

She noticed her gold wedding ring. She twirled it around her finger and eased it off, leaving a white indent. She studied the ring for some minutes, turning it over and over, remembering when they had bought it, how they had it specially designed and made. The marriage had obviously meant more to her than it did to him.

Something Kirsty had said came back to her — how keeping that secret for so long must have tormented him. Well, maybe it had tormented him. It didn't excuse the fact he had wasted five years of her life. She put the ring into a compartment in her wet pack along with the few pairs of earrings she had brought with her.

The heavy rain had abated so now was the time to drive to the supermarket to buy an electric blanket. This proved more difficult than she expected. The bed in her flat was what she would have described as queen size but apparently here it was called king size. Plus there were none available in any of the stores so she had to order one online to have it delivered the next day. Probably, because it was coming into summer, no one needed electric blankets. Except her.

Back in her flat, she attempted to order one online but came up against the unfamiliar postcode system. It was bafflingly specific with six digits and letters instead of the simple four digits she was used to, and each street seemed to have its own unique postcode. If you didn't know your exact postcode you couldn't order anything online. She resigned herself to another night cosying up to a hot water bottle.

She stared out of her living room window at the heavy, grey day, at the rows of depressing buildings just like hers, dirty beige with brown tiled roofs. Traffic sprayed up water on the wet road. People trudged along, heads down, raincoat collars turned up against the drizzle. It was not the view of Scotland she had imagined.

The aroma of curry again wafted up from the downstairs flat. She sat on her plastic couch listening to the sound of helicopters whirring overhead, and for the first time since she had arrived in Scotland, she cried.

Just as she was contemplating putting on her pyjamas and curling up in a blanket in front of the television again, she heard a knock at the door. Kirsty.

'G'day mate!' she yelled as she peeled off her waterproof jacket. 'Geez, you're rugged up like you're going to the Arctic.'

'I know. I'm frozen.'

'You don't look so good. Have you been crying?'

'Mm. Just a bit. I'm still getting used to being on my own. And things are so different here. Don't worry, I'm being a big baby. But I'm really glad to see you. How did you get here by the way?'

'I cycled. I came the back way past the hospital — took me less than ten minutes. I only got a wee bit wet.' Kirsty looked around the flat. 'Did you find out who left you the flowers?'

'Landlord, I guess. There's no name on the card.'

Kirsty sniffed, 'Are you cooking curry?'

'Not me. It's the people downstairs. Second night in a row.'

'Pooh-ee. Anyway, I thought why don't we go to the local pub for dinner and a few drinks. It's too dreich to walk though, so we'd have to drive.'

'Well, no, I'm not really … oh, all right, why not? Let's do it. Just give me a sec to put something else on.'

The pub was warm and pleasant, and a live band played background music. The wine, the atmosphere, the food and Kirsty's cheerful chatter began to lift her spirits.

'I'm goin' into the big town on Friday if you'd like to come,' Kirsty said. 'I can show you where the library is.'

'Yes, I would, thank you, sounds great. I'm keen to start exploring and researching.'

'And I can't wait to show you round the local sites,' Kirsty said. 'You have to see the castle and the Heads of Ayr.'

Morgan laughed out loud. 'Eh? Heads of …? Oh I see — Ayr. Yes of course. Funny name.'

'You think that's funny?' Kirsty said. 'Well, you know, there's a place right at the end of Lewis called the Butt of Lewis.'

'No way!'

'Yes, true, and wait till you see the Cock of Arran — it's a must-see.'

Morgan choked on her drink. 'You're shittin' me.'

'No shit. Just don't tell your ex-husband, I reckon.'

She cried tears for the second time that day, except these were tears of laughter.

'I'm getting the bill,' Kirsty said. 'It's my treat tonight, no arguing.' She brought out the little flat toad purse Morgan had given her.

Chapter 16

Morgan remade the bed with the new, essential electric blanket she had collected from the supermarket. Something about talking to Don yesterday, on Anzac Day, had made her miss Australia, just a little. It had only rated a mention in passing on the news here. Australia was literally a world away.

Rather than reheating another frozen meal she had decided to make an effort to actually cook something. She bought ingredients to make spaghetti Bolognese: a selection of vegetables, mushrooms, tinned tomatoes and a jar of spaghetti sauce. No point reinventing the wheel. And garlic — five cloves. That should disguise the smell of curry. If you can't beat 'em, join 'em. With the added bonus it was unlikely she would be bothered by vampires.

When the Bolognese sauce was ready, she dropped a handful of spaghetti into boiling water. A loud knock at the door made her jump. Kirsty again.

She was surprised to see, not Kirsty, but a tall man holding a bunch of flowers. She smiled and brushed the hair away from her face. He was handsome, in his early forties, with a boyish face, grey-green eyes and light, sandy-coloured hair swept over to one side. For a second she thought he looked familiar. But then she realised he probably had the wrong flat.

'Hello, Morgan, is it?'

He knew her name.

'Yes, that's right.'

He thrust out a hand with professionally manicured fingernails to grasp hers in a surprisingly gentle handshake.

'Ross McFarsund. Pleased to meet you. I'm sorry to arrive without warning — I thought you might need your flowers replenished by now.' He said 'floo-ers'. His soft lilting accent was gorgeous. In fact he was gorgeous.

'Really? Okay, thank you. Was it you who left me the lovely flowers?'

'Oh, I'm so sorry. Aye, I should have said. I'm the landlord here. I like to welcome the new residents, try to make them feel at home. Have you settled in all right then?'

'Yes, it's very comfortable, thank you. Would you like to come in?'

'Och, no, I don't want to disturb you. You'll be in the middle of making your dinner.' He came in anyway.

'No, you're not disturbing me at all. The spaghetti is just cooking.'

'Smells delicious. Is it spaghetti Bolognese?'

'Yes, vegetarian, one of the few things I can cook quite well. With the help of Paul Newman of course,' she said, holding up the jar.

'Aye, well, can't go wrong wi' that. At first I thought it was a curry you were making.'

She smiled. 'Ah, no, that is someone downstairs, I think. They seem to like their curry. Every night. So I thought I'd make something to disguise the pong.'

Ross looked alarmed. 'Oh, my. That's no' good. Let me have a wee word with them.'

'It's okay. I don't want to upset them at all.'

'That'll not be a bother. Maybe they're just not using their extraction fan. I'll pop in and see them.'

'Thank you, but I really don't want to offend them.'

'No bother at all. I'm their landlord too, ye see. Actually, of all the flats in this building.'

'You own the building?'

'Aye, I do. It's one of my investment properties.' He caught a glimpse of himself in the mirror over the mantelpiece and ran a hand through his hair.

'Ah. I see.' *One of?* Eek. She didn't have another vase for the flowers so she put them in the Bolognese jar. She drained the cooked spaghetti into a colander.

'So, Ross, I'm just about to serve this up. Would you like to stay for dinner, such as it is?'

'Are you sure, now? I wouldn't like to impose.'

'Absolutely. One gets tired of dining by oneself.'

'Aye, okay then, thanks very much. I'd love to.'

She placed a shaker of parmesan cheese on the tiny round dining table and ladled out two generous serves of spaghetti. He seemed to enjoy the meal. He certainly ate it heartily. It was lucky he had appeared tonight; any other night he would have been offered a frozen microwave pie.

'So Morgan, Andrew tells me you're from Australia.'

'Andrew? Oh, the real estate agent. Yes that's right, at least that's where I've been living most of my life.'

'I do like the Australian accent. Many don't, but I do.'

'I didn't know I sounded all that Australian. I often get mistaken for a Kiwi.'

'Mm. You definitely sound Australian. What do you mean *Kiwi*? A New Zealander?'

'Yes, they have a slightly different accent.'

'Do they? I never noticed any difference in the accent. It all sounds Australian to me.'

After a couple of glasses of wine, she began to relax and enjoy his company. She discovered he was a surgeon from Edinburgh and he often came down to Ayr to work. He kept a townhouse there not far from the hospital.

'Would you like another glass of wine?' she asked.

'Thank you, aye, I will. I don't usually drink if I'm working the next day but I'm not down here for work this time. Sometimes I come to Ayr just to get away from the big smoke, the noise and the people. I can breathe down here.'

She was dying to ask if he was married or attached but she didn't want to seem forward. He solved that problem for her.

'And seeing I'm happily single, I can come and go as I please. What about you? Are you on your own here in bonnie Scotland?'

'Well, yes, I don't know if Andrew told you anything. Probably not. Privacy and all that, but, yes, I'm just out of a pretty unhappy marriage.' Even now, when she mentioned her marriage, she felt her stomach begin to churn. Or maybe that was the Bolognese.

'So I've come on my own. It's a bit of an adventure, I suppose, to get away from things, see where I was born. I was born here actually — South Ayrshire Hospital. And I was hoping to find out about my real mother and father. They died in an accident somewhere here when I was four.'

'Oh, aye, I see. That is sad. It's quite a crusade you've taken on. And you've landed here in my wee flat. I'm pleased about that, I must say.'

She smiled at him. He was so good-looking she thought he wouldn't be single for long, that was for sure.

'How are you planning to find out about your parents? Do you have any photos of them?'

'I thought I'd search in the Carnegie Library and see if there are any old newspapers on microfilm. It's a start anyway.'

She handed him the photo of her parents standing in front of their car. No point showing him the other one with her mother's face crossed out.

'This is them, Isla and Jack. It's precious to me. It's the best one I have.'

He studied the photo. 'She was beautiful, your mother. You take after her.'

She felt her cheeks reddening. 'Thank you, but I don't really.'

He continued to look at the photo. 'New BMW.' He tapped his finger on her father and tilted his head to the side. His smile widened.

'*Nirvana — Nevermind.* I remember that album so well. It was the anthem to my life as a youth. I would've been sixteen when it came out in 1991 and I played it so loud I damaged my speakers. Drove my parents crazy, until they bought me headphones.'

The blood had drained from Morgan's face. She took back the photo but couldn't stop her hand from trembling. '1991 you say?'

'Aye, late 1991. I'll never forget it. It was like I hadn't grasped what my life was about until I heard that album. The raw angst of the music … it kind of represented all the emotions I couldn't express. Sixteen-year-old boys can have such a rage against the world. And I've got the tinnitus to prove it. Are you all right, Morgan?'

'Yes, thank you, just suddenly a bit tired.' She stood up, holding on to the back of the chair. 'Thank you for coming to see me, Ross, and thank you for the beautiful flowers.' She glanced over to the jar of new flowers. The other flowers, on the sideboard, were still perfectly fresh.

He stood up also. 'Thanks very much for the meal. You're a good cook. I'll just nip in and check if the downstairs neighbour's fan is working on my way out.'

She managed to keep her head together as she saw him to the door. As soon as he had gone, she grabbed up the second photo, the one with her mother holding her as a small baby and stared at it, blood pounding in her temples. If that's 1991, then that baby was not her. It couldn't be. She was three in 1991.

Chapter 17

'Why didn't you tell me, Don? Why did you not tell me my mother had another baby?'

Morgan had waited until midnight to Skype Don and Lou. At that time it was nine am in Australia. She couldn't wait until tomorrow; she knew she wouldn't be able to sleep until she had asked Don the question.

'I'm so sorry, Morgan. I really am.'

She could hear Lou beginning to cry in the background.

'We did know your mother had another baby. A baby boy — Simon. We wanted to tell you many times but you'd been through so much and you were so young. It was just never the right time. And you didn't seem to remember him at all, except sometimes in dreams. Then we thought if we told you, it was never going to help anything, it would just upset you more.'

'We're very sorry, darling,' Lou said. 'I knew we should have told you earlier, but we were anxious to give you a perfect childhood, and we didn't want you to go through any more hurt. You were so fragile. Poor little Simon. He died so young.'

Morgan's eyes blurred. 'Well, what happened to him then?'

'It was a cot death, dear,' Don said. 'He was only a few months old. We didn't even know Isla had another baby until we went over to Scotland to get you and bring you back here. We'd been in Australia for about … how long, Louie?'

'Well, I suppose it would have been thirteen years. Yes, since 1978 it was. Once we moved to Australia, we mostly lost touch with Isla. Until your uncle Mal called and asked us if we could take you after the tragedy.'

'That's right,' Don said. 'It was Malcolm who told us then that Isla had another baby who died. Of course we should have told you, I nearly did. It was my mistake; I should have thought. You were bound to find out in Ayr, you'd only have to visit the cemetery.'

'It was all so dreadful, love. We just wanted to shield you. We honestly didn't see how you knowing about Simon was going to help you. We're so very sorry, darling.' She could hear the tears in Lou's voice.

'Well, it did upset me,' she said. 'I think I would have liked to know earlier, but like you said, I guess it wouldn't really have helped. So is there anything else I should know before I go looking in the library?'

'No, dear, that is all,' Don said. 'You already know you stayed a while with your uncle Mal and auntie Jane after your parents' accident. But then soon Jane became too ill to look after you. Mal asked us to take you before she died. There was nothing anyone could do to save her life, and he thought you'd seen enough death for someone so young. It broke his heart, so it did. But how did you find out about Simon?'

'Ali had some old photos from 1991. There was one with Isla and Jack holding a baby. I thought it was me but the year was wrong. I would have been three then.'

'Ah. Did you find any photos of yourself as a baby?'

'A few, at around two years old I think, but none where I was with my parents. That was the only photo Ali had of them. So, why do you think I wasn't in the photo too?'

'You were probably staying with Mal and Jane,' Don said. 'You had your own room in their house. Jane loved you so much; she would have been happy for you to live with them. Maybe she was looking after you to make it easier for your mother with the new baby and all. I'm just guessing though.'

'Darling, why don't you Skype us back later and we'll talk more if you like,' Lou said. 'Any time. We are just on our way out now — Don has an appointment, but call us any time, all right love?'

'Yes, of course. Thank you. I will.'

'Are you very cross with us, darling?'

'No, Don.' How could she ever be cross with these beautiful people? 'I'm not cross. It's a shock, that's all. And sad as well. But I know now, so I can deal with that. Please don't feel bad, it's fine, really. I know you were only thinking of me, and I understand that. We'll talk later. Love you.'

It was close to one in the morning but her head was buzzing. Who else knew? Ali must have. That would explain her guarded reaction to seeing the photos of Isla and Jack. She must have known that baby wasn't her. She would tell Ali she already knew about Simon, so she wouldn't think it was some sort of dark secret.

+ + + +

Kirsty knocked on her door bright and early, before she had finished breakfast.

'Good morning, Cuzzie!' Kirsty was wearing a soft, pale blue cashmere roll-neck jumper and black leggings that flattered her slim figure.

'You look gorgeous,' Morgan said, giving her a hug. 'But pooh! You smell like fish.'

Kirsty laughed, 'Kippers. We had smoked kippers for breakfast. Yum, you should try them, delicious. And anyway, pooh yourself, you smell like garlic.'

'I excelled myself. I made spaghetti Bolognese with loads of garlic. It was meant to last for two nights but I had a visitor — my landlord.'

'The landlord? What's he like? I see you have more flowers. And, what? He stayed for dinner?'

'That's right. He's pretty hot actually, blond, greyish green eyes. He's a surgeon from Edinburgh. His name's Ross. He's single. And he owns this whole building.'

'Are you kidding? You just made that up.'

'No, it's dead set true! He came round to see if I'd settled in okay. Don't worry, he's highly unlikely to be interested in me. But, that's not the weirdest thing. I showed him the photo of my parents, because he asked, and he recognised the *Nirvana* album cover on my father's sweatshirt. He said it was from 1991. Which means the baby my mother was holding in the other photo wasn't me. She'd had another baby in 1991, Simon, and no one wanted to tell me.

'I asked Don and Lou about it late last night and they said it was true, and how sorry they were, but they hadn't told me because they didn't want to upset me.'

'Jesus. That's a bit … shit. What happened to the baby?'

'He died of cot death, only a few months old.'

'God, that's sad. Poor wee thing. You don't remember him at all?'

'No, not at all. But sometimes, you know, I see him in dreams — a baby boy — always trying to tell me something. I never knew who he was. Now I know.'

'Wow. Well, I should leave you in peace; you've had a shock. I did come over to ask if you wanted to go into the town with us, Ma and me. It's the anniversary of my Dad's death today, April twenty-seventh, and we always visit the cemetery. This year will be twenty years since he died. But you probably don't feel like company today.'

'Oh, Kirsty, I'm so sorry. Twenty years today. Can you remember anything about him?'

'Not much. Same as you, only in dreams. But it's always like he's not dead in the dream. I have the strong feeling he's not dead, but then I wake up and know that he is.'

'Funny things, dreams. And I would be glad to come with you to the cemetery, I was hoping to go there soon anyway.'

'Ma and I always have lunch and go shopping after we visit Pa, make a day of it.'

'Sounds great. I'll probably give the shopping a miss though. I have to go on a serious money diet. I might go to the library after lunch instead and we could meet up later.'

'Sure thing. I've got the Landy with me, so if you want to get ready, I'll wait, and then we'll go and pick up Ma.'

Morgan threw on jeans, a grey sweatshirt and a warm jacket. Then she grabbed Ross's new flowers and wrapped them in a paper bag.

'For your Dad's grave,' she said. She also plucked three red carnations from the other vase.

Chapter 18

organ took the opportunity to look around while Kirsty drove. They crossed the river into the town of Ayr. It was attractive and vibrant, a shopper's paradise, with solid sandstone buildings and pretty flower baskets hanging off what she assumed to be old gas lamp posts. History everywhere she looked.

They turned into Holmston Road and parked outside the cemetery. Walking through the impressive, white stone entrance archway she immediately sensed an atmosphere of reverence, a deep, solemn peace.

'I've brought these flowers to put on Malcolm's grave, and these other three carnations,' she said. 'One for each of my parents, and one for Simon, my brother.'

'Ah, that's lovely,' Ali said. 'So you do know about him then. I wasn't sure if you knew or not. Mal did mention his sister had two children, and that the wee boy died. Awful sad. Where did you get the flowers from?'

'She's got a secret admirer,' Kirsty said. 'Keeps giving her flowers.'

'Not true, don't listen to her, Ali. He's not an admirer, he's just a thoughtful landlord. His name's Ross. Ross McFarsund.'

'And he's gorgeous. And rich.'

'Kirsty!'

In the cemetery she saw headstones of all shapes and sizes, some modest, some elaborate topped with angel statues, some ancient and weathered. Ali and Kirsty knew exactly where Mal's grave was, in a newer section. She placed her flowers on Mal's grave and left Ali and Kirsty while she searched for her parents' graves. She had no trouble finding them, only a short distance away.

But she was unprepared for the shock when she came across two dark pink granite headstones with chiselled lettering:

In loving memory of Jack Dee,
died 14th December 1991, aged 41,
loved husband of Isla, father of Morgan
and Simon, brother of Minerva.
In loving memory of Isla Dee, née Murray,
died 14th December 1991, aged 31,
loved wife of Jack, loving mother of Morgan
and Simon, adored sister of Malcolm.

Next to them lay a smaller grave with a grey granite headstone:

*In loving memory of Simon Dee, died 31st
October 1991, aged four months
and three weeks. Taken too soon.*

She stood frozen to the spot, staring at the graves, aware of the blood pulsating through her body. The realisation overwhelmed her — under this earth were her family. All her family. Her tears flowed freely as she placed a carnation on each grave.

Some time later, she drew herself away from the headstones. Next to her mother's grave lay the four graves of her grandparents — Jack's parents, Alasdair and Christine, and Isla's parents, Graham and Beth. Graham must have been the grandfather Don said had saved his life in the war. They were all buried together. Clearly, her ancestors had all lived and died in this Ayrshire area.

Would she be buried here too? Or in Australia? She had given it no thought. Australia was second nature to her; here she felt like an alien. That might change in time. If she had not been sent to Australia at such a young age, her life would have been different. Everything would have been different.

She photographed each of the headstones with her phone, then walked back to Ali and Kirsty who were standing together, their arms around each other.

'You found them, Morgan?'

'Yes, thank you, Ali. Beautiful headstones.'

'Aye, that will be Malcolm who arranged for those. Bless him. Your aunt Jane is just here too,' Ali said, pointing to the left of Malcolm's grave.

'Oh, my God, my whole family is here.' She took an orange rose from Malcolm's bouquet and placed it on Jane's grave.

In loving memory of Jane Murray,
née Selkirk, died 8th August 1992, aged 35,
beloved wife of Malcolm.
Rest in Peace my darling.

'She was lovely, your aunt Jane,' Ali said. 'She had her moods, but then she was so very sick. Terrible thing the cancer; you watch someone waste away to skin and bone before your eyes. And you never forget the smell — sweet, yeasty, something like fermented mushrooms. Not everyone can smell it.'

Morgan recognised that smell; she had sensed it fleetingly when she saw the photo of Jane and Malcolm for the first time.

'Poor Janie. And poor Mal,' Morgan said. 'He must have suffered a rough couple of years. Losing his nephew, sister, brother-in-law and then his wife in little more than a year would have been almost unbearable.'

'Aye, it was wretched for him, right enough.'

'It was good you were there for him.'

'Well, the one happy thing to come of it was that it brought us together. And then we had this precious one,' Ali said, stroking Kirsty's hair. 'We were together for only five more years. I still miss him.'

Morgan, Ali and Kirsty left the cemetery in silence. Kirsty easily negotiated the short drive into the town centre, pointing out the Wallace Tower to Morgan on the way. 'He was born in Ayrshire, you know. William Wallace. That's his statue. And there's the Town Hall — a good landmark if you ever get lost wandering around.'

Kirsty manoeuvred the big Land Cruiser into a car park on the road. 'Here's our favourite wee coffee shop.'

Inside, the café was warm and welcoming with dark timber walls and comfortable, green tartan padded seats. They chose a cosy booth in a corner. 'We always have lunch here after visiting the cemetery,' Kirsty said. 'Are you sure you won't come shopping with us?'

'I'd like to, but another time. I'm keen to explore the library archives, especially now after visiting the graves. Do you know, it struck me today you are my only actual living relative? Apart from Minerva.'

'*Minerva*? What kind of … I mean who's *Minerva*?'

'My father's sister, apparently. Her name was on his headstone. I didn't know I have, or had, another aunt. She may not even be alive. I feel like I have the smallest family in the world.'

'You have us, dear,' Ali said.

When the toasted sandwiches arrived Morgan was delighted to see a side of chips served in a delicate china teacup. Cute as. After lunch they stepped out of the café into the sunshine. Kirsty pointed up the road. 'The library is just over the bridge on the right, it's an easy couple of minutes' walk. We're going down this way to the shops. So how about I pick you up outside the library, say, what, about four o'clock?'

'Sounds good, see you then. Happy shopping,' she said, and turned towards the bridge.

Chapter 19

The solid stone bridge railing felt warm under her hand. She stood for a few moments gazing out to the mouth of the blue, sparkling River Ayr. She could see right out to the Firth of Clyde and a tiny blue island in the distance. It was windy here, always so windy. She turned to look at the river on the other side of the bridge and was surprised to see heavy dark clouds forming. She checked her watch. Just under three hours to spend in the library.

She walked up the few steps of the impressive, red sandstone building, and up again to the first floor past a magnificent stained-glass window. She read the text in the top panel: *Let there be light.* How appropriate for a library, full of ancient books, knowledge and secrets waiting to be discovered. She found her way to the Local History section and asked one of the librarians, who looked at least eighty, where to start.

He introduced himself as Stewart. He was softly spoken, incredibly thin, and walked with a noticeable stoop. She was surprised to see that, despite having only wispy strands of white hair covering his head, a tuft of long hair tied into a ponytail hung at the back.

The library housed a mind-boggling amount of information but with Stewart's help, she soon had the *Ayrshire Post* newspaper archive for 1991 in front of her on microfilm. She already knew the date from the headstones, and before long she found what she was looking for:

Cot death tragedy. On the evening of October 31, a four-month-old baby, Simon Dee, from Ayr, was pronounced dead on presentation by his mother, Isla Dee, at the South Ayrshire Hospital. Nurse McFeeter, the duty nurse, expressed regret at the passing of the child. "It is a terrible tragedy for the family. We did everything we could but the baby had stopped breathing and sadly could not be revived."

Sudden infant death syndrome, previously called cot death, has claimed the lives of one in every 500 babies in the UK in the last decade. New research into this infant mortality problem has shown that, along with parental smoking, one of the causes involves the sleeping position of the baby. Parents are now being advised to lay their babies on their backs for sleeping. It is hoped that better public education might help avoid more tragedies such as this.

She printed a copy of the article and searched later papers in the year for any mention of her parents' accident. She found plenty of articles about the negotiations for the sale of the Prestwick airport, the future of which had seemed to be uncertain. Then she found the article:

Double drowning tragedy in Ayr. Local couple, Jack and Isla Dee were tragically killed when their car plunged off the B742 into the River Ayr late last Saturday night. Emergency Services were called by Mr McTavish, from nearby Annbank. "I was on my way home from the bowls club when this car came out of nowhere, swerving from side to side, going at a tremendous speed. He almost hit me before he crashed straight into the bridge and flipped over into the river. I didn't hear any tyres squealing either. I couldn't get anywhere near them because the river was flooded and full of ice. It was an awful thing to witness," McTavish said.

The bodies were retrieved by the emergency crew and Mr and Mrs Dee were pronounced dead at the scene. Their BMW sedan was later winched out of the river. An emergency services spokesperson said, "We don't like to see this kind of accident, especially at Christmas time. We strongly advise people to take it easy on the roads when they are icy."

This tragedy for the Dee family occurred only five weeks after the death of their infant son, Simon. This death was ruled as an unfortunate Sudden Infant Death Syndrome incident which saw Mrs Dee subsequently cleared of charges.

Mr and Mrs Dee are survived by a four-year-old daughter who is being cared for by relatives.

She read the article again. *Charges? What charges?* She printed a copy and began packing up to leave.

Stewart appeared at her side. 'I'll pack that all away for you. Did you find what you were looking for Miss?'

'Yes, thank you Stewart. I found a couple of interesting articles here.' She showed him one she'd printed.

'Oh, you're interested in that one, are you? Yes, a terrible tragedy. I remember it well. And so close on losing their baby too. So sad. She didn't do it, of course. I never believed she did.'

'Did what?'

'Well, in the early nineties there were an unusually high number of what they called cot deaths, and people became suspicious some of the deaths were really infanticide. That is what the gossip said about this. She was a local clairvoyant, you see, and the rumours accused her of practising the witchcraft, sacrificing her child intentionally because it was Halloween. Absolute nonsense, of course, very cruel. She was a perfectly lovely woman. But people love a scandal. Why would you be interested in this now?'

Morgan couldn't speak. She pointed to the article: 'survived by a four-year-old daughter.'

Stewart drew in his breath sharply. 'Oh, my! Oh no! I am so sorry. Would that be you then, the daughter? Isla's daughter? Oh my goodness, please forgive me. I thought, well, I thought you were an Australian.'

The atmosphere had become warm and stuffy; she started to feel dizzy. 'I'm sorry, do you have any water please?'

Stewart shuffled into a small lunchroom and returned with a plastic tumbler of water. 'Are you all right, Miss?'

She drank the water and took a deep breath. 'Thank you. Yes, I'm fine. Really. Just a bit of a shock. How could people be so mean?'

'Aye, indeed. There are plenty of superstitious people around here, and some have spiteful tongues.'

She picked up the article. 'Yes, I am the daughter mentioned here. I was sent to Australia to live with my godparents after my aunt became too ill to look after me. I came back over recently because I wanted to find out about my real parents, how they died.'

'Yes I see. Of course. I do remember your parents' accident. I believe it was never investigated as anything other an accident, so there may not be much information available about it. But I remember they did construct a guard rail on that bridge shortly after it happened.'

'Well I wish you the best of luck, and if you need any help digging up more information, I would be only too pleased to assist you. I'm just a volunteer here, but I come to the library to lend a hand most days. Local history is my specialty, you might say. We're open every day, except Sunday. May I ask your name?'

'Thank you, Stewart. It's Morgan. Morgan Shelford, but my maiden name was Dee.'

'Ah, Morgan, yes. I do remember that now. And Morgan, you mustn't be upset by the gossip. Your mother was not a murderer.'

'Thank you, Stewart.' She never thought she was.

She left a generous donation in the box at the entrance. She was becoming used to tipping and leaving donations. She crossed the road to wait for Kirsty and Ali.

Although her time in the library seemed to pass quickly, almost three hours had elapsed, and the weather had changed.

The wind had whipped up; gusts of squally rain blew leaves and litter in circles. The water in the river had turned black. She shivered, tucked in her scarf and zipped up her jacket.

111

Chapter 20

She was glad to climb into the back of the warm Land Cruiser, although she didn't have much room — the back seat was piled high with shopping bags.

'It looks like you two have had a productive afternoon.'

'Oh, aye, we most certainly have,' Kirsty said. 'And there's a present for you too.'

Ali turned around from the passenger seat, 'And how did you get on, love? Did you find anything interesting?'

'Yes, I did. I met a really helpful librarian. He was ancient and looked like he belonged in the Rocky Horror Picture Show but he knew where to find what I was looking for. I found articles about Simon's death and my parents' accident. Some local people apparently believed my mother murdered her own baby as a Halloween sacrifice. Can you believe that?'

'Jesus Christ, how stupid can you get!' Kirsty said. 'Come back to ours and have a cuppa before I take you home?'

In a few minutes they arrived in the driveway of Ali's russet sandstone house. To avoid getting drenched by the relentless rain they entered through the back-patio door. Morgan helped carry in the numerous shopping bags, some from exclusive boutiques. Kirsty extracted dresses, tops, leggings, jeans, shoes and bags. She handed Morgan a parcel. 'Here you go, this is for you.'

She unwrapped an aquamarine, longline cashmere jumper. 'This is gorgeous, Kirsty, thank you. I'll pay you for it though. It must have been expensive.'

'No, you will not. It's a present, and anyway it wasn't expensive at all. It was in the bin for leftovers from the winter styles. The shops all have the summer fashions in now. But I figured this weather is probably like your winter so I thought you might be glad of it.'

'It's beautiful, I love it. Thank you, but you didn't need to buy me anything.'

'Not me, actually. Ma paid for everything. She's always buying me things. She says money is for enjoying now; you cannot take it with you. And if it makes her happy, I'm not going to complain, am I? So what did you find out at the library? Did you get any printouts?'

Morgan unfolded the two articles and handed them to Kirsty.

'Shit, Morgan, that is really sad. First your wee brother and then your parents. It sounds like … I mean … no brakes … why would he be speeding, and out of control? You don't think your dad drove into the river deliberately, do you? Sorry, no, I shouldn't have said that. I'm sure it would've been an accident. Those icy roads can be so deceptive. Maybe he had a heart attack or something.' Kirsty's cheeks flushed pink.

'How would anyone know?' Morgan said. 'It doesn't bear thinking about. I haven't had time to process it all yet. The old guy at the library said it was only ever investigated as an accident, nothing more sinister, so there won't be much information about it. But apparently a guard rail went up afterwards.'

'I wonder whereabouts on the river that would have been,' Kirsty said. 'Your old bloke could probably show us on a map. And *charges*. What does that mean? Was your mother really accused of killing her own baby? I can't believe any of that. It's ghastly.'

Ali came in carrying a tray of tea and homemade chocolate slice.

'Ma, look at these articles Morgan got from the library.'

Ali read the articles. 'What a wretched tragedy. You poor thing, having to find out like this. What were you saying in the car about the gossip, love?'

She repeated what Stewart had told her.

'That's interesting. I mean it's awful, but it makes me wonder if that's what Jane thought too.'

'*Jane?* Really … why?'

'Well, remember I told you I was caring for Jane during the last two months of her life. It was not a good time … for anyone. She was in a lot of pain, and most of the time she was on powerful drugs, opioids. She often slipped in and out of delirium. And she would ramble, blether in gibberish sometimes, and blurt out things I mostly ignored. I thought it was the drugs affecting her moods; she did have some manic moods.'

'What did she say? Can you remember?'

'Well, it was twenty-six years ago, but I do remember Jane talked about you quite a lot; she loved you dearly. She desperately wanted children herself but could never have any, and I think she was angry at the unfairness of it all, and maybe jealous. I suspect it was Jane who crossed out that photo of your mother you found. In fact, it could only have been Jane. It makes sense to me now, because, if she had been aware of the rumours, it's possible she also blamed Isla for wee Simon's death.'

'Wow. My poor mother. Fancy being accused of that. It's hard to believe people can be so gullible, and hateful.'

'Aye, you like to think we've moved on from the dark ages but, if you scratch the surface, some of those old superstitions are still deeply ingrained. Most people wouldn't have any idea why they believe what they do. But don't judge her too harshly, pet. You wouldn't have known but she would probably never have been allowed to adopt you. Before the cancer took hold, she had been taking medication for what is called borderline schizophrenia, possibly brought on by smoking too much marijuana when she was young. I know they used to smoke a lot of pot. And on top of that, the drugs she was taking for the cancer would have stoned an elephant.'

'God, poor Janie.'

'What do you think you'll do now, love?'

'Well, I'm not sure. I'd like to understand what happened, I suppose, so I can move on. Closure, I guess. But I don't want to spend all my time stewing over it. I want to enjoy my time here and start exploring more of Scotland. Oh, and thank you for this gorgeous jumper. It's absolutely lovely. It will be getting lots of use, for sure.'

'Maybe when you go out with your new boyfriend,' Kirsty said.

She tutted. 'Landlord.'

'What is his name again?' Ali asked.

'Ross McFarsund.'

'Sounds Scandinavian. Is it?'

'I don't know. He is tall and blond.'

'Unusual. I can't help feeling I recognise his name from somewhere. Don't know where. It will come to me.'

Back in her flat, she was pleasantly surprised to notice she couldn't smell curry. Maybe Ross had come through with the extractor fan like he promised. She had refused Ali's offer of dinner, having really just wanted to be alone with her own thoughts.

She spread out the two articles and the photos of her parents and studied them. This was her whole family, all gone, and she knew hardly anything about them. She searched the faces for any trace of resemblance to herself. Although she had blue eyes like her mother, they were not so strikingly sapphire, and she hadn't inherited her mother's beauty.

She gazed at her mother with a sad longing. Her heart ached to know her. She had been cheated of a life with the parents she had never known and would never know. Only occasionally in dreams did her mother appear, but more as a vague presence than a person. Strangely, she had never had any such sense of her father's presence.

She thought back to what Ali had said about Aunt Jane

— Janie, who had loved her and cared for her for six months until she was too sick to carry on. How was it possible she believed something as ludicrous as her own sister-in-law having murdered her four-month-old baby because it was Halloween?

She didn't want to believe her aunt Janie was capable of anything so malicious. But, if she had actually been mentally ill, as Ali suggested, she may not have been in control of her emotions or her actions; delusional enough to believe anything. And how well can we ever really know another person, to say for certain what they would, or would not be capable of? She was fully aware a person could conceal aspects of their true character, even from someone they had lived with for five years.

But it didn't explain the eager willingness of the public to blame her mother for Simon's death. She recalled what she'd read about that abominable miscarriage of justice, the Lindy Chamberlain case, where the public and the media had ghoulishly seized on it as a chance for a witch hunt. There had been suggestions of ritual child sacrifice as part of the family's cultish religious beliefs. They were Seventh Day Adventists.

Is that what her mother had been — the victim of a witch hunt because she'd been a spiritualist, accused of meddling with the occult? Incredible to think, in this modern day, ignorance and superstition still drove people to fear anything other than the mainstream.

The emotion of the day had wearied her; she was having trouble staying awake. She stared at the photo of her father, mother, and baby Simon, taken outside a white bungalow.

She looked more closely at the background. It looked like many other suburban Scottish streets she'd seen — narrow roads lined with small brick and stone houses with chimneys, but she noticed for the first time the street that crossed behind them, and what appeared to be a street sign attached to a stone wall. She had nothing to magnify it with so she photographed it with her phone and tried to increase the size, but it was too pixelated to read.

If it was possible to find their house, the one she had lived in until she was four years old, maybe there was a chance of finding neighbours who might remember their family. Although she doubted anything much was to be gained by interviewing neighbours, and despite having told Ali that she wanted to move on, she couldn't ignore the insistent curiosity gnawing at her.

Chapter 21

She carried her breakfast dishes into the kitchen and glanced through the window at a silver late-model Jaguar which had pulled up in the car park outside. She watched with interest and then shock as Ross climbed out of the driver's side door.

She raced into the bathroom and hurriedly brushed her teeth, combed her hair and applied a pink lipstick. Just in case. She rinsed her breakfast things and stacked them on the draining board. A few moments later, Ross knocked at her door. Her pulse quickened but she opened the door in a leisurely manner.

'Oh, hello, Ross. How are you?'

'Never been better, thank you, Morgan.' No flowers this time.

She opened the door wider. 'Come in. Join me for a coffee? I've got this pretty snazzy, new little espresso machine.'

'Oh, aye, sounds tempting. Are you sure I'm not interrupting?'

As if. 'No, of course not. I was just about to make myself a second cup.' Even though she had just brushed her teeth.

'Well okay then, thank you, that would be grand.' Ross stood in the kitchen while she made the coffee. 'Nice and warm in here.'

'I like it warm. It's a good heater.' She didn't tell him she never turned it off. 'Talking about snazzy machines, is that your silver beastie out there in the car park?'

'Oh, aye, she's a wee beauty. Only a month old, F-type Jaguar, all leather upholstery. I'm still running her in.'

'It's gorgeous. I bet it turns some heads.'

'That it does. But nowhere much to drive properly round here, mind. I'm looking forward to taking her out onto the open roads, you know, up in the highlands.' He pronounced it 'hee-lands'. She was smitten but she just nodded and threw him a casual smile. There was no way he would be interested in her.

'I'll take you out for a spin sometime, if you'd like.'

Oh my God. 'Sounds good.' Casual.

She placed two cups of coffee on the minuscule, round dining table that barely fitted the four chairs. Ross ran a hand through his hair. 'I came round to tell you I've fixed your downstairs neighbour's extraction fan. Easy job — just a loose connection inside the unit; the fan made a hell of a din so he never used it. He's a nice young chap, Pakistani or something, I think. His English isn't great, but he seemed grateful to me for fixing it. You shouldn't have any more trouble with the pongy Punjabi.'

She laughed. 'Oh, that's great. Thank you. I love the aroma

of a good curry but only if you're going to eat it. There's something depressing about smelling someone else's dinner.'

'I couldn't agree more. And while we're on the subject, would you like to come out and have dinner with me? I was thinking I'd like to try a seafood restaurant near me, maybe Friday night? I'm not too keen on going out to eat on my own — looks a bit sad somehow.'

Really? A date? She had not expected that. She smiled at him. 'Friday night. Yes, I believe I have room on my dance card then. Sounds lovely.'

He grinned. 'Okay, grand. It's no' very posh or anything, but I hear the food's excellent and it has a great view over the river. Seven o'clock? I'll pick you up a wee while before, about ten to seven, okay?'

'Sure thing. I will look forward to it.'

She watched as Ross opened the door of his Jag and drove away. She let out a long breath. Oh my God. The sun was attempting to filter down onto the houses and trees she could see from her kitchen window. What's today? Monday. Okay, four days. She knew straight away she would wear the new jumper Kirsty, or rather Ali, had bought her.

She looked in the full-length mirror at her small breasts, wide hips, dull, mousey hair, and sighed. Was it such a good idea to go out with Ross? What on earth did a man like that see in her? He would soon find out she was ordinary, uninteresting. He was way out of her league.

Still, he had asked her, and she had accepted. It was only dinner after all; there was no need to read more into it. Perhaps she could get her hair streaked to make it less boring.

She made an appointment with a hairdresser for Thursday. Then she brushed her teeth again and collected up the photos she'd been looking at the night before. Outside, she unlocked the door of her little blue Polo. Cute little car. Not exactly in the class of a Jaguar F-Type.

She drove the few minutes to Kirsty's house. It was only a mile away. Maybe she should get a bike and cycle like Kirsty does. She should probably get more exercise. She asked Kirsty if she had a high resolution scanner, she could use to scan the photo of her parents' street.

'I do have a scanner, but it's no' a high-end one. Tell you what, though, I have a loupe.'

Morgan arranged the photos on the coffee table while she waited in the lounge. Iain sat nearby in his armchair. Ali was out grocery shopping. Kirsty rummaged upstairs and brought down the loupe in a small fabric case, then positioned it over the photo and peered through it. 'It looks like something hill Crescent.'

'What have you got there, pet?' Iain asked.

'Just a wee designer's loupe. We're trying to work out the name of a street here in the background.'

'Let me see.'

Iain squinted through the loupe at the photo. 'Oh aye, I recognise this. That would be Forthill Crescent. It runs off the Forthill Road. Down past the train station and Morrisons.'

'Ah, yes, the big supermarket. You're right. I know where that is now. I'll show you on my phone.' Kirsty quickly found the location on her app for Morgan.

'Wow, that's it. That's the house, with the bus stop outside.

I have this crazy idea to see if I can contact any neighbours who might remember back to the time we lived there. How would you feel about coming with me?'

'Of course I will. Whenever you like.'

'Today?'

'Yep. I'll be ready in a bit. What's the weather dooin'?' Kirsty checked her weather app. 'Not too bad. Sunny, a few sprinkles, twelve degrees max. I'll just get my jacket.'

In the car Kirsty said, 'Hey, while I think of it, there's a Burns festival on next weekend if you'd like to come with me. It's part of *Burns an' a' that!* He's a local hero around here you may have noticed. It's a long weekend too.'

'Ah. Maybe. What day is it on? Not Friday?'

'No, Saturday afternoon and evening. Why not Friday?'

'Well … I have a date on Friday.'

Kirsty squealed. 'What? A date! Why did you no' tell me first thing! With Ross is it?'

'Yes, it took me by surprise. He came around this morning and asked me to go out to dinner with him on Friday.'

'Oh, that's great. I thought you seemed a bit chirpy. Where are you going for dinner?'

'I don't know the name but he said it was a seafood place, and near the river I think.'

'That sounds super. Be sure to take a photo of him for me.'

'I will. I'm getting foils in my hair on Thursday and I'll wear the lovely jumper you gave me. And I'd love to come to the festival with you on Saturday.'

'Brilliant! So what's his shaggability rating?'

'Pardon?'

'You heard. Out of ten.'

'Well … Jesus, Kirsty what a question. I guess I would have to say … eleven.'

Chapter 22

With Kirsty navigating they drove down Forthill Road until they located the side street Forthill Crescent. Morgan parked and they walked the short distance to the corner. 'I'm loving these old stone walls. The stones are all different sizes but the top of the wall is level. You just don't see this kind of thing in Australia unless it is an extremely historic building. And here, you see this wonderful stonework everywhere.'

The houses, either white render or dark brown stone, were all similar in style with a bay window and a chimney. Morgan's old house, second from the corner, was a neat white one with green window frames. Kirsty photographed it with her phone. 'What's the plan? Are we just going to knock on doors and ask if they knew your family when you lived here?'

'Pretty much,' Morgan said. 'I'm feeling a bit nervous, I must admit. Just seeing the house gives me butterflies. I guess there's no point asking the people who live here now.

But I'm curious to see inside it. Do you think that would be appropriate?'

'Only one way to find out. Shall we start with the neighbours or with the house?'

'Geez, I haven't thought this through at all. Neighbours probably.'

They walked back to the immediate neighbour on the corner, a white bungalow with a well-tended garden and a cracked concrete ramp at the front. They walked up five steps leading to the dark brown door and knocked.

After a few minutes Kirsty said, 'No one home. Try the one on the other side?' But then the door opened. They were met by a stout, dark skinned woman in her seventies with short, tight curly grey hair and a wide smile.

'Hello there, can I help you?' She had a curious accent, half Scottish, half something like Jamaican.

Morgan smiled back. 'Hello. I'm sorry to bother you. My name is Morgan. This is Kirsty. I believe my family used to live in the house next door to you, in the early 1990s.' She pointed to the little white rendered house next door. 'And I was hoping to find any neighbours who might remember them. Their name was Dee — Jack and Isla Dee.'

'Oh my goodness gracious. Isla, yes, and you're Morgan! Oh my, oh my. Yes, we knew them. We've lived here for de last, well, it would be thirty-one years now. Won't you come in? I'm Mrs Paterson — Bella.'

They entered the old-fashioned cottage and saw a long, dingy central corridor with rooms either side. Bella ushered them into a sitting room with an open, unlit fireplace, and fresh flowers on the mantelpiece. She grabbed Morgan by the arms. 'Little Morgan! I can hardly believe it.' She gave her a crushing hug. She smelled of antiseptic.

'I remember you so well, poor little pet. You always called me Mizz P. You must have been only about three years old then.'

'I'm amazed,' she said. 'I really didn't expect anyone to still be living in the same place.' She glanced at Kirsty who was, for once, lost for words, and staring transfixed at something at the back of the room. Morgan turned around and with a shock saw a profoundly disabled man sitting in a wheelchair. His head lolled to one side, and a blanket covered his knees. He had a wide grin on his face.

'I wonder if you remember Evan?' Bella said. 'Look at his smile — he recognises you. He remembers you. You're about the same age. It's all coming back to me.' Bella wiped a tear from her eye. 'You and he always seemed to be able to communicate. You never even noticed he was different — the two of you used to play together so nicely when you were wee.'

Did they? She walked over to Evan and picked up his hand. He squeezed her hand with an unexpectedly firm grip. His skin was pale, almost translucent. 'Hello, Evan, it's Morgan.' Evan's head rolled to the other side and a dribble escaped from the corner of his smiling mouth. She fought back the tears. She didn't remember him at all.

She turned to Bella, her eyes glistening. 'Do you look after Evan on your own, Bella?'

'Oh, aye. I always have. I used to have the help of my dear husband, Ted, but he's passed away de last ten years.

Nowadays someone comes in to help me three days a week. They take him for a walk or help with the washing and such. It lets me get out to the shops. We bought this house specially when Evan was born. It suited us with the bus stop just outside the door, the hospital so handy, and shops just a short walk. Ted put in the ramp outside once Evan was big enough for the chair.'

Bella wheeled Evan closer to them. 'Sit yourselves down and I'll make some tea.'

Morgan and Kirsty sat on the sofa. Kirsty sat on her hands. Evan grinned and nodded. Morgan had no idea what to say to him so she said, 'You're looking well, Evan.' He laughed. 'I used to live next door to you. I've been in Australia for twenty-six years. This is the first time I've been back here in Scotland. You and I are the same age, I think. Do you remember when we used to play together when we were children?' Evan closed and opened his eyes, as if to answer yes, and made a mumbling noise.

Kirsty stood up to look more closely at the framed photographs on the sideboard as Bella came in with tea and homemade shortbread on a tray. 'He understands everything you say, you know,' Bella said. 'He's very intelligent. He loves the tellie — he laughs at it all the time. Especially at rude things, the ruder the better.'

'Like my cousin Kirsty here.'

Kirsty tutted, then spoke for the first time, 'We didn't think you were home, Bella. Yours was the first house we tried. We thought we'd have to knock on many more doors before we found someone who might remember Morgan's family. We were hoping to maybe see inside her old house.'

'Well dat house is exactly the same as this one inside. I'll show you through if you like. It was a stroke of luck you came here first. I know for a fact that everyone else in this street has moved away. And I think most of the new people work. A young couple live in your old house now but they seem to work long hours. But Evan and me, we always here.'

Bella noticed Kirsty holding one of her photographs. 'That's a photo of the three of us soon after we moved in here. I think your mother might have taken it, Morgan. I have more photos, of you and Evan when you were wee. Let me go and have a quick look.'

Bella left the room, and Kirsty showed Morgan the photo. She saw a white man with ginger hair turning grey, a slimmer Bella with darker hair and little Evan between them. They were each holding one of his hands, propping him up. It was clear Bella was not a young woman even then. Kirsty replaced the photo while Morgan brought out her own photos.

Bella returned holding an album, the old kind which used transparent film to hold the photos in place on a sticky background. 'Here you are. There are a few pages to look at. Here's a nice one of you and your mum together. And here's one of you and Evan playing in the paddling pool we set up in the back garden one summer.'

Morgan showed Bella the photos she had — the one of her parents standing in front of their car outside the house next door, and two of herself as a baby.

'Oh yes, there you are,' Bella said. 'That is how I remember you. And de car. He was so proud of that car, your dad. He bought it new. Would have cost him a packet too ...' Bella abruptly stopped talking.

Morgan realised she was afraid she might say something wrong. She said, 'Bella, I know this was the car my parents were killed in. And I know I had a brother who died. I was hoping you might be able to tell me anything about them, anything at all. It's okay, I really want to know.'

Chapter 23

'Okay, aye, well. Your mother was a beautiful lady with a beautiful nature. She helped me a lot with Evan. He was a surprise to us you know; I wasn't really expecting to ever have a child at my age. And your mother was a great comfort to people. She would do the readings, you see. They would come to the house and she would read their energy and connect to those passed over. She had a gift that way.

'But your father, he was different. He was a troubled soul. He was a businessman, did well in his business too, ambitious. But he was such a violent man. We could always hear him shouting. He used to take out his anger on your beautiful mum, and on you too, poor little thing you were. You were so wee, but you always had some bruise or other on you. I cannot believe anybody would bash a wee child so, but he had a terrible rage in him. I never understood what your mother saw in him. He was a good-looking man, of course, but what a temper.'

Bella stopped and studied Morgan, who had turned pale. 'I'm sorry, is this news to you, dear?'

'It is,' she said, 'but I came over from Australia to find out about my parents, and I'm prepared to hear the truth.'

'Okay, well. You used to spend a lot of time over here playing with Evan, especially when your father was home. And you stayed with your auntie quite a bit too, I think. Funny thing though, when your wee brother was born … what was his name again, dear?'

'Simon.'

'Yes of course, wee Simon. We used to hear him crying all de time. Well, then your father seemed to calm down. The shouting stopped for a while. It was a son, you see, maybe that's why. But then, the poor wee mite died in his sleep. Awful sad that was.

'And instead of quietly grieving like you would expect, he became more violent than ever. He gave your mother bruises on her face, and you were covered in bruises head to foot.' Bella shook her head at the memory. 'We called the polis — we thought he was going to kill someone. He spent a few nights away somewhere, to calm down like, maybe the jail, I'm not sure. But it didn't change him. And after that you went to stay with your auntie for a month.

'The folk in de town, they stayed away, so that was the end of your mother's little clairvoyant and healing practice. Then there was that nasty business when she was suspected of killing the baby. As if she would ever do that. The local gossipmongers were cruel, aye, and superstitious too. Your mother was accused of performing black magic or some such bunk. There was a terrible time when both our houses were egged, nearly every day. It was persecution, like a witch hunt. Your poor mum didn't like to go into the town anymore.

'We suffered our share of the gossip as well, me and Ted, when we first moved here. You'd think people are not prejudiced these days, but they are, or they were then anyway. I remember I was in the fruit shop one day and I overheard a woman say our son being disabled was our punishment — you know, black woman, white man.' Bella shook her head. 'It's hard to believe how hateful some folk can be.

'And then, as if that wasn't enough, your mother and father were killed in that dreadful accident in the river. It's no wonder you don't remember anything about all this, dear. You've probably, you know, repressed all the bad stuff.'

Morgan sat silently, staring at Bella.

Bella continued, 'But, there were good times too. You spent a lot of time over here with us. You were such a lovely, quiet wee thing, never made a fuss, and you were never naughty. Visitors would sometimes say "that one's been here before", meaning you looked old and wise. But I used to think you looked more haunted. I remember thinking you might be the same as your mum too, because you would say things like, "answer the phone Mizz P", right before the phone rang. Or you'd sing the tune to a song before it came on de radio.

'We missed you when you were taken away. Evan was always looking for you. He was so sad, we had to get him a little dog, Molly. Dogs don't live forever though; she lived to eighteen years old, and it broke his heart when his little

Molly died, about eight years ago now. I thought he wasn't going to recover from the grief, so I never got him another one. Couldn't let him go through that again. Molly was what he called you, by the way. He couldn't say "Morgan" properly.'

Evan was nodding but not smiling. Morgan's eyes overflowed with tears. She scrabbled in her bag for a tissue.

Kirsty came to her rescue. 'You've done an amazing job, Bella, coping all this time on your own. I don't suppose you've been able to get away much for holidays either.'

'Right enough, dear. I have a sister in Jamaica. That's where I'm from, you know, Montego Bay. She keeps asking me to come over and stay with them, but I've never been able to manage it. Maybe one day. But I'm kept busy here, and I love my gardening.'

'We noticed your lovely garden at the front.' Kirsty held up her phone, 'Would you mind if I took photos of your pictures of Morgan and Evan when they were little? Those few photos we showed you are the only ones Morgan has of herself or her parents. And I'd like to get a photo of you, Evan and Morgan all together if that's okay.'

'Of course you can. Come over here, dear,' Bella said, motioning to Morgan.

She dried her eyes and went to sit beside Bella and Evan. She picked up Evan's hand and held it while Kirsty took a photo of the three of them, Bella with her arm around Morgan. Then she angled the photo album and took copies of all the old photos she could find. Evan had started smiling again.

'I'm sorry, there aren't too many of your mother and father,'

Bella said. 'I'm trying to think who else might have any. Your mum had a brother.'

'Yes, that's right, Uncle Mal. He was Kirsty's dad.'

'Oh aye, Mal and Janie, your uncle and aunt. You did mention you were cousins.'

'He died when I was only four,' Kirsty said.

'Oh, I'm sorry to hear that, dear. I'm thinking there was a sister too — your father's sister that would be. Now, she lived up north somewhere, on an island. Maybe Skye. I'm sorry, dear, I can't remember much else about your family. Would you like to see through de house while you're here? The houses along this side of the street are all the same inside.'

They followed Bella through the little bungalow. On the opposite side of the dark corridor were two small bedrooms, separated by a modified bathroom. At the back was a worn kitchen with black and white vinyl tiled flooring, a claustrophobic dining room with peeling wallpaper, and a tiny utility room which housed the washing machine and dryer.

But stepping down into a conservatory which opened onto her garden, both girls gasped at an unexpected pageant of yellow, purple, pink, blue, red and orange flowers. Bella said, 'You can see daffodils, rhododendrons, bluebells, roses, bell heather, lavender — all de spring flowers.'

'Oh, Bella. This is spectacular. What an incredible display.' Apart from the roses Morgan knew none of the flowers by name. She breathed in the air, sweet with rich perfume. 'And so fragrant. It's a secret garden. No one would ever expect to find such beauty ... hidden away like this.' Her first thought had been to say, 'in such a depressing place.'

'I spend all de time I can out here, it gives me a lot of peace.'

Morgan peered through a hedge to the back yard of her old house. There was no conservatory and it looked bare and neglected compared with Bella's magnificent garden. It triggered no memories or feelings in her at all.

On the way out, she kissed Evan on the cheek and hugged and thanked Bella. 'It was lovely meeting you and Evan, Bella. Thank you so much for showing us your house and filling the blanks about my childhood. It doesn't sound like a happy time, quite the opposite, but now I know, and that helps me.'

'Don't dwell on it too much, dear, it's over — it's all in the past now. We move on. How long are you staying in Scotland? I hope you will be able to come back and pay us a wee visit again. It's made Evan's day.'

'I have no plans to go back to Australia, really. It's all a bit open-ended. And I'll most definitely come back and visit you.'

As Kirsty and Morgan were leaving through the front door, they heard Evan distinctly say, 'Love you, mum.'

Bella smiled broadly at them. 'Did you hear that? You see, that makes everything worthwhile.'

Kirsty and Morgan walked back to the car. Morgan said, 'Do you think you'd be able to drive? I feel a bit shaky.'

'No bother, of course I will. Jeez, that was heavy stuff. Do you want to talk to any other neighbours? We didn't get to look through your old house and we'd have to come back on a weekend when they're not at work, but it sounds like most of them have moved away anyway. It was nearly thirty years ago.'

'Yeah, we were lucky to come across her. I probably don't feel I need to look through the old house now. I've seen it, that's enough. Great thinking to get copies of those photos from her album, by the way. Will you send them to me? I'll have a good look at them later. I don't think I need to know any more; I don't know if I even want to. My father sounds like a real prick. My poor mother sure picked a rotten one. I wonder why she didn't leave him?'

'She must have had her reasons. Maybe she didn't think she had any options. And it sounds like you were lucky to escape with your life. Poor little you. Fancy anyone hitting a wee child like that. Makes my blood boil.'

'That explains why I spent a lot of time staying with Jane and Mal.'

'Do you still know things before they happen?'

'Not really. Well, occasionally. I think I did when I was little, but I might have grown out of it.'

Chapter 24

As promised, Kirsty emailed the dozen photos: the one she took yesterday of the house, the one of Morgan, Bella and Evan together, one of Bella and Ted helping Evan to stand, seven showing Morgan and Evan playing at about two or three years old, a tender one of her mother holding her hand, and one showing her mother holding a baby wrapped in the same yellow blanket, a baby she now knew was Simon.

She spent time zooming in and out of the photos and gazing at herself as a young child. Small and thin with dark pigmentation around her eyes, she understood what Bella meant by looking haunted. She had thought the same thing herself. With no memory at all beyond age four, it was like looking at someone else. Being beaten for just existing, and safer with a schizophrenic aunt than her own father, it must have been a traumatic time for a little kid.

Bella had no photos of her father in her album. She stared at the only two printed photos she had of him. There he was, standing proudly in front of his new car. What had made him so angry? Had he always been like that or did he change during the course of their marriage?

How could you hurt a child, you bastard. And her mother. She resented the injustice, frustrated that she would never be able to confront him or get any answers from him. One thing she couldn't understand was why Mal hadn't intervened if he'd been aware his sister and niece were being abused. He must have known, surely. The thought had occurred to her yesterday but, because she hadn't wanted to upset Kirsty, she had kept it to herself. Perhaps he was too doped to be motivated. Great gene pool. A stoner and a psychopath.

She remembered Bella's words, 'It's all in the past now. We move on.' Wise words. Bella was right; there was nothing she could do now. What was the point of being angry about something that happened long ago? And it affected no one else anymore, only her.

Still, something niggled at her: the treatment of her mother by the local gossips. How dare they destroy her business, her reputation, and possibly her life. Who were 'they' anyway? Who were these narrow-minded stupid people, who had egged her mother's and Bella's houses? She realised she was grinding her teeth.

What would Lindy do? What *had* Lindy done? Incredibly, she had tried to find ways to make the best of the situation, forgiven everyone, moved on with her life, and become an inspiration to others.

She tried to find a positive thing to come out of her mother's victimisation. The only thing she could think of was that she had spent an idyllic childhood being looked after by her loving godparents, Don and Lou.

Kirsty was right, she was probably lucky to be alive. And now, she had to move on with her life, as her mother would have wanted, not wallow in regret. She would put it out of her mind. Besides, she had a date with Ross to get ready for. The thought of it excited her into action.

She smiled as she glanced at the clock: eleven-eleven, her favourite time. She planned out her days. Thursday was the hairdresser, so today she would drive into Ayr to shop for new clothes. Dammit, Kirsty was right again, she should have gone shopping with them last week.

She drove into the town and parked in an underground car park. It cost four pounds for the whole day which she thought was cheap until she reminded herself again, these were pounds, silly. Normally she would have taken the elevator to the shopping mall but instead, thinking the exercise would do her good, she took the stairs.

The clothes she had brought with her from Australia were casual, comfortable and baggy. Last time she'd bought jeans they were low on the hips and had wide legs. Now the style was high-rise with skinny legs. When had the fashion changed? She mooched through the unfamiliar shops, buying new makeup, jeans, a stylish jacket and boots.

After loading her purchases into the car she decided to leave it in the car park while she explored the town. It was a fine but cloudy, cool day with a sea breeze; a perfect day for walking. She wandered for twenty minutes down to the seafront, recognising the Wallace Tower Kirsty had shown her. She hadn't intended to walk so far, but the sea glimpse in the distance was enticing.

She sat on a low stone wall and breathed the bracing, salty air. There was even a sandy beach. She became absorbed in watching the sea birds, waders she didn't recognise, and a variety of gulls who rapidly lost interest in her once they realised, she wasn't a food source.

Walking back she noticed how ancient the buildings were. She stood in awe at the crumbling citadel walls, still visible, dating back to Cromwell's invasion of Scotland. Ayr was big enough without being too large a town — about the size of Bundaberg, a friendly size. It was alive, and she liked it. The people smiled at her. Or was that because she was actually smiling at them?

Not being used to much physical activity, by the time she reached the car her feet were sore. She must make an effort to get herself into better shape. On the short drive home, she became aware how even the traffic lights were different from those in Australia: the amber light flashed on before the green light. Get ready to go. Love it.

She laid out her new clothes on the bed and held up the aquamarine jumper she planned to wear on Friday night. The blue enhanced the colour of her eyes, although, as she regarded her own eyes in the mirror, she knew they weren't pure blue, rather a murky blue-green, the colour of the sea on a cloudy day.

The next day was her hair appointment in Prestwick. As the salon was only fifteen minutes away and, as she felt motivated to increase her fitness, she decided to walk, taking an umbrella just in case.

The blonde streaks had long since grown out of her straggly hair. Had it really been a year since she'd visited a hairdresser? After three hours of listening to the hairdresser relate her whole family history, and how she'd been a hairdresser in the same salon for thirty years, and how much they had drunk at her fiftieth birthday party, she emerged with a head of spectacular copper foils and a fashionable cut, not too short, just below shoulder length.

Her new hairstyle swung in a pleasing way as she bounced along the road back to her flat. The many people she met walking their dogs nodded at her. She didn't know if she had lost any weight with all the walking but she certainly felt fitter.

Friday finally arrived. She epilated, washed, exfoliated, tweezed, moisturised, and dressed in her new skinny leg jeans and long, blue cashmere jumper. By six-thirty she was primped, preened, primed and ready to go.

Chapter 25

At exactly ten to seven she heard the low growl of Ross's Jaguar. Should she go downstairs to meet him? No, she didn't want to appear too eager. After a minute or two he knocked on the door. She delayed for a few moments and then casually opened it.

He was wearing trendy jeans, an open-necked white shirt, a casual oversize pinstriped jacket and dark blue sneakers with white soles. She sensed his outfit was expensive.

'Gidday mate!' he said. 'I've been practising.'

She laughed, 'Gidday yourself, mate.' Funny how the Australian accent seemed to invite mockery.

He presented her with a bunch of flowers. 'You look lovely. You've done something to your hair.'

She accepted the flowers. 'Thank you, they're beautiful. Yes I thought I'd try some foils.' She swung her head from side to side. 'I'm glad you like it. I'll put these in water.'

He followed her down the stairs and out to the waiting

car. 'Is this your Polo?' She nodded. 'Good choice, they're good wee cars.'

He opened the door of the Jag for her and she snuggled into the luxurious leather seat. It smelled new. 'What a gorgeous car.'

'Aye, it's not too shabby. Top of the range. How do you like the ambient lighting?' He touched something on the dashboard and the internal lights changed colour from light blue to red.

'Impressive.'

'Aye, I'm still getting used to driving it. Apparently top speed is about 155 miles per hour. I could have had the V6 which can do 160 but I thought, why bother? Where could you drive at that speed? On a German autobahn maybe, but no' around here. The fuel consumption's better on this model, too. Still about twice the consumption of your wee Polo, mind.'

Ross spent the ten or so minutes it took to drive to the restaurant talking about the features of his car. Outside the restaurant he said, 'Och, I'm sorry, listen to me blethering on the whole time.'

She didn't mind at all; his happy chatter took the pressure off her to make conversation. She also loved that he was knowledgeable about cars, a masculine trait she found attractive.

The restaurant was located in a prime position right on the riverbank. He ushered her in ahead of him, and she was relieved to find it warm and cosy inside. As they were shown to their table, heads turned. It was like she'd walked in with a celebrity. She was aware the other diners were looking at him, not her.

He had booked a window table with a panoramic view of the river, boats, and stone houses on the bank beyond. Towards the mouth of the river a stunning sunset lit the sky with an orange glow.

They sat, and he perused the wine menu.

'Would you like a New Zealand Sauvignon blanc or Australian Chardonnay? Just to make you feel at home.'

'Is it from Marlborough?'

He looked surprised. 'Aye, it is. You know your wine then.'

'No, not really, but I know it will be a good one.'

She snapped a sneaky photo of him with her phone, then studied the menu. She chose scallops followed by salmon. He chose prawns followed by lamb.

He poured her a generous glass of Sauvignon blanc. 'So, Morgan, have you been up to anything interesting?'

'Yes, Kirsty and I found a neighbour who remembered my family, and she had photos of me as a child. I also discovered my mother had another baby who died. He was in a photo taken on the same day as the one you saw, and I assumed it was me. But when you mentioned that photo was taken in 1991, I realised it wasn't me at all.'

'Oh, aye, I thought something had upset you that night. You didn't know then. Family secrets, eh? All families have them. Did you find out any more about how your parents died?'

She told him she had learned her parents had drowned in the river on a winter's night, according to the library articles but she avoided mentioning her father had been a violent abuser, not wanting to spoil the mood of the evening. Instead she talked about her sightseeing walk around Ayr, and Kirsty's and her plans to go to the Burns festival tomorrow.

'Are you going to be around for the festival?' she asked.

'Och, there's always something being celebrated around here; we're big on festivals in this country. But no, I'm needing to get back to Edinburgh this weekend so I'll be missing it, unfortunately. And Kirsty, she's a friend of yours?'

'She's my cousin. As far as I can tell, she's my only living blood relative. It's a strange feeling, like being on the end of the last twig on the family tree. Oh, that is apart from Minerva, my father's sister. But I don't know if she's even alive.'

'Never heard of anyone called Minerva before. I remember there was an old car called a Minerva. Belgian, might have been, had an unusual large flat boot. I remember because my father was into vintage cars in a big way and we were always off on some rally or other when we were kids. I've inherited his love of cars, you might say.'

'Do you like go-karts?' she asked.

'Go-karts? Oh aye, we used to play with them when we were wee. Good fun, for a kid. There used to be a popular go-kart track near here but it closed down. It turned out to be really a front for a cannabis farm. Why? Is it something you would like to do?'

'No, not at all. I don't know why I asked.'

'I'm partial to the Formula One, mind. Go-kart racing for big boys.'

She was keen to steer him away from the subject of cars. 'Are your parents still living?'

'Aye, they live in Spain now, and my brother lives in Canada. Just the two of us boys, Craig and me.'

Their entrées arrived. 'Look at the size of these scallops. They're delicious, so fresh.'

'So are these prawns ... swap some?'

'Of course.' They exchanged parts of their meals. She began to unwind and feel at ease. 'I know this sounds weird, but I can't help feeling I know you from somewhere. Or maybe you just remind me of a movie or television star. You should be on TV you know; you'd be in demand.' She instantly felt her face blushing. Now she was gabbling and saying stupid things.

He didn't seem phased though, 'Well, thank you for the compliment but I have no desire to show my ugly mug on television.' He ran a hand through his hair, deliberately styled in casual disarray. 'And it's funny you should say that because the morning I first met you, I was trying to remember where I knew you from. I didn't mention it at the time — it sounded like a lame pick-up line.'

As the meal progressed, she became more comfortable with him and more mellow. They had a similar sense of humour and taste in music; they laughed and shared their stories. But she was careful not to speak too loudly. Her Australian accent was noticed everywhere she went, and the other diners were still stealing furtive glances at them.

Ross, however, appeared to be enjoying the attention her accent attracted, and encouraged her to talk. 'Australia is a place I'd always thought I'd like to visit. Whereabouts are you from again?'

'Brisbane … well, halfway between Brisbane and the Gold Coast.'

'Oh, aye, the Gold Coast. Surfers Paradise, is that right?'

'Yes, that's part of it.'

He wanted to know all about Australia. 'What's it like living there?'

Where to start? 'It's great,' she said. 'Different lifestyle from here, different buildings, different everything. Where I live, it's new and modern. We have glorious beaches and scenery, but it's not as green.

'It's more casual than here, I guess, because of the weather. People wear thongs, even to the shops — not usually in the city though.' She thought back to Kirsty's barrage of questions at the airport. 'I'll show you photos later if you like. It's really hard to describe; it might not be what you expect. Sometimes we have bushfires, droughts and flooding, all at the same time. It depends where you live. Pretty much any kind of life you want you can get in Australia.'

It was like six blind men trying to describe an elephant by feeling one part. She could not capture the vast, diverse country and culture in a few words. It was not possible to do it justice.

'Thongs? They would be flip flops?'

'Ha, ha, sorry, yes, flip flops.' She liked 'thongs' better.

'And what do you think of our fair Scotland?'

'I love it, although I haven't seen much of it yet. I love that everything is so close, and it's easy to get around. I love the

Scottish accent and being surrounded by history. Funny though, I expected to see tartan kilts and hear bagpipes. I haven't even heard one yet.'

He ordered a cocktail. She was tipsy already but couldn't resist the temptation of something called *Nectar of the Gods*. Outside the restaurant after the meal, she shivered in the chill air, despite her jacket. He noticed and put his arm around her.

'Would you like to walk down to the seafront or are you feeling the cold too much?'

'I'm fine, really, it's just the difference in the temperature from inside. I'd love to walk to the seafront.'

He took her hand and they walked to the esplanade. The sky was aflame with remnants of the spectacular sunset, turning the water to liquid gold. They came to a sandy beach and an old low concrete wall — the same wall she had sat on two days ago. She breathed deeply the fresh air scented with seaweed and salt. Cold air filled her lungs.

They walked hand in hand along the esplanade while the sun disappeared behind the island of Arran. There was something romantic about the setting. She looked up at him and smiled.

Abruptly, he stopped. 'Well, this is me. Would you like to come in for a drink, or a coffee?'

For a moment she was confused. She looked to where he was pointing and saw a lovely old white rendered cottage with a dark slate roof and a low stone wall at the front. It had two bay windows and looked directly over a park to the sea.

'This is you? You mean you live here? I thought you lived in a townhouse.'

'Aye. Well, when I'm down here in Ayr I live here. It's a nice little holiday type house — a house in the town I suppose.'

She loved the way he pronounced it 'hoose'.

'It's handy to the shops and I can be at the hospital in under ten minutes. And it's nice and warm inside.'

She hesitated. It seemed a little too coincidental. But then she realised it was no coincidence, just convenient — he had planned this.

'Okay, thank you,' she said. 'Maybe a coffee would be nice. I'll come in for just a short while though.'

Chapter 26

Ross led the way down the path to the front door. Morgan turned to looked back over the esplanade. The house would have a magnificent view. As promised, inside was cosy and warm. A wood burning heater sat in the fireplace but it wasn't lit.

'No fire? How come it's so warm?'

'Central heating. Much easier, especially if I've done a late shift. The last thing I want is to have to poke around lighting a fire.' He must have turned it on earlier.

All the furniture in the room was made of quality oak timber. She laid her jacket over the back of a pale grey fabric lounge chair. Heavy apricot coloured drapes covered the side window but the front window revealed a vista of dark pink sky and an expansive view of the sea.

He motioned for her to sit on the sumptuous grey sofa. 'Have a seat … what can I get you? A coffee? Or, even better, I have this lovely old port.' He held up a bottle. 'I've been saving this for a special occasion. And tonight is pretty special.' He flashed his irresistible smile at her.

'Well, why not? Sounds lovely.'

He poured out two measures of port and handed her one. It had a delicious, rich plum flavour, aged and mellow.

He sat beside her on the couch, placed his drink on the coffee table and put his arm around her. With his other hand he tilted her head upwards, leant in and kissed her full on the mouth, surprising her. Her whole body melted under his touch.

He pulled back and said, 'You're gorgeous.' There was that adorable Scottish accent. He took the port from her hand, put it on the table, and kissed her again. She responded willingly. He ran his hand slowly down her arm and said, 'This is beautiful, so soft. There's nothing sexier than cashmere.' His hand stroked her silky jumper over the swelling of her breasts. Then he slid his hand up inside her jumper and inside her bra. This was a bit sudden but she was completely overwhelmed by him, unable to resist. She didn't really *want* to resist.

He fondled her nipple with his soft hands, and then expertly unclipped the bra at the back. His warm hands explored both breasts. Her nipples had grown hard in response and she moaned softly. He lifted up the jumper at the front and took one of her breasts into his mouth, sucking and caressing the nipple with his tongue.

Without speaking he stood up, took her by the hand and led her into the dimly lit bedroom. He gently pushed her onto the bed and lay beside her. He undressed her and ran his hands all over her body. She felt exposed and vulnerable but she loved every second of it. He said, 'You're beautiful; you turn me on something fierce. I'm so hard for you — feel.' He took her hand and pressed it to himself. She felt his hardness, insistent through his jeans. He wriggled out of his clothes.

She was highly aroused and her heart beat rapidly. She hadn't meant to sleep with him but she had gone without for some time and she found she wanted him badly. She ran her hands over his naked body. He was toned and very fit.

He flipped back the quilt and they slid between the cool, cotton sheets. His hands and mouth explored every part of her. She gasped. She would have let him do anything. She moaned and dug her fingers into his back. He was so deft and agile, and moved with such power she was completely consumed by him. She let herself be taken and responded to his every motion. Her excitement rose to breaking point. She remembered he was a surgeon; he clearly knew his way around the female body. This thought thrilled her even more. She closed her eyes and completely abandoned herself. The feeling was like nothing else she had ever experienced. She gasped at the intensity of the pleasure as her world exploded.

Then he also moaned and lowered himself gently beside her. She stroked him and held him close to her as they both came down from the height of their passion. He was covered in a fine film of sweat. Her body pulsated, warm, and her nerves tingled. 'Oh my God, you are amazing.'

He kissed her and said, 'You have such a wonderful body. Curvy, not like those skinny young skelfs you see everywhere.'

'I never thought it was. You do though. So fit.'

'Aye, well, I work out at the gym whenever I can.'

They lay for a long time, wrapped in each other's arms. He covered her with the quilt and she fell into a deep and blissful sleep.

When she awoke in the morning, she could smell eggs and coffee. Oh God, did that really happen? She eased herself over the edge of the bed. He had placed a white robe on the bedside table for her. She draped the robe around herself and made for the en suite bathroom. Jesus, what did she look like? She washed her face in the basin and decided to have a quick shower. She used some of Ross's deodorant. She didn't have much makeup with her in her small handbag but she combed her hair and applied a light smear of lipstick. She slid the robe back on and went to find the kitchen.

'Hello, gorgeous,' he said. 'Will you have some scrambled eggs for breakfast? I've made coffee there for you. I let you sleep on, you looked so peaceful. I didn't want to wake you.'

'Thank you, that was kind. And that smells delicious.' She took a sip of the milky coffee he had made with his upscale model of her own machine. 'Mm, perfect, just how I like it.'

He was wearing a loose shirt over baggy linen trousers. Somehow, he still managed to look like he'd just stepped from a fashion magazine.

'How are you feeling this morning?' he asked.

'I feel wonderful — I must have slept like a log. Last night was sensational, you're incredible. And persuasive. I was only going to come inside for a quick coffee.'

'Hee hee. Well I couldn't help myself. You are so sexy. But I'm glad you stayed.'

'Me too.' She had a sudden thought. 'Where's the car?'

'Outside the restaurant where we left it. You have your breakfast and I'll nip round and get it. I have to get back to Edinburgh this morning. Not for surgery, otherwise I wouldn't have been drinking last night. I'd rather not have to go but I need to be there for supervision of students. I'll drop you off at the flat on the way.'

She ate scrambled eggs and hot buttered toast, then she loaded the dishes into the dishwasher and switched it on. She dressed back into her jumper and jeans and waited for Ross to return with the Jaguar.

Outside her flat he leant over to kiss her. He picked up her hand and kissed that too. 'Thank you for a wonderful night. I hope you'll want to see me again?'

'Yes, of course. I'd love to. When will you be back?'

'I'm on call for the next two weeks in Edinburgh, so I'll be back down here on the Monday. Twenty-first I think that is. I'll call you then.' He picked up his phone. 'Here, you'd better send me your number.'

'Just tell me one thing?' she said.

'Okay.'

'Are you by any chance bisexual?'

'*Eh?* No, of course not. Why on earth would you ask that? You ask some funny questions. Do I look bisexual?'

'I honestly wouldn't know.'

She watched as the Jag pulled out of the driveway and purred up the road. She spun around and almost collided with an Indian man wearing a grey turban.

'I'm so sorry ma'am,' he said. He joined his two hands like he was praying and bowed his head.

'No problem, my fault. Do you live here?'

'Yes, ma'am, I'm living here in the downstairs flat.'

She thought about saying, *Yes, I've smelled your curries*, but instead she held out her hand and said, 'I'm Morgan, I live in the flat above you. Pleased to meet you.'

'Pleased to meet you also, Morgan ma'am. I am Harish.' He did the bowing thing again. 'I'm on my way to the festival. Maybe you have heard of it? It is called Burnsfest. Burns was an important poet here in your country I believe.'

Her country. Was this her country? She nearly said *Australia is my country*. But she nodded and said, 'Yes, I'll be going there soon with my cousin.'

'Oh that is marvellous. Then you must come to my van. We will be making the curries, same as in our restaurant, you know? Delicious tandoori, you will like. Come to the van and I will give you a free curry, for neighbour, yes?'

'Thank you, Harish, that is kind, I'll look out for you.'

He bowed again, so she did the same. He walked over to his van and she searched in her handbag for her front door keys. She wanted to be dressed and ready before Kirsty arrived.

Chapter 27

Too late. Kirsty pulled up on her bicycle. 'Hiya. You look nice. You ready to go already? I love what you've done with your hair. But you'll need to take a warmer jacket and maybe wear hiking shoes instead of ...' She stopped abruptly and scrutinised Morgan more closely.

'You're no' just coming home!' she shouted.

The blood coloured Morgan's cheeks. 'Yes, actually. Come up.' She hastily ushered Kirsty into the foyer and up the stairs before the whole street heard.

Inside the flat Kirsty hopped from one foot to the other. 'Oh my God, Morgan, what happened?'

'Here, sit down,' she said pulling out one of the dining chairs. 'Well, we went to this lovely restaurant, as planned, and then we went for a romantic walk along the esplanade. His house was right there and we went in just for a coffee, but I ended up staying the night. Accidentally.'

Kirsty's dark brown eyes were like two shiny chocolate

marbles. 'When you say "staying the night", you mean … you shagged him?'

'Yep, I'm afraid so. It wasn't planned. It just happened somehow. But, boy, was it good.'

Kirsty squealed. 'That's some quick work! You've met him, what three times? I know you said 'eleven' but … Jesus. Did you get a picture of him?'

She showed her the photograph she'd secretly taken while he'd been looking at the wine menu.

'Wow, yeah, I do see the attraction. He's a pretty-boy, isn't he? Looks like something straight out of *Vogue* magazine.' She studied Morgan for a moment. 'Did you say he lives on the esplanade?'

'Yes, pretty little cottage, really nice inside. He calls it his town house.'

'On the waterfront.'

'Yes.'

'Fuck me, do you know how much those houses are worth? Is he loaded or what?'

'I did kind of get that impression. But I didn't want to ask if he was wealthy or anything — that would seem a bit rude, wouldn't you think?'

'Yeah, I guess so.' Kirsty was shaking her head, 'You lucky bitch!'

'*Anyway*. What's the go with this festival?'

'Okay, well, I thought we should get an Uber, then neither of us needs to drive. It's supposed to stay fine and sunny like this, not too cold, but you might feel it chilly, being from *Queensland*, so take a warm jacket, and maybe scarf. And it's in a park so don't be wearing them fancy wee booties.'

The festival was a relaxed and casual family afternoon in the grounds of a mansion. People milled around food and craft stalls, and various tents offered kids' activities, music and poetry readings.

They bought wine in plastic cups and sat on hay bales listening to folk music. One female artist, with only an acoustic guitar for accompaniment, sang with the voice of an angel, causing the hair on Morgan's arms to stand on end. Other bands played energetic Celtic music with fiddles, tin whistles, banjos and harmonicas, and at last a bagpipe! It was so similar to Australian bush music she realised this was where it had obviously originated.

They migrated to listen to readings of Burns' and local original poetry. She couldn't remember ever having attended a poetry event before. She expected it to be a yawn but she was surprised how much she enjoyed the rich language and the humour of the old poetry. Here was a poet who had been celebrated for over two hundred years, who had been born nearly thirty years before the first fleet had even landed in Australia.

Giggling, Kirsty pointed out a young fellow wearing a t-shirt displaying the words, *Cock up your Beaver.*

'Hey, Morgan, there's a good shirt for you.'

'Oh, choice … thanks. You've got a one-track mind, girl.'

When the t-shirt guy turned around they saw the whole two verses of the poem written on the back. They weren't the only ones laughing.

'Funny thing is,' Kirsty said, 'it's not even a rude poem

— it's something to do with sticking a feather in a hat, I think. But some of his poems are downright filthy. There's one called, *Nine Inch Will Please a Lady*, and another where he laments how a penis goes flaccid after sex. I'll see if I can find a copy of his bawdy poems for you. You'll love them, they're hilarious.'

They drifted towards the food stalls. Morgan spotted Harish busily serving from his curry van. A tantalising, spicy aroma wafted towards them.

'Hello, Morgan, ma'am,' he called. 'Special tandoori curry skewer for you?'

'Yes please, Harish. And one for my cousin Kirsty please.'

'Hello, Kirsty, ma'am.' Harish handed over two tandoori chicken skewers. 'No charge for you, ma'ams. Will you like a card from our restaurant? Maybe you would come for dinner one time?'

'Certainly, thank you Harish. If it's as good as it smells, we'll definitely come to your restaurant.'

'He's the guy who lives downstairs from me,' Morgan said. 'You know, the one always making pongy curries. But, tell you what, these are delicious. Let's get a couple more. And more wine.'

Over at the bar, a grizzled, unshaven middle-aged man sat hunched on a hay bale, holding a beer with two hands. He heard Morgan ordering two cups of wine and looked up. He called out to her, 'Far aboots ye fae, hen?'

Kirsty translated. He says, 'where are you from'.

'Oh. I come from Brisbane.'

'Brrusbun! Tha's braw. Yer a lang wae fae hame.'

'Yes, I am. I'm Scottish though. I was born here in Ayr.'

'Oh aye, right.' He lost interest then and went back to peering into his beer.

They listened to more lively music in the tent. She enjoyed the fun atmosphere of the festival but her mind continually strayed to Ross. She had an aching desire to see him again. She could still feel his touch on her skin. The next two weeks were going to be interminable. She sighed.

Kirsty read her thoughts. 'When are you seeing Mr Vogue again?'

'Not for two weeks. He has to work at the hospital in Edinburgh.'

'I know how you feel. I miss Callum while he's studying. I can't see him again until he finishes his degree; apparently I'm too much of a *distraction*.'

'How long have you and Callum been going out?'

'Two years, but it's a bit more than going out. We were living together. We talk on the phone every week but it's hardly the same. I'll be going up to Edinburgh to see him again at the end of June for about six weeks … can't wait. Hey, your Ross is a doctor in Edinburgh, isn't he? I wonder if Callum has heard of him?'

'Maybe … it's possible. He's a surgeon. I believe he supervises students too. I think that's what he said, anyway.'

'I'll ask him when I see him again.'

'Yeah, it would be funny if he knew him. Tell you what, I'm loving these long days, I can't believe it's nine o'clock and still sunny.'

Kirsty ordered an Uber to take them home, dropping Morgan off first. She climbed out of the car and said, 'I'll ride your bike back for you tomorrow. I'm thinking I should get more exercise, anyway.'

Kirsty laughed. 'Yes, I've heard of that: sexercise. Good for you. Mr Vogue will be impressed.'

Chapter 28

Morgan cycled along the quieter back streets of Prestwick to return Kirsty's bike, enjoying the sensation of the cool wind on her face. She was getting better at navigating her way around the town. When she arrived Kirsty was waiting for her with another bicycle.

'This is Ma's,' Kirsty said. 'She doesn't ride it anymore so she said you might as well use it. There's a helmet too.'

'That's great. Thanks, Kirsty. I'm looking forward to exploring right along that wonderful seafront.'

'I'll come with you if you like. I've a bit of work on at the moment, but maybe in a few days I can join you. Actually, some website design work has just come my way. I could pass it on to you if you're interested — bit of extra pocket money for you. I've got more work than I can handle. I like the print work better anyway.'

'Sure, I'll be happy to help out. I like to keep my hand in.'

And it would help take her mind off Ross, fill in the long,

empty days. She felt like a child impatiently waiting for Christmas.

'I've got the place to myself for a wee while,' Kirsty said. 'Ma and Iain have taken a ferry over to Arran for a holiday. It's good timing. I can get stuck into the work in peace. It can get quite loud around here when we're all home.'

Kirsty went through the brief with her for the website and copied the files onto a USB stick. 'Okay, that's everything you need. Call me if you get stuck with anything.'

Back in her flat, she made a start on the website, but became distracted by Googling Ross's name. She searched for doctors and surgeons at Edinburgh hospitals. There were a number of them, and the names of individual doctors weren't easy to find.

Eventually she found his name under a list of consultants. It displayed his photo and listed his medical qualifications but gave no further information or personal profile. Neither was he active on Facebook or any other social media. They certainly like to protect their privacy, these doctors.

She gazed at his photo for a while and then turned her attention back to the website she was supposed to be designing. It felt good to get into the coding again; she'd forgotten how much she enjoyed the process.

After a few days she was satisfied with the result, and the site was ready to go live pending the client's approval. She was about to call Kirsty when her phone rang. Ross. Her heart missed a beat. She took a deep breath.

'Well hello, stranger.'

'Hello bonnie lass. I've been thinking about you.'

'I've been thinking about you too. How's it going? Are you busy at the hospital?'

'Aye, constant, and mental. Short staffed. I've only a couple of hours off and then back to it tonight. It's only the thought of seeing you again that's keeping me going.'

'Poor you. I could be there with you if you wanted me to.'

'It'd be no fun for you here, believe me. What're you up to?'

'I'm keeping out of trouble. Kirsty's given me a bike to borrow so we'll be doing some riding, and I've just finished designing a website. We went to the Burnsfest on Saturday. I met the guy from downstairs who was selling curries from a van.'

'Oh, aye, that Pakistani bloke who couldn't work out the exhaust fan.'

'Yeah, that's him, except he's Indian, not Pakistani.'

'Oh, okay, well I wouldn't know the difference. I miss you — I miss your sexy body. I'm sitting here by myself feeling lonely. I cannot wait to kiss you again, on the mouth and everywhere else. I want to strip you naked and lie you down on the bed and caress you all over. Just thinking about your hot, naked body, all soft and luscious, it's making me deed horny. I've got this raging hard-on.'

'Ooh, stop it. I wish you were here now.'

'Aye, me too, bonnie lass. What are you wearing the noo? *... eh? ... what?* Och, sorry, some fucker's bangin' at my door. I'll have to go. I'll call you soon.'

He ended the call. She sat staring at the wall, seeing nothing, feeling her blood pulsating. Finally she came back down to ground level and remembered what she'd been doing.

Website. Kirsty. She emailed the link, then called her to say she had done it.

'Oh that's grand, Morgan. They'll love it.' Kirsty looked over the pages. 'I'll send them the link soon. Are you feeling like a day out riding tomorrow? We've been cooped up working for nearly a week, shame to waste this glorious weather.'

The following afternoon Morgan and Kirsty rode along the Prestwick promenade and then south to the end of the Ayr esplanade. It was getting warmer by the day.

She loved how dramatic the sky always looked over the sea, brooding and changeable. Today the sea sparkled blue in the sun.

'What colour would you call the sea today, Kirsty? Azure? Cobalt?'

'I'd call it … Pantone 301.' She laughed. 'Sorry, occupational hazard.'

The esplanade took them past Ross's house on the waterfront. Morgan pointed it out to Kirsty and they pulled their bikes up outside.

'Oh, aye, there it is, the cute little love nest,' Kirsty said. 'Isn't it lovely? Looks really old. Probably worth a fortune.'

The apricot curtains were drawn closed across all the windows, as they had left them. Memories of the passionate night she had spent with Ross immediately flooded back. She yearned for him.

On the way home they also passed Harish's restaurant and, as it was after five pm, and Morgan's rear end was suffering from the hard bike seat, they decided to call in for dinner.

Harish, wearing his grey turban, smiled widely, and bowed to each of them enthusiastically.

'Welcome Morgan ma'am and Kirsty ma'am. Thank you for coming to our restaurant. Take a seat anywhere and I'll bring you menus and some drinks pronto.'

The food was tasty and plentiful, and the drinks were cheap. Riding in the fresh air had given them ravenous appetites. Somehow between them they drank the best part of two bottles of wine.

By the time they stumbled out of the restaurant onto the esplanade, the sunset had transformed into a breathtaking display of pink and purple hues, colours no Pantone chart could come close to describing.

'Magnificent — sunset over Arran. Where Ma and Iain are.'

'Ow, geez this bike seat's hard,' Morgan said. 'I hope there aren't any drunk-cycling laws here.'

Kirsty hiccupped and waved at the island. 'Just as well they can't see us. Better hop on these bikes and get home pronto.'

Chapter 29

'You must get over to Arran sometime, Morgan,' Ali said. 'It's beautiful and quiet, and there's so much history to see, wonderful walks, great food. We had a ripper time as you Aussies might say.' She laughed. 'So what have you girls been up to?'

'Well, apart from working hard,' Kirsty said, 'we've been riding our bikes, we went to the Burnsfest, eaten lots of Indian food, oh … and Morgan got laid.'

Morgan closed her eyes and shook her head.

Ali laughed. 'Did you dear? Well that's lovely.'

Her cheeks burned. 'Thanks Kirsty.'

'Och, no bother.'

Ali smiled. 'Don't worry dear, I think it's great you've met someone. Kirsty, you're a naughty wee thing.'

Ali took the scones she had bought on the island out of the oven and they moved into the lounge room where Iain had already settled into an armchair with a whisky.

'Would you like a wee dram, Morgan?' he asked holding up the bottle.

'Er, no thanks Iain, I'm cycling.'

Kirsty said to Iain in her powerful voice, 'Did you know Morgan's got a new boyfriend?'

Morgan looked at Kirsty in alarm.

'Aye, he's a surgeon from Edinburgh, he drives a Jaguar, he has a waterfront house, and a block of flats, he's rich and he's handsome, and he's single. If I didn't have Callum, I'd be jealous.'

'Goodness me. Well, that's good news you've met a young man,' Iain said.

'He's not all that young. He's forty-two,' she said.

'Eh? *forty-two* and no' married? He must be divorced, is he?'

She realised she didn't even know. 'Not sure, he just said he was single, is all.'

'He sounds too good to be true. If he starts asking you for money, run a mile!'

'Don't worry, Iain, it wouldn't do him much good being after my money, seeing I don't have any. And I'm awake to that one anyway.'

'I've remembered where I heard that unusual name before — McFarsund,' Ali said. 'It was possibly your young fellow's grandfather who made a fortune from developing real estate here and in the north. I think he started out with old family money, made around the time of the clearances. I've got a mind they were a large land-owning family. There's a good chance your Ross has inherited his money, rather than earned it as a surgeon. I couldn't say for sure though.'

'That's interesting. I tried Googling him but those doctors seem to like to keep to themselves. I'll bring it up, casually, next time I see him.'

'Which is?' Kirsty asked.

'He said he'll be back down here on Monday, so I guess sometime next week.'

'What kind of car did you say your young man drives?' Iain asked.

'It's an F-type Jag.'

'Oh, aye. Very nice. In my day, that kind o' motor would have been called a fanny magnet. Probably what the 'F' stands for.'

'*Iain!*' Ali said with a burst of laughter. 'Sorry, Morgan, too much whisky.'

✦   ✦   ✦   ✦

Monday came and went. She heard nothing from Ross. By Wednesday she was checking her phone every ten minutes but she resisted the temptation to call him.

She tried to keep herself occupied by searching the internet for Ross's family name to see if Ali had been right about his wealthy land-developer ancestor.

Evidently, she was. She found references to the name affiliated with horrific accounts of small land tenants who had been brutally evicted from their homes to make way for sheep. Apparently, some large landowners, including the McFarsunds, had become even more wealthy from sheep farming than by renting their land to families.

Looking at the dates, this could not have been in Ross's grandfather's time though, more like two or three generations before him. Old money indeed.

She became aware of a reverberation outside. She jumped up and raced to the window. Ross. In his fanny magnet. She quickly gargled some mouth wash, tidied her hair and checked her face in the mirror.

He arrived bearing flowers. 'I'm sorry I didn't call earlier, bonnie lass. Things were hectic at the hospital. I was hoping to get down here on Monday but I've only just managed to get here the noo. Could not get away. I'm fair scunnered.'

He dropped down onto the couch and held out his arms to her. She went to him immediately. He embraced her tightly and pinned her to the couch in a long passionate kiss. He was clearly aroused, but she wanted to take it more slowly, to savour the moment. She wriggled out of his hold and stood up.

'Shall I pour us some wine?' She wanted to talk — ask him about his work, about him.

'No, no thank you, nothing like that. All I want is you. Come back.'

She sat back down on the couch and he clutched at her with an urgency. In an attempt to slow things down she undid his shirt and stroked and kissed his chest. She undid his belt and loosened his trousers, going down on her knees in front of him.

She caressed and massaged and kissed him until he could not contain himself any longer. He raised her up and pushed her backwards onto the couch. He lifted her top and squeezed and kissed her breasts, then took her greedily, forcefully, the vinyl squeaking beneath her. After about twenty seconds he cried out in ecstasy and collapsed, spent, on top of her.

She stroked his hair and lay still, waiting for him to recover. Eventually he propped himself up, kissed her and started to dress. He laughed a funny little chuckle. 'Ah, bonnie lass, you've no idea how bad I've been wanting you these last two weeks.'

She stood up and straightened out the couch.

'Did we ruin the couch?' he said. 'Och, never mind about that, I'll buy a new one.'

Chapter 30

Morgan reclined on the feather sofa in Ross's lounge room, mesmerised by the view over the Firth of Clyde. She had been staying at his house (his 'toon hoose') for the past two weeks. The sex had improved. It was less frantic, but no less frequent. He wanted her every night, and at least it lasted more than twenty seconds.

One night after they had made love, she summoned up the courage to ask him why he was single. 'You know I'm divorced, or rather getting a divorce, but you've never told me if you were ever married or if you've always been single.'

He yawned, 'No, bonnie lass, never been married. I've had plenty of relationships, mind. Some lasted longer than others, but I've never really seen the point in getting married. Unless you want children. Which I don't.' He yawned again and kissed her. 'Night, night, bonnie lass.'

It was now late June and the weather had grown significantly warmer. Her fitness had improved, and her skin had taken on a brighter glow. She smiled to herself, something she had been doing more frequently. Her smile broadened when Ross came in from the kitchen and handed her a glass of wine.

'Darlin',' I've been thinking, I need to be back in Edinburgh mid-July but I'm having some time off before that, so maybe if you're free, we might do some travelling. I fancy a wee trip into the highlands to get away from everything for a while. If you're interested in coming with me that is.'

'Are you kidding? Of course I'm interested. I'd love to.'

'Brilliant. Okay then, I'll make arrangements.'

At last she would see more of Scotland. 'Where were you thinking of going?'

'I'm keen to keep away from the big towns. I had a mind to stay on Skye a wee while, it will only be for a week or so, and maybe a night at Loch Lomond on the way through.'

'Sounds fantastic, can you show me where it is?'

He picked up a driving map of Scotland. 'Here's us, and here's the Isle of Skye.'

'That's quite a distance. So do we get across there by ferry?'

'Aye, there is a bridge now so it's possible to drive, but I think the ferry would be more fun, and less driving. I need to book everything ahead because we're into the high season and the place will be hoachin' with tourists.'

'When do you want to leave?'

'My consulting work down here finishes in about a week or so. How about Monday next, does that suit you?'

'Absolutely, I can't wait, I'm excited already. It'll take me five minutes to pack — everything I have fits into one suitcase.'

She stayed another week with Ross, then returned to her

own flat on the weekend to pack and make preparations for travelling. She was looking forward to a couple of relaxing days on her own. She opened her front door and glanced around. Cooler and darker than Ross's place, it was much more basic, but it was her own space. Although she reminded herself that, technically, this flat also belonged to Ross.

She started a load of washing. With a sudden rush of guilt, she realised it had been more than a month since she had spoken to Don and Lou. She checked the world time app on her phone. It would be about eight-thirty pm in Brisbane, not too late, so she immediately set up Skype.

Lou was so excited to hear from her she felt even more guilty.

'How are you both?'

'Oh we're fine dear, except Don had a short spell in hospital, but he's better now.'

'Is he okay? What was wrong?'

'There were some palpitations of the heart, misfiring — something like that, but he's taking medication for it and he's right as rain. Just a minute, dear, I'll get him for you.'

Don appeared with Lou on the screen. He looked a little thinner, but otherwise seemed as normal. 'We're so glad to hear from you, love, we wondered how you're getting on.'

She told them about the articles she'd found in the library, about visiting Bella Paterson and Evan, and finally, about meeting Ross and their plans for travelling.

'Oh, that has made my day, dear,' Don said. 'You've met someone nice. That is the best news ever. I'm so pleased it's all worked out. And have you found out everything you wanted to know about your parents?'

'Pretty much, I guess. My father sounds like a person who should never have had children at all, but the good thing to come of it was that I grew up with you two, and I couldn't be more grateful to you both.' She wanted to ask them if they'd seen Anton, but then decided she really didn't care what he did.

After talking with Don and Lou, something stirred in her memory. Ross had mentioned travelling to Skye and Bella Paterson had suggested Jack Dee's sister might live on Skye. Had she really found out everything she wanted to know? She debated whether it was even something worth pursuing. Despite thinking it was probably a waste of time, she looked up Minerva Dee's name on an online phone directory. She was surprised when the search returned an address on Skye and a phone number. She transferred the contact details to her phone.

She also felt guilty about neglecting Kirsty, who had told her she was tired of being the one getting no sex, so she had travelled by train to Edinburgh to stay with Callum three weeks earlier than planned.

She phoned Kirsty to tell her about Ross's plan to holiday on Skye for a week.

'Oh, that's brilliant,' she said. 'You'll get to see more of Scotland, and I assume you'll be travelling in that gorgeous car of his. What a way to go! You'll have a fabulous time. I'm envious.'

'Are you having a good time in Edinburgh?'

'Aye, I certainly am. I'm trying to keep out of Callum's way, but that's easy in the city, it's so exciting, so much to do.'

'It's a pity we're not going near there; Ross said he'd rather keep away from big towns. Reminds him of work, I guess. But I was going to ask you — I've found a phone number for my father's sister who lives on Skye. Do you think I should contact her?'

'Of course, why not? She'd be your aunt, why wouldn't she want to see you. She's Athena or something isn't she?'

'Minerva. Goddess of wisdom and war if I remember rightly. Actually, I think you're right though. Didn't the Romans pinch that goddess Athena and change her name to Minerva?'

'Aye, probably, sounds like something the Romans would do.'

✦ ✦ ✦ ✦

She stared at the number on her phone; her fingertips sweated. Finally she found the courage to tap the number.

'Helloo,' said a voice with a sing-song lilt.

'Oh, hello. Would that be Minerva?'

'Yes, speaking.'

'Hi, my name is Morgan. Morgan … Dee, and I believe I might be your niece.'

There was a squeal over the phone. 'Really, noo? Morgan! Oh my goodness me. I never thought I would ever hear from you again. You are in … Australia, isn't it?'

'Yes, that's right, I was. I'm in Scotland now and I'll be travelling over to Skye soon. So … I wondered if you would maybe like to meet and have a cup of coffee, a chat, and catch up?' She wiped her fingers on her jeans.

'Oh, yes, indeed. Jack's daughter noo, that is amazing. Yes, I think that would be lovely, we will have loads to talk about. Where are you staying on the island? Would you like to stay here? We have room.'

'Thank you, that's kind of you to offer, but we have accommodation already booked. I'm travelling with my, er, boyfriend you see, and he's made all the arrangements.'

'Oh, yes, I see, well that's grand, pet. Just give us a call when you're on the island and I'll give you the directions. We're home most days. We'll meet up and have a natter. Goodness, gracious me … wee Morgan … what a surprise.'

Chapter 31

Morgan drove to Ross's house with her packed suitcase on the back seat. She had been able to fit all the clothes she owned into the case, but she left out her daggier outfits. She took a small day bag containing her laptop, and also the coffee machine, as the quality of the coffee, she had discovered, could be hit-and-miss.

It was considerate of him to garage the Polo while they travelled. Undercover parking was not such a rarity in Australia, and she didn't like to think of her car sitting in the unprotected car park in all weathers.

'All ready, bonnie lass.' Ross lugged out a suitcase bigger than hers and another smaller case. 'We'll be going in your car, if that's okay. I've put the Jag away in the garage. There's no room in it for all these cases, being a two-seater. And what with getting on and off ferries, the salt air and such, it's no' really a car to go knocking about the countryside in, ye ken.'

She managed a feeble smile. She thought the whole idea had been to give the Jag a run on the country roads. 'Okay, I wasn't expecting that, but I guess it makes sense. It will need petrol — the tank's not full.'

'Aye, no bother. I'll pay for all the fuel, and I'll drive, so you can sit and admire the scenery. Back in a tick, I just need to check a loose window is shut properly.' He disappeared behind the house.

'Sure.' She opened the boot of the Polo. It was too small for his suitcase so she dragged hers off the back seat and transferred it to the boot with his smaller case.

He returned. 'All good.' He loaded his huge suitcase onto the back seat alongside her day bag. He adjusted the seat and mirror and lurched out of the driveway. Instead of travelling through Prestwick, he drove past the cemetery and readily navigated his way onto the A77, the double-lane bypass road. She followed their route on her phone. They turned off near Monkton for fuel and then continued on a different highway, not the main one to Glasgow.

'This is a scenic way to go and the road's less busy,' he said.

She began to relax with Ross driving. He was a good driver, a bit fast, but precise and decisive. She turned to steal a secretive look at him. He looked too tall for the tiny car. He was immaculately dressed and groomed, as always. She turned her head further to look at the bulging giant suitcase on the back seat and wondered how many outfits he'd brought with him. She stifled a snort of laughter, and pretended it was a sneeze.

The day was idyllic for driving, twenty-four degrees and sunny. She was seeing Scotland at its finest. The road narrowed to single lane with periodic passing points. Again she was delighted by the vibrant green fields as high hedges gave way to views of fertile, incredibly lush open farmland.

At about halfway through their journey they pulled off the main road for lunch at Lochwinnoch, on the shore of a loch with a spectacular view across the water. Then they turned north near Glasgow Airport and headed towards Loch Lomond. He had booked a night in a self-contained guesthouse in Luss, a historic village on the shore of the loch. Old, neatly-kept stone cottages with charcoal grey slate tile roofs lined narrow streets leading down to the waterfront. The dark water of the loch was still and calm but heavy clouds hung over the opposite shore.

They held hands and walked around the village, stopping at an information sign which proclaimed Luss to be Scotland's loveliest village. 'I especially wanted to show you this pretty village,' he said. 'I thought you would like it.'

'It's stunning, so much character. On the bonnie banks of Loch Lomond.'

'Aye, exactly. This is where they filmed that television series: *Take the High Road*. Do you know it? It was popular here.'

'No, but what a great name. *Where me and my true love will never meet again*. From the song — sad song.'

After dinner in the cosy local pub, they walked down to the waterfront again, this time with a bottle of wine and two glasses. They strolled along the rough sand to a bench seat. The dark clouds had dispersed and a wonderful moon had risen, not full, but bright enough to illuminate a path over the water. He draped his arm around her as they drank a toast to the moon. 'And here's to you, bonnie lass,' he said, smiling at her.

He was so handsome; she loved the way his eyes crinkled at the corners when he smiled. She leant into him and felt the warmth of his body. She couldn't remember ever having been so happy. She was aware she was falling in love with him but she was careful to keep that to herself.

Their guest house was a short walk back up the village street. It wasn't just a room; it was a whole cottage with modern furnishings and a full kitchen stocked with everything they would need for breakfast. He had spared no expense with the accommodation; it was clearly a luxury guest house.

The bed was large and comfortable. Before they fell asleep holding each other, in the afterglow of their lovemaking, she wished she could stay in this place with him, like this, forever.

In the morning they set off on the road north. He was wearing a completely different outfit from yesterday's; he had even changed his shoes. She wore a different jumper but the same pair of jeans, jacket, shoes and her tartan scarf.

After about three hours driving through dramatic scenery, they arrived at the colourful fishing village and port of Mallaig. The busy ferry terminal was fragrant with the distinctive maritime scent of fish and diesel. He had pre-booked and paid the fare, so all she had to do was hand over the booking slip to swap for the tickets.

They drove onto the large ferry, *The Lord of the Isles*. Although she still wasn't ecstatic about taking her little car on a long journey, she realised driving Ross's car would probably have been asking for trouble. No one looked twice at her little Polo.

During the half-hour trip they had time for a cup of tea and a sandwich in the cafeteria. Passengers weren't allowed to remain in their cars but he wanted his tweed cap — he called it his 'bunnet' — out of his small case so he sneaked back down to the vehicle deck. He returned a few minutes later, annoyed, red in the face. 'Some glaikit bampot in a Hyundai has parked so close to us I cannot get the boot open.'

Despite being grumpy and petulant, he still turned heads, particularly women's heads. Secretly, she was glad he wasn't able to get his cap; it would have attracted even more female attention. As soon as they disembarked at Armadale, on went the cap. He glared at the glaikit bampot who was completely oblivious to the aggravation he had caused.

She was awed by the size of the island. They would need to drive for nearly two hours to reach the cottage Ross had booked for them. The land, lacking many high trees, was covered in tough-looking vegetation. It was rugged and mountainous in parts but they were never far from a spectacular sea view. The cottages were mostly similar in style — white with dark slate roofs, and no eaves. They stopped at the main town, Portree, to stretch their legs and to pick up supplies.

The vibrant town had an abundance of quaint craft and tea shops and breathtaking views of the harbour, with a row of brightly painted houses lining the seafront. It was the kind of town she could have happily mooched around for hours.

They found a space in the crammed car park. Ross

disappeared into a newsagent while she walked to the co-op to buy enough groceries for the week. She handed over her Visa card; it was her contribution as he had paid for everything else. The woman at the checkout scanned her card and then motioned with her head towards her scarf. 'Would that be a MacLeod tartan you're wearing?'

'I believe it is,' she replied, surprised. 'I'm not a MacLeod though.'

'More like one o' MacLeod's Daughters,' sniggered a Scottish female voice in the checkout line behind her. A male voice joined in, singing to the tune of a Rolling Stones song, 'Hey, MacLeod, get off o' my ewe.' And this witticism was followed by general derision and giggling. She could not turn around to look at the jokesters. She put her head down and picked up her groceries.

The checkout woman said something that sounded like, 'Aw wheesht,' but it could also have been something in Gaelic; it was hard to tell.

'What do you think she meant?' she asked Ross, back in the car.

'Och, who knows. There's a considerable MacLeod presence here on the island. Maybe she thought you were a pretender.'

'A pretender? Really? I just chose it because I liked the colours. I was really embarrassed. Now I'm going to be self-conscious wearing it.'

'No, don't be. Some folk identify strongly with their clan tartan. Maybe she thought you might have relatives here. Just wear it and tell them to stick it up their arse.'

They drove the final thirty minutes north to the guest house that was to be their home for the week. It was at the other end of the island in a secluded spot. Apparently, he really did want to get away from everything. What everything? The stress of the hospital, presumably. 'I guess there's no internet,' she said.

Ross looked at his phone. 'Actually, there is, I cannot promise it's very fast, but there's definitely a solid signal.'

The cottage looked sweet, white with a dark slate roof. No surprises there. It sat at the end of a single lane road which narrowed to become a driveway. It was directly on the waterfront, no road in front, with a breathtaking north-east view to open water.

'Do you like it?' he asked.

'It's gorgeous, I love it.'

'It's a wee place called Staffin. We're even further north here than Inverness.'

'Geez, no wonder I'm cold. Let's light the fire.'

He busied himself stacking and lighting the fire while she unpacked the groceries and made up the bed with the sheets that had been left for them. She gazed out of the kitchen window across to the blue water, sparkling with the last of the sunlight. She opened a bottle of red wine and handed Ross a glass as he knelt down in front of the fireplace. She ran her hand through his blond hair and massaged his neck.

'This is heaven on earth, it really is,' she said. He needed no further encouragement. He pulled her down onto the fluffy sheepskin rug in front of the crackling fire and peeled off all her clothes, slowly and deliberately.

Chapter 32

Ross, up bright and early, wearing his bunnet and collecting firewood, looked like a model in a photoshoot for the cover of *Country Life*. He was wearing yet another outfit: casual chinos, green jumper and soft brown loafers. He didn't even own a tracksuit or Ugg boots.

'What would you like to do today?' she asked.

'Nothing much, I might go for a wee walk along the shore later. I have a few phone calls and business to take care of.'

Sensing he wanted to be alone she said, 'Okay, well I was thinking I'd like to look around the shops in Portree. Do you want to come or would you rather have some time by yourself?'

'No, you go, I just feel like staying here the day, to unwind, and enjoy the nature and the peace and quiet.'

She smiled. 'How's the serenity?'

'Eh?'

'No, nothing. It's from *The Castle*. I mean it's remote and restful — good for the soul.' An Aussie would have got it.

'Exactly. And you've reminded me. Tomorrow, how would you like to take a trip over to Dunvegan Castle?'

'Absolutely.' She kissed him. 'See you later, then. Have you got other shoes for walking along the beach?'

'Oh, aye, I've some plodging boots I'll change into.'

She wondered what his plodging boots looked like; designer Wellington boots maybe. He took an hour to get ready every morning, even if he wasn't going out. She found this ritual endearing; she could believe he was making the effort for her. In response, she paid more attention to her own appearance. She wore full makeup every day, painted her fingernails, took time with her hair, and chose her outfits, such as they were, carefully.

Once in her own car, driving south along the A855 towards Portree, she pressed down the electric window to enjoy breathing in fresh, cool air. There was a wildness to the scenery — open green fields dotted with sheep and purple heather, lakes, groves of pine trees, distant mountains, and sea views. Strangely, the soft, muted light had the effect of intensifying the colours. This could be nowhere else but Scotland. She remembered words Don used to say years ago: a sight for sore eyes. It described Skye perfectly.

Half an hour later she arrived in Portree, and eventually found a car park; tourists with cameras outnumbered locals in the lively town. Two hours browsing, shopping and picking up extra supplies passed like minutes. She had deliberately not worn her tartan scarf. She bought an innocuous soft pale-grey scarf, two woollen jumpers and leggings, which seemed to be the current fashionable attire of choice. These should help pad out her wardrobe somewhat.

She looked up Minerva's address on her phone app while she had tea and a toasted cheese and tomato melt in a café with a sweeping view of the harbour. Minerva lived in Carbost, on the other side of Skye in the hills behind a distillery; an hour's drive away from their cottage in Staffin. Tonight she had plans for a roast chicken dinner; she would have to see her aunt another day. It gave her an idea though. She'd been puzzling over what to buy Ross as a gift. Around the corner she found a whisky emporium and bought a bottle of the local distillery whisky.

Just as she was opening her car door to put her packages on the backseat she noticed a family of four taking photos of the harbour. The father, wearing glasses with five-millimetre thick lenses, approached her and asked her, in hesitant English, if she would take a photo of all of them together. Then she noticed the Hyundai. It was the glaikit bampot from the ferry.

'Aye, no bother at all, ah'll tak' some wee photies fer ye, hoots mon.' she said in a dreadful Scottish accent.

'Thank you, thank you. We are from Taiwan. Your country … very beautiful.'

'Och, aye, it's bonnie, and braw. All squish up thegither noo a wee bit, ye ken.'

She took a few photos of them with the harbour in the background and handed him back the camera.

'Thank you very much,' he said, nodding and bowing his head.

'Aye, no bother at all. And remember to tell everyone you meet "och aye the noo". It means "good luck" in Scottish.'

'Okay … thank you. Ock-eye-de-noo. Thank you.'

'Aye. Och aye the noo to you. Cheerio.'

The family practised saying it as they jumped in their car.

She smiled. She felt guilty but, if she was to really fit in properly, she would have to participate in the apparently local custom of taking the piss out of tourists.

✦　✦　✦　✦

After lunch the next afternoon Ross drove to Dunvegan Castle. This time the landscape was rugged and bare, covered only with sparse vegetation. They passed several ruined and abandoned stone croft houses.

'They look so sad,' she said. 'It's heartbreaking to think these were once people's lives and livelihoods. That reminds me — Ali said she recognised your name. She thought your ancestors might have been large landowners who had something to do with the highland clearances. Do you know if that's true? Was your family involved?'

'Aye, that's right. Not something we'd be proud of now, ye ken. But that's what they did back then. Made a fortune out of the cheviot sheep.'

'And is that where your money comes from? Sorry, I don't mean to be nosy. I was just interested, is all.'

'Aye, that would be right too. My pa was a doctor before me, in Glasgow, where I grew up. But he wasn't keen on working too hard, and as soon as my grandpa died my folks flitted off to a villa in sunny Spain, Mallorca, and they've been there ever since. They have a good life now, always off travelling somewhere.

'But my grandpa was a canny chap, I think. He hadn't left all his booty to my pa — he divided it three ways between my pa, my brother and me. He had the foresight to realise Pa would probably as likely blow it all. So aye, in answer to your question, I didn't really need to work, but I wanted to be a surgeon, and that's what I did. I wanted to prove I could make it with or without my family's money.'

She reached over to gently massage his shoulder. 'I admire you, being a surgeon. I don't know how you do it. Even if I get the smallest cut, I feel lightheaded. I have an aversion to blood, even in meat. I always go for the sausages at barbecues.'

Dunvegan was an impressive, well-preserved castle with a commanding view of the loch beyond. Inside they inspected macabre, cruel dungeons and a collection of artefacts including Bonnie Prince Charlie's waistcoat and a clipping of his hair taken by Flora MacDonald.

She grabbed Ross's arm and whispered, 'I'm glad I didn't wear my MacLeod tartan scarf today — there are MacLeods everywhere.'

'Aye, right enough, it's their ancestral home, and there's enough pretenders represented here already.'

Outside they strolled through the extensive gardens featuring waterfalls, bridges, ferns and exotic species. Surrounded by such peaceful beauty, it was almost possible to forget about the unspeakable horror of grisly clan feuding the eight-hundred-year-old castle had witnessed.

They dined in a restaurant in the small town of Dunvegan where, feeling adventurous, she had her first taste of haggis. It was interesting, like chewy mince with a subtle liver flavour. Fortunately it was served with a creamy whisky sauce. At least now she knew what the national dish of Scotland tasted like.

Afterwards they climbed a steep hill, dominated by a large single megalith, standing nearly five metres high. By the time they reached the rock they were both puffing, but it was worth the effort; from this vantage the view stretched miles into the distance in every direction. Although it was after eight, the filtered sun accentuated the green, lush vegetation and illuminated the white houses below them with a magical light.

'Is this an ancient monument?' she asked, laying her hand on the pitted and cracked surface of the standing stone.

'Not sure,' he said. 'It's cemented in — I think it's a fake.'

'That'd be right. My first standing stone, and it's a Clayton's.'

'A what?'

'A phoney. But the rock is genuinely old though.'

'Oh aye, and I wouldn't want to be up here in an electrical thunderstorm.'

Further down the hill he found an information board. 'Well, how about that? Apparently, on midsummer's day in the year 2000 the locals held a Millennium cultural festival and erected this stone by traditional means. It's meant to be a marker of time.'

'That's extraordinary. What a wonderful thing to do. See, it's not a fake, it's as valid as any other monument — it marks two thousand years.'

'Aye, it's undoubtedly special, right enough. It would have been no mean feat getting it all the way up here.'

They wandered through an ancient cemetery and ruined chapel dating back to Saint Columba. The whole area was eerily quiet and suffused with a spiritual quality, an atmosphere that affected them both. They walked in silence, hand-in-hand, back down to the bottom of the hill to their waiting car.

Chapter 33

Friday — the morning Morgan had planned to meet Minerva. Ross was keen to go riding on a bicycle he had found, so he chose not to come with her. In a way she was glad to visit her aunt by herself, at least for their first meeting.

The narrow single lane road to the west took her through vast bare fields and cleared land. So empty. She noticed another derelict stone house, standing as a forlorn memorial of a crueller time. Lou had once mentioned her ancestors had relocated from Scotland to Australia and New Zealand around the time of the clearances. She wondered if Lou's family had once lived in stone croft houses such as these.

After driving for nearly an hour, she passed through a small but thriving township of Skye houses clustered around the distillery. Soon afterwards she pulled up in the driveway of Minerva's bright, white cottage in the surrounding hills. She was greeted by a boisterous border collie, obviously excited to see a visitor.

Minerva appeared in the doorway. 'Wheesht, Angus, away noo.'

'Hello … Minerva?'

Minerva embraced her in a powerful grip. 'Morrrgan! It's grand to see you. And please, call me Minnie. No one ever calls me Minerva.'

She was Minnie by name, but there was nothing mini about her — she was a large, robust woman with closely cropped, greying hair, cut longer on the top.

'Come inside, you'll be feeling the chill no doubt.'

'What a magnificent view you have. You live in a beautiful place,' Morgan said.

'Aye, we like it. It's quiet. And close to the distillery. We help out there sometimes so it's nice and handy for the work.'

Morgan entered the cosy cottage through which wafted a tantalising aroma of baking, and raisin toast.

A smaller, but also rotund woman with neatly trimmed short brown hair and a round smiling face entered from the kitchen, drying her hands on a towel.

'This is my partner, Petra,' Minnie said. 'Petra MacLeod.' Petra opened her arms to give Morgan a warm hug.

'Hello, Petra. MacLeod hey? I've noticed your mob have quite a presence here — we saw all the history up in Dunvegan Castle yesterday.'

Petra laughed, 'Oh aye, ye cannot get away from us MacLeods here on this island.'

Minnie ushered Morgan to sit on a soft, old leather couch

in the front room where a fire blazed in the fireplace. She couldn't help thinking it was specifically for her benefit, as both ladies were in short sleeves.

Angus, the dog sat at her feet and looked up at her expectantly, so she patted him on the head. He was smelly and, once she realised this, tried to wipe her hand on her jeans.

'Away now, Angus, ye big sook. Sorry, he loves attention. So, Morgan, tell me all about yourself. How do ye come to being here on Skye?'

Petra came into the room with hot scones, cream, jam and tea. Morgan thought she'd eaten more scones since she'd been in Scotland, than she had in her whole life. They were delicious though, and as they ate, she told them about being looked after by Don and Lou in Australia, coming to Scotland, finding the newspaper articles, meeting the neighbours Bella and Evan, and about discovering her father had a violent temper. She was aware she had to mention this sensitively; her father was Minnie's brother. She showed them the few printed photos she had, but not the crossed-out face one.

Petra sat silently, occasionally stroking Minnie on the arm. Minnie nodded and sighed. 'I can see why you'd want to know about your parents — it's only natural. I have more photos you might be interested in. There are some of your mother and the early days, still in the packet your uncle Mal gave me.'

So Mal hadn't destroyed the photos of his sister after all — he had passed them on to Minnie.

Petra stood up. 'I'll get them, love. I know where they are.'

Minnie's large face looked sombre. 'Aye, it's true. Jack was an angry young man. We say here in Scotland, "thrawn". He had a temper on him, even as a child. I remember meeting you only once. You weren't yet walking, so maybe you were somewhere around one year old. Your mother brought you to me but she didn't tell Jack. He and I didn't talk, you see. We were estranged for many years.'

'Can you say why, or you'd rather not …?'

Minnie fondled Angus's ears. A long, elastic dribble escaped from the dog's mouth and landed on the rug.

'Oh aye, it was all a long time ago noo. But I still feel the hurt of it. He would torment me, I was three years younger. He'd always find a way to upset me, pushing or tripping. I was wee then — if it was now, I'd give him a good wallop right back. And he had a cruel streak, that's no lie. He used to catch insects and small animals, mice and such, and kill them. He seemed to be fascinated with watching them die.

'But one day he went too far and he killed the little dog I had. He tied it up and cut it deeply with a kitchen knife and just watched, and timed it, to see how long it would take for the blood to leak out before he died. I was inconsolable and I wanted to have nothing to do with him ever again. It was a relief when he left home and got a job.'

'Didn't your parents do anything?'

'He was beyond their control, really. My dad, your grandfather, Alasdair, was a dear man, kind and sensitive, but he was weak, always did what Ma wanted. Now I think of it, he was possibly gay. Like me, ye ken.'

Morgan nodded. She'd already worked that one out.

'But our mother, Christine, was another thing altogether. She was a self-centred, bossy woman. She controlled the household, including my pa. Jack was always her favourite, and she made excuses for him all the time. She maintained it would have been an accident, not his fault. She and I never really got on. I don't think I was the daughter she wanted.'

Petra came back in with photo albums, and a packet of loose photos, labelled *Isla*. She put them on the coffee table and cleared away the tea things. Minnie smiled up at her. 'Thanks darlin'.' She handed Morgan the packet. 'These ones are for you to keep.'

Inside were a dozen or so photos of her mother, taken when she was a teenager, probably by Mal. She blinked her moist eyes a few times and returned the photos to the packet; she would look at them closely later.

Minnie opened one of the albums. 'Ah, now here are some pictures I took at your mother's and father's wedding. I didn't want to be there but I was obliged to, so I kept out the way by taking photos.'

Minnie pointed out Morgan's meek grandfather and her imposing grandmother. Then she saw her father and mother together, smiling, happy on their wedding day. They were undeniably an attractive couple.

'And there's your poor mother. I never understood what she saw in him, but I suppose he was good looking. I always wondered if she knew what she was getting herself in for. I knew him better than she did, of course, and I hoped he'd changed. He hadn't.'

'Were my other grandparents there, do you remember? On my mother's side?'

Minnie turned a few pages. 'Let me see — yes, here's the

fellow, what was his name? Graham maybe. I remember he was quite old at the wedding, a military bloke, very proper. He'd been somebody important in the war — army, I think. He had an air of authority about him, domineering, demanding. He spoke to people as if he was in command of them. I didn't take to him, anyway, maybe because he reminded me of my own mother.

'And his wife, your grandmother, well she wasn't there. She'd already died. She died quite young, poor thing, probably worn out by attending on him. Your mother was only young when her mother died, I remember now. She was lovely, your mother, by the way. I always felt I should warn her about Jack but I couldn't bring myself to spoil her happiness. Happiness — that's a joke. And anyway, I'd only met her once before they married. I kept as far away from my brother as I could.'

'They look so happy there. Why do you think he started abusing her and me — was that just part of his nature?'

'I couldn't say, pet, I'm sure he didn't hit her at first. Maybe it was because when you were born you took your mother's attention away from him. He was self-centred, narcissistic, ye ken, like our mother. And then the wee boy dying, well that must have tipped him over the edge.'

'I wonder why my mother didn't stand up for herself. Bella, the neighbour said she wouldn't leave him.'

'I really cannot think why. She could have if she'd really wanted to. Maybe she thought she could fix him, or maybe she thought because she had chosen him, that was her lot, and she should stick by him. Who knows?'

'What I can't understand is why her brother, my uncle Mal, wouldn't have stepped in to help her.'

'I believe he did try, dear, but like you said, she was goin' nowhere. My theory is she was meek and compliant like her mother. She was beautiful, Isla, but I got the impression she had low self-esteem. Her father, that military bloke, was overbearing, a strict disciplinarian, and possibly she was drawn to Jack, weirdly, because he was the same. Perhaps it's an attraction to the familiar, or the subconscious trying to put something to right, but it does seem to happen that way, doesn't it? Patterns repeat through the generations.'

Chapter 34

Morgan asked to borrow all Minnie's albums so she could study them in more detail and take copies of the pictures she was interested in.

'Aye, no bother at all, pet, take them for as long as you like.'

The hour's drive back to the cottage gave her time to reflect. Minnie had confirmed Bella's account of her father having been abusive. But more than abusive, downright evil. Could she have inherited any of her father's malevolence? She didn't think so; she had never had any desire to hurt people, and especially not animals. She was more like her mother, a bit meek.

Perhaps he was an aberration, a freak of nature, or had sustained damage as a result of some childhood incident. Whatever it was, he had certainly held a powerful grip over her mother. Her eyes misted thinking about her mother — a sensitive, gentle soul who deserved respect, not abuse. And, like her mother before her, she was too oppressed to escape the black hole of her husband's control.

Minnie had said something about patterns being repeated, and her thoughts turned to Anton. Could that explain why she had been attracted to him, an angry, dominant type? But how did that work? She had only just discovered her father had been abusive; she had no conscious memory of him. It was alarming to think that, as a three-year-old, she had registered enough of his behaviour to influence her choice of marriage partner.

Staffin Bay came into view as she rounded the corner leading to their little cottage. For some inexplicable reason, her mother had chosen to stay with her father. She had determined her own destiny and, tragic though it was, these were other people, with other lives, who had made choices. It was all in the past and brooding about them wasn't helpful; it wouldn't change anything. In the end, knowing was better than not knowing. She would try not to dwell on it.

Ross had already started making dinner. He had taken some trouble to cook a salmon pie but she wasn't hungry, having eaten several of Petra's scones. His pie was tasty though and, not wanting to hurt his feelings, she ate as much as she could.

'What were your uncle and aunt like?' he asked.

'Well, my aunt Minnie is living with her partner, Petra, so no uncle involved. She's never been married.'

'You mean they're lezzos?'

She nodded.

'Ah well, each to their own. Did you find out anything interesting about your parents?'

'I did, but it's not great. Apparently, my father had a cruel streak. He tormented and killed animals when he was a child, he beat Minnie up when she was little, and then when he married my mother started bashing her, and me too. He was attractive but he had a violent and uncontrollable temper. I didn't mention it to you before but the next-door neighbour we visited told me I was often covered in bruises. At age three. Can you believe it? I'm sorry my mother died, but I'm not sorry to have missed out on being brought up by that monster.'

'Sounds like a right bastard.'

After dinner she brought the albums to the table so they might look through them together. He immediately recognised her mother. 'She was a beautiful lady, your ma. And here's your pa — handsome chap. I can see why she was attracted to him. Pity he was such a prick.'

He looked at a few more pages but soon yawned. 'Maybe I'll look at more later, bonnie lass. I'm just feeling like watching television the night. My bum's a bit sore from the long bike ride. I could do with a nice massage.'

She decided the photos could wait until tomorrow.

✦ ✦ ✦ ✦

Next morning they walked briskly along the shoreline strewn with volcanic rocks. She was gradually getting used to the constant cool temperature and the bracing, moist air, and walking fast was a good way to keep warm. Ross wore his plodging boots, nubuck leather with rubber soles. No green plastic Wellies for him.

They watched fat, grey seals basking on a flat rock, and

caught sight of a swimming sea otter. He pointed out the unfamiliar seabirds she had seen before but had not been able to name: redshank, sandpiper, and a wader called a yellowlegs. A few heavy spots of rain splattered on them and, reluctantly, they returned to the cottage.

'Why don't you go through your albums and just relax here,' he said. 'I want to nip down to the gym in Portree this afternoon, make a few calls, and do a couple of things in the town. I'll see you later on.'

Clear enough. But the day had turned cool, and with rain forecast for the rest of the week, she was happy to laze around the cosy cottage by herself, fire lit, enjoying the solitude.

She arranged the photos of her mother and gazed at them for a long time. She looked happy and carefree. Sadly, she had been only one year older than Morgan was now when she died. What a waste of a life.

She had no idea who most of the people were in Minnie's albums, but she pored over the pictures for hours. Seeing a photo of Don and Lou at the wedding, eight years younger than when she first knew them, made her realise how much she missed them. She was glad Ross had gone out; it was impossible to look at old photos and not become melancholy.

One photo fascinated her: the one showing her grandfather, Graham — Major Murray — proudly wearing his military medals. He still looked formidable and imposing at nearly eighty. But according to Don, he also had a sixth sense which had saved him, as a young cadet, from being blown to pieces.

If it hadn't been for Graham, she would never have known Don or gone to Australia. Her life would have been completely different. Or would it? She could have been brought up by Minnie as a Scottish girl living on Skye. In fact, it was possible she could have ended up exactly where she was today. A different path to the same destination.

On the day they were due to leave Skye, she had to return the photo albums to Minnie, and it was pelting with rain.

'I've seen on the map where your aunt lives — close to the Talisker distillery,' Ross said. 'So how about you just drop me at the distillery on the way to visit her and pick me up after.'

'Sounds like a plan,' she said. 'I'll drive and you can sit and enjoy the scenery for a change.' Not that he would see much through the downpour.

She was actually relieved not to drag him up to her aunt's place. She knew he wasn't really interested in meeting her family. They packed the car and said goodbye to the little cottage, their cosy haven for the past week.

At Minnie and Petra's whitewashed cottage on the hill, Angus bounded out, barking and running in circles. He jumped up, covering her with slobber and mud.

'Where's your young man?' asked Minnie.

She didn't feel inclined to enlighten her as to Ross's age. 'He's down at the distillery doing a tasting tour. I'll pick him up on the way home.' Now she regretted he hadn't come to meet them; she was afraid it might seem like a snub.

Petra had baked shortbread for their journey home. 'That's so kind of you, Petra, thank you. We've got a long drive ahead of us, so we'll be glad of it.' In return, she gave them a batch of Anzac biscuits she had made yesterday in the cottage.

'Where are you off to now? Back home or more travelling?' Minnie asked.

'We're heading back home to Ayr but we're booked in to stay the night in Oban.'

'Mm.' Minnie looked at her watch, then out the window at the teeming rain. 'That'll take you a good four hours, even by the bridge, in this weather. And what then? Are you planning on staying in Scotland?'

'Yes, I feel settled in Ayr — Prestwick to be precise. Kirsty lives there and, apart from seeing Don and Lou, I've got no reason to go back to Australia.'

Petra beamed at her. She had the kind of smile that turned up at both corners like a crescent moon. It was impossible not to like her.

'Oh, that's brilliant,' Minnie said. 'Then we can see each other more often. How did you get on with the albums, were they interesting to you?'

'Yes, fascinating, thank you. A lot of the people I didn't know, of course, but I did recognise the grandparents in many of them, and the ones when you were a child, and my godparents Don and Lou. I took copies of them on my phone. It made me realise how important physical photos are — digital photos are so easily deleted or lost — and they could be all we have left to remember someone once they're gone.'

'And before I forget, I've something for you.' Minnie picked up an old biscuit tin painted with a Bonnie Prince Charlie highland scene. She prised open the lid and handed Morgan an antique silver pendant made of Celtic spiral knotwork, set with a huge, golden, translucent stone in the centre.

'Oh my God, it's beautiful. Is it really old?'

'Oh aye, it came from your grandmother — your mother's mother that is. Beth was her name. We think it's from the eighteenth century or even earlier because it would have been handed down to her too. That stone is a cairngorm. It could do with a good clean, but it should polish up nicely. It's for you, dear — it's from your uncle Mal.'

'Really?' She took the heavy pendant from Minnie. The stone, a warm, amber colour cut in an unusual seven-sided shape, sparkled with many facets. A smaller, flat, central face, of a darker shade, gave the whole stone the appearance of an eye. It had an alluring depth and when she turned it, she could see different shapes and patterns like a kaleidoscope. As she touched the stone, the hairs on her arms stood on end. She felt a perceptible vibration coming from it. And it wasn't just that her hand was shaking.

'When did Mal give you this?'

'It was at Jack and Isla's joint funeral, back in 1991, a bitterly cold day, I remember. There's more jewellery in the tin. It all went to him but he passed it on to me because he was afraid his wife … Janet?'

'Jane.'

'Oh, aye, Jane. He was worried she might take it into her head to destroy Isla's jewellery, like she destroyed some photographs. She seemed like a nice enough lady to me but I think she might have been schizophrenic or something.'

'Yes, I heard about that.'

'And there's more … right at the bottom of the tin I found this.' Minnie fished out an old black-and-white photograph showing an imposing man in military uniform standing beside a small woman.'

'This is your grandfather, Graham, I was right about his name, and your grandmother, Beth. Your mother's parents on their wedding day in 1946 — it's written on the back.'

'Fantastic, Minnie, that's great. I couldn't find any photos of them in the album, apart from the one of him where he was elderly at my mother and father's wedding. Makes sense I suppose, they're not your relatives. So, wow, look at them, taken just after the war. He looks much older than her, do you think?'

'Yes, I believe so, but he still outlived her. But that's not all. Have a close look at what she's wearing — if I'm not mistaken, she's wearing that pendant.'

She peered at the photo then photographed it with her phone to zoom in closer. 'You're right you know, it's the same pendant.' She showed Minnie and Petra the closeup.

'Amazing contraptions these things,' Petra said, holding the phone close to her eyes.

'But, do you know what? I've got a feeling ...' She took back the phone and found the photos of her mother she had copied. 'There you are.' She showed Minnie and Petra a photo, zoomed in. Her mother was wearing the same pendant with the golden stone.

'That gives me goosebumps,' she said. 'I have to say, when I first touched that stone, I felt a tingling going up my arm.'

'That must mean you are the rightful heir of it,' Petra said, nodding. 'Cairngorm is a crystal you know, often used in healing because of its energy.'

'I don't know what to say. It's beautiful. Thank you so much. I'll look after it well.'

'And wear it,' Minnie said. 'Jewellery should be worn and seen, not hidden away in some old tin. There are other things in here too — bracelets, rings, brooches.'

'I will. I promise. This is wonderful. These are the only things I have of my mother's. I shall treasure them.'

She kissed and hugged them both and patted smelly Angus. Then she navigated carefully through the rain down the narrow driveway towards the distillery.

Chapter 35

Like many of the buildings on Skye, the distillery was a large whitewashed building with a dark roof. Ross was nowhere to be seen so she sat in the car park with the windscreen wipers on for a few minutes. She tried calling him but his phone was off. She reached behind her for the two umbrellas on the floor; she would have to make a dash through the rain to collect him.

Once through the front door she shook her umbrella and entered the foyer, rich with golden timber flooring, oak wall panels and barrels, all illuminated with warm lighting. A distinctive malty aroma mixed with smoky peat hung in the air. She spotted Ross in a far corner engaged in close conversation with a pencil-slim blonde woman wearing a short yellow skirt suit.

A knot formed in her stomach. Despite being wet, muddy and bedraggled, she assumed a confident facade and sauntered up to them casually.

'Oh, hello bonnie lass. Finished with the rellies then?'

She smiled. 'Yes, all done and ready to go.' Confident.

'Aye, well thank you Jacinta,' he said to the guide, holding out his hand. 'That was a most enjoyable tour.'

Jacinta pushed her hair behind her ear and beamed a dazzling smile at him as she shook his hand. 'No bother at all, Ross, you're most welcome. Any time.'

She attempted to smile at Jacinta but she suspected it came across as more of a sneer. He collected his four bottles of single malt, handing two to Morgan to carry. He had seemingly developed a liking for this whisky, already having finished the gift bottle she'd bought him.

'Ah'm glad you're driving, bonnie lass. There weren't many people in the tour so they were more than usually generous with the tasting whiskies,' he said, chuckling. 'And, man, that Jacinta was a cracker — very tidy. Nice to see someone wearin' a skirt for a change.'

He yawned. 'I might just have a wee snooze. You okay to drive? It's quite easy — main road all the way.'

He shoved the cases on the back seat over to her side and reclined the passenger seat. Driving through the rain and mist while contending with an overabundance of motorhomes took some concentration. After an hour she passed the picturesque Eilean Donan castle which, disappointingly, was obscured by the weather. After another hour he woke up when she stopped at a hotel in Invergarry for lunch and to stretch their legs.

She made a beeline for the ladies where she resurrected her makeup and hair. She smoothed her jumper down over her hips and frowned at her muddy jeans in the long mirror.

Despite the rain she had enjoyed driving, but after lunch she reluctantly let him take the wheel, as he knew where their accommodation was for the night. They arrived at a charming bed and breakfast high on the hill in Oban overlooking the harbour. It wasn't a poky room in a creaky house, but a luxuriously appointed, separate private annexe.

'Boy, you sure can pick 'em,' she said. 'So many gorgeous places. You know, I honestly don't think I would be able to choose where to live in Scotland. Every place has been more beautiful than the last. I would have to live like a gypsy, travelling indefinitely. What a pity we have to go back so soon.'

'Aye, well, unfortunately I need to be back in Edinburgh on Monday otherwise we could have done a longer trip.'

They had packed only the things they needed for the night into his small case and her day bag; the rest they left in the car. But she did bring in the tin of jewellery to show him. She handed him the pendant and he examined it closely.

'Well, look at that — a heptagon. Heavy, isn't it? Genuine antique — could be hundreds of years old. Nice to have some vintage bling to wear.'

As a break from home cooking they planned to eat in a restaurant. She lounged on the sofa while he was getting ready. After the long drive she was struggling to keep her eyes open. She yawned and reached for the cairngorm pendant. It intrigued her and she couldn't leave it alone. She wanted to touch it, hold it and wonder about it. The stone was translucent and open at the back, letting the light shine through. She held it up close to her eye to look through it.

Everything in the room became suffused with a golden

glow, distorting her vision. She could make out only shapes. The light enveloped her with a curious frisson, giving her goosebumps. Suddenly her vision cleared and she could see straight through the gemstone as if a mist had been lifted. But the scene she saw was not of the living room she was in. Her pulse quickened. It was a Roman military camp, as real as if she was actually there.

She was looking down at dozens of leather tents and wooden structures, surrounded by high timber walls built upon raised earth ramparts. Lookout towers stood at each corner. A few soldiers stationed outside the enclosure wore metal armour, others inside wore tunics that looked like leather, and shoes tied up with laces. Her heart beat rapidly. She could hear the murmur of their voices, horses neighing, and smell the smoke from the fire. It was the same scene she had sometimes dreamed about. She dropped the pendant in fright.

When Ross came back into the room, he found her sitting bolt upright on the sofa, staring straight ahead. 'What's up bonnie lass? You're lookin' like you've seen a ghost.'

'No, I'm fine, just tired, is all.'

'Okay, are we ready to go out?'

She replaced the pendant in the tin with a shaking hand. The rain had abated but the air was still moist and chilly. She threw on her new grey scarf and they walked down the hill to the marina where they splurged on an extravagant seafood dinner in a restaurant converted from an old boat house.

Afterwards, back in the guest house, she even joined him in a few drams of the Talisker. It was different from other whiskies she'd tasted — peatier. She found it went well together with Petra's shortbread.

In bed that night as he leant over her and ran his soft, but strong hands all over her body, making her ache with desire for him, she wanted to never forget this moment, this place, this experience. And she wanted never to lose him. He cupped her breasts, caressing and kissing them. 'I just love how your tits are so responsive,' he said as he gently bit her nipples.'

Ecstasy. 'I'm glad you like them.' She laughed. 'My ex-husband used to call them east-west tits. He criticised that they weren't proper because they should point straight ahead, not side to side, and he claimed that he would know because, apparently, he was a connoisseur of tits.'

'Was he now? Nice fellow. Sounds like a right twally. Nothin' wrong with them at all. He squeezed both her breasts together and examined them. Nothing that couldn't be fixed, anyhoo.'

Chapter 36

They arrived back at Ross's house in Ayr mid-afternoon the next day. She hadn't mentioned the vision she'd seen through the cairngorm. She wasn't even sure she'd really seen it. He was pragmatic, scientific, a doctor. He would ridicule the notion of anything paranormal, and say she'd had a hallucination or she'd fallen asleep momentarily and dreamt it.

She hadn't wanted to wear the pendant again either. The thought had been playing on her mind: had her mother been wearing it when she died? Perhaps it was a bad omen; it didn't seem to have done her mother or grandmother much good. One part of her was telling her not to be silly and superstitious about an inanimate piece of jewellery, but another part was attracted to its strange energy.

She helped him out of the car with his cases. 'Do you want me to stay tonight?'

'Maybe not the night, bonnie lass. I've a few things to do, washing clothes, bits and pieces. I'll call you in a wee while, before I have to get back up to Edinburgh.'

Returning to her own flat after being in such close contact with Ross for so long felt wrong. It was cold, dark, and smelt musty. Even though it was mid-summer it was still only nineteen degrees — winter daytime temperature for Brisbane. She turned on the heater.

She unpacked, put on a load of washing, then opened her laptop to transfer the holiday photos from her phone. She looked back at the photos of Loch Lomond, Skye, Portree, their little cottage in Staffin, the Millennium standing stone, Dunvegan Castle, Oban, Minnie and Petra, dozens of old photos from Minnie's albums and dozens more of Ross in various poses and outfits. They had been away for only nine days. She sincerely wished they could have travelled for longer, but he had pressing commitments at the hospital.

Now she had a better picture of Scotland, the highlands, the lochs, the villages. Had she seen the *real* Scotland though — the Scotland she had imagined and fantasised about? It occurred to her that she hadn't, and she never would. It didn't exist, any more than the 'real' Australia existed. It was a construct, an illusion.

She placed the shortbread tin of jewellery on the sideboard without looking in it, and heard a knock at the door. Her heart leapt. Ross? She opened the door, smiling, but it was Harish.

'Hello, Morgan, ma'am. I hope you had a nice holiday.'

'Yes thank you Harish, it was really lovely. Would you like to come in?'

'Oh, no thank you ma'am, I have to go to work at the restaurant pronto, but I wanted to give you your letters. I collected your post for you while you were away so it didn't fall on the ground and get wet.' He handed over the bundle.

'Thank you, Harish, that's thoughtful of you.'

He smiled showing his white teeth, did his little prayer bow to her, and went back down the stairs, his turban bobbing as he descended. She took the mail inside and spread it out on the table. He needn't have bothered. There were only advertising leaflets, retail catalogues, and a news sheet from a local politician. Nothing addressed to her personally at all. Of course, why would there be?

What should she do now? Phone Ross? No, he said he would call. So she phoned Kirsty in Edinburgh and then read a magazine until she determined it to be drink-o'clock. Her fingers itched to call him but she resisted. Later in the evening she Skyped Don and Lou to tell them all about their travels — well, not all, but enough.

Despite the electric blanket she had trouble sleeping; she missed Ross's warm body next to hers. She reached out her hand but his side of the bed was cold.

She awoke late, washed, dressed and applied full makeup as she had become accustomed to doing. Would he be up or had he slept in like she had? Checking her account online she saw the payment for the website work she'd done had been deposited. Not a bad little earn. And it gave her an idea. The day being fine, she wheeled her bike out from the downstairs locker and cycled into Prestwick. A ride in the fresh air always lifted her spirits.

First, she took the pendant, bracelets, rings and brooches into a local jeweller. He peered at them closely with a loupe, similar to Kirsty's designer's loupe, and scratched his large nose. 'These are exquisite. This pendant, in particular, I would date around 1700. Thereabouts. I can see small, faint markings on the back of the chain. But then again I'm not really sure — I'm not an antiques expert but I have the feeling the stone could be much older.' He balanced the pendant in his palm as if testing the weight.

'This would certainly come up nicely after cleaning. We use an ultrasonic method, so it causes no damage to expensive or delicate jewellery.' He examined the pendant again. 'This is unusual — this spiral pattern and the knotwork, it almost has a Norse influence. Can I ask where you got it from?'

'It was my mother's and my grandmother's before her.' She could tell the jeweller was impressed with the pendant. 'Is it valuable, do you think?'

'Valuable — I should say it is. The collection probably belongs in a museum.'

'I did want to wear it once it's cleaned.'

'It's certainly sturdy enough, nothing flimsy about it.'

'How long will it take for you to clean them?'

'Come back in three hours, they should be ready then.'

He gave her a receipt slip and she collected her bike from outside the shop. Ross would be interested to know the jeweller thought the pendant and other pieces should be in a museum. She cycled further on to a travel agency. The travel agent, a smartly dressed mature lady with a friendly face took off her headset and smiled. Her name tag said 'Trudy'.

'I'd like to open an account on someone else's behalf if that's possible please,' Morgan said.

'Of course you can,' Trudy said. 'What did you have in mind?'

'I'd like to deposit enough money so a friend of mine can book a flight to Jamaica for her and her son, and maybe a week's accommodation for them. The son is disabled and confined to a wheelchair, a fairly substantial one, so are there flights which can accommodate that?'

'Absolutely. Usually wheelchairs go at the back of the plane. If it's an electric wheelchair they have to store it as luggage but there are special seats available to accommodate disabled passengers. As long as we have plenty of notice we can organise something that will work.'

'Great. Shall I get my friend to call you once she knows when she'd like to travel?'

'Yes, please do. Here's my card. I'll arrange everything for them directly and we'll draw from the funds you leave for them. That's a kind thing you're doing, by the way.'

'Thank you. They well and truly deserve it.' Using her phone, she electronically transferred an amount Trudy suggested would cover all the expenses. Then, given she had a couple of hours to spare, she cycled to Ali and Iain's house. Iain was out playing golf but Ali was delighted to see her.

'Hello, pet! How lovely to see you. Come in. You're looking glamorous.'

She laughed. 'Glamorous! I think that's the first time in my life I've ever been called glamorous.'

'Oh but you are. You've lost some weight, and your hair is pretty — lovely copper streaks — it really suits you. So, how was your trip away? When did you get back? Tell me all about it.'

'It was wonderful, and romantic, could have been longer though. We got back only yesterday. You were right about his family — he didn't seem to mind telling me. It was an old family that made a fortune out of some kind of sheep. His grandfather divided the estate between his brother and him as well as his father, so he received his inheritance early. He doesn't really have to work but he chose to be a surgeon.'

'He sounds like a fine young man ... well, maybe not so young.'

'He is, he's great. He has to go back up to the hospital soon, unfortunately. So I've just been catching up on housekeeping and stuff. I phoned Kirsty. I'm looking forward to her coming back.'

'Oh aye, I know, I'm missing her too. She'll no' be coming back for another month. She's having too much fun distracting Callum from his studies.'

They laughed and chatted until she realised it was already four o'clock and the jeweller closed at four-thirty. She hugged Ali goodbye and pedalled back to the jeweller.

'Ah, here you are,' he said. 'The pieces are all ready for you. They've come up quite nicely.' He displayed the jewellery on a velvet cloth for her inspection. The silver gleamed and the stones sparkled. 'It's some collection you have here. These brooches could possibly be French — there's a tiny fleur de lis hidden in the knotwork. At a guess, they are maybe sixteenth century.'

'Oh, yes, they're beautiful. They've been transformed.'

She picked up a chunky black bracelet she hadn't taken much notice of before.

'That's jet,' the jeweller said. 'Real jet. One way you can tell is by the temperature — it's warm, not cool like glass. This kind of design was popular in Roman times.' He looked at her with a curious expression as if to say 'where did you really get this stuff?'

'Roman, wow. Pretty old then.'

'Aye, and jet was supposed to have a protective power, to help ward off the evil eye.'

'Okay.' You never know when that might come in handy. She picked up the pendant and inspected it.

'Ah, now, that one's interesting,' he said. 'I discovered the silver chain is a later addition, but the central cairngorm and spiral knotwork is much older. Older than I first thought. It might originally have been a brooch. It's an exquisite specimen of cairngorm you have here, no flaws I can see. It's a type of quartz, which can produce a small electrical current, or a vibration. I cleaned it as well as I could but my machine stopped working halfway through, so I polished it by hand. It's come up well though.'

He wrapped each piece in tissue paper and handed her the tin. 'I think you should consider insuring this jewellery. You'd need to get it valued first.' He gave her a valuer's business card.

'Thanks, that's good advice.'

'But I don't think you should be carrying it round in a biscuit tin. Here's my card too. If you ever want to sell any of these pieces, please do call me.'

She pedalled away from the shop and glanced back to see him staring out the window after her.

Chapter 37

Although Morgan was tired after another night of broken sleep, she dressed to go out early. She badly wanted to phone Ross but restrained herself; he did say he would call. A whole day and two nights had passed without talking to him. She thought about him constantly and couldn't wait to see him again. Trying not to think about him made her think about him even more. How was she going to manage when he went back to work? Maybe she'd have to relocate to Edinburgh. That wouldn't be so bad.

On her way out the door, as an afterthought, she took the cairngorm pendant from the tin, unwrapped it and slipped it over her head. The silver chain felt cold where it touched her neck.

It was a dreary day, too wet to cycle, so she drove to Bella and Evan's house. She knew the way without needing to consult a map. Bella opened the door and immediately squashed her in a bear hug. Evan grinned and said something that sounded like 'Molly'. Morgan kissed him and sat down to give them the travel documentation.

'This is a gift from Kirsty and me. Two flights to Jamaica. It's all paid for. Here's Trudy's number — all you need to do is call her and tell her when you'd like to go. And here's Kirsty's and my email addresses, and phone numbers in case there's anything you need us to do for you.

'I know you said your sister would have you stay with her but there's a week's accommodation for you and Evan in Montego Bay so you have the choice, and you can decide how long you'd like to stay. When you want to come back, just contact Trudy by email and she'll arrange it. I've checked the flights and accommodation are all suitable for Evan's chair, and there will be people to help with the whole trip. It's all organised. All you need to do is call Trudy, and then pack.'

Tears glistened in Bella's eyes. 'This is too good of you Morgan. I thought I would not see my sister for a long, long time. I don't know how I can repay you.'

'You're not going to repay it. It's the least I could do for you.' She handed Evan a glossy travel brochure on Jamaica. He grasped it in his twisted hand but his eyes never left her face.

'I don't know how to thank you, dear, it is very generous.' She turned to Evan, 'We're going to see Auntie Hannah in Jamaica. It will be sunny and warm — look at de beautiful beaches.'

She turned back to Morgan, 'This is a dream come true. It really is. We'll go as soon as I call my sister and let her know the good news. Is your cousin Kirsty no' with you today?'

'No, she's staying in Edinburgh for a while, she'll be back next month.'

Bella said, 'Will you thank her for me?'

'Of course I will.'

Then Bella noticed her pendant. 'Oh, my goodness. Is that your mother's?'

'Yes, my aunt Minnie gave it to me. You were right — she lives on Skye. She gave me all my mother's jewellery. She was keeping it in a shortbread tin.'

'That is wonderful. I'm so glad it wasn't lost. It was precious to her — her keek stane.'

'Sorry? What? Her keek stane?'

'Oh yes indeed. She always kept it with her.'

'You mean like a crystal ball?'

'Something similar, yes.'

'How did she use it, do you know?'

'Well, she did many readings for me when I knew her. The pendant would stay around her neck and she would hold the stone in her two hands and just look at it, for a while. And then she would change, sort of go somewhere else. She would receive messages and be able to tell you things about yourself and your past, and also your future. That is what most people wanted to know I think.'

Morgan felt a chill in the air. 'Did she ever look through it?'

'Only once or twice I saw her do that. Mostly she just stared at it. I think the spiral pattern kind of put her into a trance, hypnotised like.'

'Oh, wow. That's how she did it. Do you know, Bella, did she wear it all the time or did she wear it only to conduct readings?'

'All de time. I never saw her without it.'

Back in her flat Morgan looked up 'keek stane' on the internet. She found it was a well-known and ancient way of inducing an altered state of consciousness in order to see visions. The skill lay in the ability to interpret those visions. Naturally, in early times, anyone with this skill was labelled a witch.

She was fascinated by the pendant but she was also wary. She traced the interwoven knotwork with her finger — no beginning and no end. She held it up to the light but there was no way she was going to look through it again.

It was smooth and cool on her cheek. To think her mother had worn it and touched it and treasured it. Now knowing what it was, should she wear it? Would her mother have wanted her to? Petra had said she was the rightful heir. She felt sure she was meant to have it. One thing she knew for certain — she had no intention of getting it valued for insurance; she couldn't put a monetary value on something that had meant so much to her mother.

She wrapped the pendant in the tissue and replaced it in the tin. Would Ross be interested to know the cairngorm pendant was her mother's keek stane or would he think she was a fruitcake?

Anyway, now it had been two days since they'd spoken and she wanted to see if he had plans for them for the weekend, before he had to be back at the hospital. She could no longer resist phoning him. She smiled as she touched his name in her contacts. Her heart quickened when she heard his voice.

'Hello … Morgan.'

'Hi bonnie lad, how are you this dreich afternoon? See, I'm

picking up the lingo brawlie. I just thought I'd call and see what you're up to.' *Brawlie?* Did anybody actually say that?

'Oh, aye, fine, fine. I'm back in Edinburgh the noo, back to the usual dramas and incompetent wankers. How are you doin'?'

'Yeah, okay … but I thought you weren't going back until Monday.'

'Aye, that's right, but I decided I'd better come up sooner. And lucky I did, this place is a nut house.'

She could hear clanging and shouting in the background. 'Sounds like it. I could drive up and stay there with you.' Her stomach began to constrict.

'Oh no, it's no' a good idea. Look, I'll call you when I've more time to talk. Sorry I have to go now … you take care. Cheerio.'

She blinked at her phone as he ended the call. Her heart pounded. She stared out the window at the wet, grey day. What was wrong? That must have been the first time he hadn't called her 'bonnie lass'. She had hoped to see him before he travelled up to the hospital again, but obviously that wasn't going to happen, and he hadn't given any indication when he would be back.

It was clear enough — he didn't want to see her in Edinburgh. Had he gone off her? Had the novelty of her being Australian worn off or was she overreacting? She began to feel sick.

Chapter 38

She awoke at two am. No point trying to sleep. Thoughts of Ross kept flooding into her mind — the touch of him, the smell of him, the taste of him, his sexy accent, his funny little mannerisms like his chuckle, and how he combed his hair at every opportunity. She missed him with a physical ache.

She wrapped herself in her dressing gown and opened her laptop. The garden centre she had designed the website for had sent through a list of changes. Of course there would be changes, there always are. She made a coffee and settled down in front of the laptop to work.

It was a cool morning and she watched the sun rise just before six. What time do the shops open, she wondered. According to Google the small Spar nearby opened at seven am. She needed supplies, and fresh air to clear her head, so instead of driving to the big supermarket she cycled along the walkway to the Spar. It took less than two minutes.

In the store AC/DC's *It's a long way to the top* played

through the speakers in the ceiling. She stood still, listening to the song. The memory of Anton singing 'It's a long way to the shop if you want a sausage roll', made her smile. She had never for a second suspected how appropriately AC/DC also applied to his sexuality.

AC/DC, the quintessential Australian rock group. Except half of them had been born in Scotland. It had been the annoying music of choice for the yobbos across the road back home, but here, it reminded her of Australia. She sighed.

Back home — why did she think that? Probably because Scotland didn't feel like home yet. How long would it take? Should she try to copy the accent? Possibly not, if her effort in Portree was anything to go by.

'Helloo, let me know if I can help ye find anything.'

'Yeah, gidday — ta, no worries.' She would clearly need to work on her Scottish accent.

She bought a selection of frozen meals and, as the store was also an off-licence, she bought several bottles of wine. How civilised, they sell alcohol.

'Anything else, pet?'

'Ah, yeah, a sausage roll please.'

She managed to balance the two plastic bags on her handlebars for the journey home. As she approached her front door, dismounted and lifted the bags from the bike, one caught on the front mudguard and tore, spilling the contents onto the bitumen path.

Harish opened the front door as she was picking up the groceries. 'Morgan, ma'am, let me help you.' He rushed to pick up the meals and replaced them in the torn bag. He also took the other bag with the wine while she manoeuvred the bike through the door and into the storage locker.

'Thank you, Harish. Lucky it wasn't the bag of wine that fell.' She looked at his mop of messy, dark brown hair. 'It took me a moment to recognise you without your turban. You don't always wear it then?'

He laughed. 'No, hardly ever. I only wear it to the restaurant because it keeps hair out of the food, and also people think you're not a proper Indian if you don't wear one. Let me help you upstairs with these groceries.'

He carried the bags up and put them on her kitchen counter. He looked at the frozen meals she had bought, and the limp sausage roll.

'You like to eat this stuff? I should bring you some good meals from the restaurant. Free, I mean, no cost. We have meals left over sometimes after a weekend. Next time I bring some for you.'

◆　◆　◆　◆

After more than a week of sleepless nights later she had still heard nothing from Ross. Early in the dark hours of the morning she sat in front of her laptop as usual. She saw again the photos she had transferred — her parents smiling on their wedding day, standing in front of their house, proudly holding their baby. Which was not her. She zoomed in as far as she could on the baby but she couldn't see his face. Why were there no other photos of Simon? There must have been some.

She tried hard to remember that time — sometime late

in 1991— but her memory turned up nothing at all. It just didn't go back that far. Her thoughts drifted again to Ross. She tried to picture him as a teenager in 1991 listening to *Nirvana*. No matter what she tried to think of, her mind would inevitably meander back to him.

Afraid of turning into a nocturnal animal, she considered making an appointment to consult a doctor for her sleeping problem, but it was three am. So she logged on to a domain she knew, searched for sleeping remedies, and navigated to a website offering all kinds of drugs to treat a myriad of health problems, with no need for a prescription. Free shipping, secure online payment.

She clicked on 'Sleeping aid' and read the description. It sounded like an effective treatment for insomnia, and it might offer the added benefit of stopping her from missing Ross so much. She ordered two boxes of the first product on the list. Great. Now she wouldn't have to get dressed and contend with some nosy doctor who would be bound to ask a whole lot of questions and might not give her what she wanted anyway.

The company must have been based in the UK because, incredibly, her package arrived that same afternoon. The recommended medical dose was one milligram. Why were the tablets three milligrams then? That evening she swallowed a three-milligram tablet. She had the best sleep ever, and awoke feeling refreshed at seven am.

She resolved to waste no more time moping. She came here to find out about her parents, and she had the persistent feeling she was missing something. Not only that, she knew exactly nothing about her baby brother. She took out the library articles and re-read them.

Local couple, Jack and Isla Dee were tragically killed when their car plunged off the B742 into the River Ayr …

How could she identify where it had happened on that road? Stewart, the librarian, at least the volunteer, had mentioned a guard rail was added later. And he had offered to help her further.

Nurse McFeeter, the duty nurse, expressed regret at the passing of the child.

Nurse McFeeter. Could it be worth asking if she still worked at the South Ayrshire Hospital? It was unlikely; it would depend on how old she had been in 1991, and she could be anywhere by now. She decided to revisit the Carnegie Library.

She dressed and was surprised to find her jeans hung loose on her. She opened the shortbread tin of jewellery and put on the pendant, the jet bracelet, the silver bracelet and four silver rings. There was a fifth ring, a gold one, probably her mother's wedding ring, and this she had no desire to wear.

The other jewellery consisted of three brooches: one set with a green stone, one with a blue stone, and the third, a gold cloak clasp, was set with a red garnet. She didn't want to wear any of those either. Not her style. She looked at herself in a mirror. Her hair was all right but her face had taken on a gaunt look.

As she rummaged in her handbag for the car keys, her phone rang. Her heart stood still. It was Ross. 'Hello, bonnie lass.'

She just melted. 'Hello bonnie lad, long time no blether.'

'Aye, I'm sorry, I've been up to my oxters in work, and problems, and people no' turnin' up on time. Usual shite. What are you up to?'

'Not a lot — I caught up on some web work, and I took my mother's jewellery to be cleaned. The jeweller said he thought it was valuable and should be in a museum. I'm going to wear it though. I'm wearing it all now in fact.'

'I wish I could see it on you … just the jewellery mind, nothing else. I'm picturing your luscious and sexy naked body draped with silver and jewels cascading down all over your breasts, making your nipples stand out hard. I would bend you over and make that jewellery rattle.'

She laughed. 'Okay, I'll keep that kooky image in my mind until I see you again. Which is when by the way?'

'Er … that would be about three weeks, just after the school holidays.'

'Three weeks. I can't wait that long to see you. I could easily drive up to Edinburgh you know, I won't get in your way.'

'No, no, it wouldn't work, trust me. I miss you too, but it cannot be helped. The time will pass quickly enough. I'll call you again as soon as I'm back down in Ayr. In the meantime, you keep that jewellery polished.'

Chapter 39

She smiled and sighed. Of course he hadn't gone off her. He was obviously just really busy. He sounded as normal and as horny as ever. She looked at the CalMac ferry calendar on her wall. Three weeks. An eternity. But her plan to investigate further in the Carnegie Library would help take up the time.

Driving to the library took less than ten minutes. She should probably have ridden her bike seeing it was only two miles away. Back in the local history section she began searching for names in the archive files: Simon Dee, Isla Dee or Murray, Jack Dee.

She found the obituaries, and in a local business article she found reference to her father as highest earning salesman in 1990 for a car dealership. Her mother was also mentioned in an advertisement for psychic services.

What she really wanted was to talk to Stewart. Right now he was occupied with a small group of children. She waited until he was free and caught his eye. He smiled and shuffled over to her. He wore a long dark suit coat, at least one size too large, possibly to disguise his skeletal, almost concave body.

'Nice to see you again, Morgan.'

'Hello Stewart,' she said, impressed he had remembered her name.

'Is there something I can help you find?'

'I think I've found all the articles that are useful, but actually, I was hoping just to talk to you.'

He sat on the chair beside her. 'Of course, happy to oblige.'

'Thank you. I like your little ponytail by the way.'

He twirled his hair around his finger and laughed. 'Aye, thank you. I've always worn it like this. I had much more hair back in the day, you know, the summer of love. America had Monterey; we had the Isle of Wight festival. I was there at the first one, would you believe. I'm still an old hippie at heart.'

She grinned. She could almost imagine him as a young, long-haired flower child, wearing a kaftan and headband, smoke from a joint drifting up between his fingers.

'I suppose you'll be wanting to know about your parents, especially your mother,' he said.

His acuity surprised her. 'You're right. I was hoping to ask if you remembered anything about them, and particularly where exactly they were killed on that B742 road.'

'Let me think now.' He called up an online map and pointed to a spot on the map where the road crossed the river. 'Here is the place, I believe. The river happened to be in flood and, from memory, he was speeding and out of control. There's a sharp ninety-degree bend approaching the bridge and I think the car hit the bridge and flipped over before it landed upside down in the river, and sank.

'If it's any consolation, I think the impact would have killed them instantly. What I mean is, they probably didn't suffer, if that's any consolation at all.' Stewart looked at her closely as if to make sure she wasn't distressed. 'I'm sorry,' he said, 'I hope this isn't upsetting you. It is what you wanted to know, isn't it?'

'Yes, thank you Stewart. That's exactly what I was hoping to find out. I'd like to visit the place, and maybe put a memorial wreath or something there. To give it a finality, to move on I suppose.'

'Closure, yes I understand.'

'I miss my mother even though I have no memory of her. I wish I could remember at least something about her.'

'I think that is entirely natural. I remember your mother well. I first met her in my history class at the high school when I used to teach. She was a bright, lovely girl. You could describe her as having a beautiful soul. I notice you're wearing her keek stane.'

She started. 'Oh you know about that do you?'

'Aye, she treasured it; she never went anywhere without it. And she was a valued member of our group.'

'Your group? What kind of group?'

'Well, it is a group of like-minded souls, people in tune with their psychic natures, you might say. We have healers, psychics, clairvoyants, and … others like me.'

She looked at him with full attention. 'What do you do in the group?'

'It's a kind of support group. It doesn't have a name or

anything. We just enjoy getting together with other people who are aware, open-minded, who know there is more than the physical world we can see. We share a connection — to each other, to nature, to the otherworld.'

'What — like a coven or something?'

'No, no, nothing like that, we have no religious affiliation. It has more to do with channelling positive energy, to heal and enhance life. We discuss issues and explore ideas. Maybe you'd like to come along one night and see what we do. You'd be very welcome. There's a meeting tomorrow night, being full moon — a blood moon because of the eclipse.'

Eek, that'd definitely be a no. 'Thanks Stewart, but it's not really my scene. I am glad you knew my mother, and I'm happy to know she had some good friends. What I can't come to terms with is how unfair it all seems. Like, what was it all for? Why was her life wasted so young, and why did she choose to stay with an abuser? I presume you knew about that too.'

'Aye, I did.'

Her eyes glistened. 'My aunt — my father's sister, Minnie, told me he had always had a sadistic, cruel temperament from a young age. I just can't believe my beautiful mother would throw her life away on such an undeserving person.'

Stewart laid his bony hand on her arm. 'Just a minute, I'll be back.' He stood up and shuffled over to the counter, then returned holding an A5 leaflet.

'I know you think you don't have the same clairvoyant ability as your mother,' he said, 'but you do have something. Probably more than you know. I can sense it. Here's a brochure from a friend of mine and, even if it doesn't appeal to you right now, I know you will benefit from a session with him. His name is Philip. Please do call him, Morgan, even just for curiosity. Will you do that?'

She looked down at the leaflet. It was a flyer advertising a psychiatrist who specialised in hypnosis and past life regressions. That again.

'Thanks Stewart. I'll think about it.'

'Would you like to leave me your phone number and, if I turn up any other information about your family you might be interested in, I can let you know.'

'Okay, if it's no trouble, thank you.' She wrote her name and number on her notepad and tore off the page for him.

She walked towards the stairs. As she descended, she saw Stewart already at the circulation counter, holding the desk phone to his ear.

Chapter 40

She hadn't meant to confide in Stewart; she almost wished she hadn't. But he was so easy to talk to, encouraging. Plus, he had known her mother — she wasn't telling him anything he didn't already know.

She wandered into a nearby sandwich bar for lunch. She thought about Stewart's group. Don might have been interested in it but, to her, it sounded like a weird, nature-worshipping new age love-in. Maybe they held séances. Definitely nudists.

Her plan had been to seek out Nurse McFeeter this afternoon but she hadn't expected to feel so drained after seeing where her parents' accident had happened and talking to Stewart. She didn't think she could face talking to the nurse today if, in fact, she could even track her down. Now she was glad she hadn't cycled; she would hardly have had the energy to ride back.

She had also wanted to visit the accident location but she couldn't cope with that either, not today. She yawned and decided to go home, study the route on her map app, and organise some flowers or a plaque, before she tackled the drive. She wished she had someone to go with her — Kirsty, or Ross.

Back inside her flat, she looked at Stewart's leaflet and groaned. She left it on the kitchen benchtop. Without much enthusiasm for doing anything else, she watched television — *Eggheads, Hairy Bikers*, and a program discussing the problem of a million feral camels spreading across Australia. Who knew? She would have to tell Kirsty. She took one of her sleeping pills and had an early night.

◆　◆　◆　◆

Next morning, she drove to the South Ayrshire Hospital and enquired at the front counter if a Nurse McFeeter had worked there, and if they knew where she might find her now. The receptionist looked up and said, 'Oh, aye, there is a Nurse McFeeter, quite right. But she's no' a nurse here anymore. She's actually a patient.'

'Would I be able to visit her?'

'I think she would love that. She doesn't get many visitors.' The receptionist gave her the ward and room number, and instructions how to get there.

'By the way,' Morgan said, 'do you have a Doctor Ross McFarsund working here?'

The receptionist searched on her computer database. 'No, not at this hospital. There are several other hospitals in Ayr — maybe try a private one. Would you like me to contact them for you?'

'No, that's okay. Thank you. Is there a gift shop or a florist here?'

'Aye, you will pass a wee florist shop on the way up this corridor if you would like to take her some flowers. That will make her day, I'm sure.'

She smiled at the receptionist, or rather at her pronunciation of 'flooers'. She was still enchanted by that accent. She bought a bunch of irises, dahlias and peonies. They were expensive and, given Nurse McFeeter wouldn't even know who she was, probably a bit over the top.

It was already a warm day but the hospital was even warmer, and permeated with a sweet, almost sickly disinfectant smell. She found her way to the ward and picked up an empty jar from a small kitchen, in case there was no vase in the room.

She knocked on Nurse McFeeter's open door and tiptoed in. The old nurse, the sole occupant of the room, lay on the bed with the mattress angled to a slightly raised position. Her eyes were closed, and a drip fed into her arm. She appeared to be around eighty, with thin yellow hair. Morgan wondered if she dyed it that colour; it didn't look natural.

She stood for a few moments, unsure whether or not to wake her up. She filled the jar with water, arranged the flowers and set it beside the bed. Then she sat down in the chair and waited. Nothing happened for several minutes so she spoke.

'Nurse McFeeter, are you awake?'

The nurse's eyelids fluttered. She turned her head towards Morgan and opened her eyes, surprisingly intense brown eyes, which she locked on Morgan.

'Oh, I'm sorry if I woke you,' she said. 'You don't know me — I'm Morgan Dee. I hope you don't mind me visiting you. I brought you some flowers.' She held the jar of flowers in front of the nurse so she didn't have to twist to see them.

'Hello dear. They're lovely,' she said, staring, unblinking, at Morgan.

It was strangely unnerving and she wasn't sure how to proceed. 'I'd like to talk to you … would that be okay? If we had a chat?'

'Aye, okay, for a wee while. Would you just press that wee button there on the side, dear? It raises the bed so I can sit up better.'

She pressed the button until the bed was in a reclining sitting position. 'Are you comfortable? Is there anything I can get you?'

'No, no, I'm fine thank you, dear. I have this drip here filling me with pain killers so I'm quite comfortable.'

'Are you in hospital for an operation, or …?'

'Well, we don't know yet, I might need an operation on a disc. I've been getting injections in my spine, but we're waiting for the inflammation to subside first. It's sciatica, horrendously painful. I blame standing for hours on end in surgery and lifting patients. I was a senior theatre nurse you know.'

Now the nurse was sitting up, Morgan could see she wasn't as old as she had first thought; she was probably not even seventy. She had a strong face, one which suggested she was used to giving orders. She would have been formidable in her day.

Nurse McFeeter's eyes travelled down to her pendant and

then back to her face. Morgan felt they bored deep into her, reading her thoughts, seeing into her soul. She smiled, cleared her throat and shifted in her chair.

The nurse said, 'What did you say your name was again, dear?'

'Morgan … Morgan Dee, well it was before I got married.'

'You've been here before.'

'So people keep telling me.'

'Ah, indeed. No, I mean you've actually been here before, in this hospital. I know who you are.'

'You do? Really? You remember my name?'

'Oh, aye. I remember fine.'

Morgan started to feel spacey. Maybe the cloying smell of disinfectant was getting to her. 'Well, that's great because I was hoping to ask you about an incident that happened back in 1991. And I wondered if, by some miracle, you might remember it.'

Nurse McFeeter lifted her chin slightly. 'Oh yes?'

'I came back to Scotland, from Australia you see, because I wanted information about my parents, and when I was researching, I discovered I had a baby brother I didn't know about. A newspaper article I found in the library said he died of SIDS, and it also mentioned your name as the nurse on duty the night my mother brought him in to the hospital.'

She squirmed in the chair. 'I thought it was a long shot, but I wanted to try to find you, because there doesn't seem to be any other record of him, or even any photos, which is weird. And I hoped you might be able to tell me anything more about it.' Her cheeks were burning.

'Are you sure, dear?'
 Strange question. 'Am I sure about what?'
'Are you sure you want to know?'

242

Chapter 41

'Absolutely, yes please, I do want to know. Anything you can tell me will help me.'

'I doubt that, dear, but since you have come all this way, I will tell you.' Nurse McFeeter wriggled slightly in the bed to make herself more comfortable.

'I don't remember every patient or incident of course — there have been thousands. You tend to remember the children, and I do remember that one.

'Peter, that is Doctor Morrow, and I had both finished our shifts and we were on our way to a Halloween party. He was dressed as Dracula with slicked back hair and a black cape and I was done up as Little Red Riding Hood wearing — well, you know — a red hood and cape. Dressed like that we should have gone out the back exit, but it was a quiet night, it was late, and we had a taxi waiting so we decided to slip out the front.

'We'd almost made it out the door when your mother screeched up in a car and ran in, frantic, a baby in her arms and a little girl — that was you — running along behind her. She should have gone in the Emergency entrance but she was panicked and went in the first door she came to. She was crying and saying her baby has stopped breathing and she couldn't revive him.

'Peter made a hasty retreat to Emergency to warn the staff and prepare the equipment, and I took the baby from her and ran down the corridor after him.'

'Dressed as Little Red Riding Hood?'

'Yes, I'm afraid so, but there was no time to think about my costume. I just grabbed the baby and ran. Your mother followed me and you trotted along behind her, still holding your teddy bear. I remember thinking thank goodness Peter had disappeared before you saw him dressed as Dracula.

'We tried our best to resuscitate the wee boy but he was already dead, poor little soul. He was only a few months old. There was nothing more we could do. Your mother was distraught. We asked her what happened and she said she had gone into the nursery to check he was asleep, and you were in there standing on a chair beside his cot, holding your teddy bear over his face, pressing it down so he couldn't breathe. When she picked him up, he had turned blue and wasn't breathing.

'Your father was out at a work party or something, and she didn't want to waste time calling the ambulance. She thought it would be quicker to drive to the hospital because you lived only a mile or so away.'

The red from Morgan's cheeks had drained away. Her voice cracked. 'Me? Are you saying I killed him?'

'Yes, I'm afraid so, dear. I can't tell you why. You were only about three, I think. Maybe you were trying to play with the baby, or maybe it was an accident. Who knows? Some children are jealous of their siblings.

'She said you were smiling when she first went into the room. She told us she screamed at you, and asked what you had done, but she couldn't get any sense out of you, and there was no time to lose asking questions. She bundled the baby and you into the car as fast as she could.'

Morgan stood up and poured herself a glass of water. Her hand shook. 'I'm sorry, I can't believe what you're telling me. Surely I would remember something as traumatic as that.'

'That's just it. Because it was so traumatic you've probably repressed it completely. But that is exactly what happened.'

'The article I found in the library said my mother was cleared of charges. I wondered what that meant, and the librarian told me my mother was a victim of malicious local gossip. But it was SIDS. He died of SIDS.'

'He didn't, dear. The PF, Procurator Fiscal that is, ordered a post-mortem, and that found fibres matching those of your teddy bear in his lungs and air passage. He died of asphyxiation. The PF investigated and deemed there was to be no criminal intent recorded, given the perpetrator was three years old.

'SIDS was what the press were told. But at that time suspicion already surrounded cot death cases because there were so many of them. And some of the local gossips took it into their heads your mother killed her own son as a sacrifice, because it was Halloween, or some such utter nonsense.

'No one, apart from Peter, myself and the PF team ever

knew what really happened, and to this day there has never been any reason to speak about it. Your mother could have stopped all the gossip by declaring it was you, but she never said a word. I can't remember your brother's name now …'

Morgan's eyes had filled with tears. 'Simon. It was Simon. How do I deal with this now?'

'Simon, yes. Don't think on it too much, dear. You can't possibly be held responsible for something you do when you're an infant. But I think it's best to confront the truth, acknowledge it, and move on. What doesn't kill you makes you stronger, so they say.

'Now you know, and whatever else you find out about your parents, you can be assured that your mother loved you dearly and wanted to protect you at all costs. You can check in the National Records if you want to see the documentation. The death certificate for wee Simon said "Asphyxiation", not SIDS.'

Nurse McFeeter shifted again in the bed. 'I think you'll need to lower me down again please, dear. I can only sit at that angle for a short while.'

As she was lowering the bed, a young nurse came into the room wheeling Nurse McFeeter's lunch on a trolley. 'Oh what beautiful flooers.' She smiled at Morgan. 'They brighten up the room, don't they?'

Morgan thanked Nurse McFeeter and left her to eat her lunch. Her walk back through the hospital corridors was surreal. Registering nothing, and unaware of any sound, she walked blindly, mechanically, feeling as if she was not really in her own body.

She found her car and sat leaning her head on the steering wheel. She would have had a brother. They would have grown up together, shared a childhood, and memories. She could have had a mate to do things with. But she didn't. She was alone, and it was her fault.

He hadn't died of SIDS. She had done it. Stupid, stupid child. There had to be something wrong with her, some inherited evil from her father. Had she been trying to see how long it would take for the baby to stop breathing and die, watching, fascinated, like her father used to do to animals? Being young was no excuse; even a three-year-old has a sense of right and wrong.

She searched in herself for any evidence, any trace of malice. She couldn't find any, but then her memories started unusually late. The earliest thing she could actually remember was floating in the sea in a black inner tube from a tyre and being hot. Hot like she'd never felt before. She must have been four, nearly five. Lou was with her, wearing a rubber bathing cap covered in yellow flowers, laughing and twirling her around on the tyre.

She must be able to remember something else, surely. Think, think. Nothing. Her brain simply would not go back that far. She had blanked it all out. Except, she suddenly remembered the dream she sometimes had — the one where a small boy is saying it's all right, he's happy. Hot tears burned her eyes.

Chapter 42

She couldn't sit in the car park all afternoon so eventually she started the engine and headed south. She didn't know why; she only knew she couldn't face going home to her flat. She needed to soothe her head with the familiar, comforting ritual of driving. So she drove. Past open green fields towards the coast where windswept rocky beaches and the round hump of Ailsa Craig came into view.

With no idea where she was going, she drove on and on down the coast until she felt compelled to turn inland. She aimlessly followed narrow single lane roads through picturesque towns and stunning scenery without noticing what she was seeing.

More than an hour later she came upon a Historic Scotland sign indicating a chambered cairn and standing stones. Instinctively she turned into this road and followed it to the end, beyond which no vehicles were allowed. Leaving the car, she stretched her legs and plodded her way over the grass to the circle of standing stones in the distance, pleased to see no other people at the site.

Close up they were an impressive array of large, sharp-edged stones covered in lichen, similar to the Dunvegan millennium stone, only erected four thousand years earlier. Ancient, majestic and formidable, they had an enticing quality that invited her to touch their rough surface. She threw her arms around one and rested her cheek on the cool, gritty stone. Then, with a shock, she saw the chambered cairns were open, vandalised. This was wrong. The sacred tombs had been knocked to the ground and raided.

Only then she turned to look at her surroundings. How did she end up at this place? She had no clue. She had just followed the roads, driving without thinking, but she couldn't shake off the eerie feeling she had been there before.

She sat down on the grass and leant back against one of the tall stones. Aware of its power and magnificence, somehow she could feel its energy coursing through her body. By squinting through the afternoon sun she could see a bay or a sea. Which was it? She didn't know — she had left her phone in the car. From the angle of the sun to her right she figured the water was south. Jesus, had she driven to the end of Scotland?

Finally, she thought back to her conversation with Nurse McFeeter. Now she knew the origin of the woman in the red cloak dream, and that soapy smell, hospital disinfectant. It had been a memory — probably her earliest memory. She could recall nothing more detailed.

Her baby brother had died because of her. And nobody

knew. Who could she share that burden with? Not Ross, or Kirsty or even Don and Lou. She couldn't share that disturbing information with anybody. If she did it would become part of their knowledge about her, and she couldn't bear for anyone to think she might harbour some deeply repressed aberration in her nature, some inherited demon.

The best thing to do would be to keep it to herself.

Nurse McFeeter's advice was probably wise — acknowledge it as a fact and move on. She closed her eyes and lay back, letting the unexpectedly comforting stone cradle her. She wept until she fell asleep, exhausted.

Sometime later she was awoken by a Scottish terrier licking her hand. The dog was attached to a lead which was attached to a wizened, stocky man wearing a tweed cap and Wellington boots. He had similar prominent eyebrows to the dog, making them look like they were related. She was surprised to see the sun already low in the sky.

'Helloo there,' the man called, 'sorry about the dug.'

'That's all right,' she said, wiping her wet hand on her jeans.

'Just, you'll be wanting to get away soon I'm thinking.'

'Yes, you're right. I fell asleep. I didn't realise how late it was.'

'Aye, and you'll be wanting to get away before the eclipse, noo. You might not find yer way back in the dark.'

'Yes, I remember, total eclipse, isn't it? A blood moon I believe.'

'Aye, right enough. And just a friendly word of caution — you shouldn't be lying up against them stanes.'

'Oh, sorry, are they protected or something?'

'No, they're no'. But they will sap energy out of you. Into the ground, ye ken.'

'I see. I thought you somehow got energy from them.'

'Oh, no, quite the opposite. They have a magnetic property to attract energy into the earth, and they'll get it from the sun and the atmosphere, and even you if you touch them for too long.'

'Okay, thank you for the warning. I had no idea.'

'Aye, no bother. And not only that …,' he warmed to his subject, 'the energy is even more concentrated when the stanes are all together like that, especially if they're in a circle. They have been known to cause folk to see things that are no' there, hallucinations, ye ken. The ancients would use the stanes to induce a trance and connect to their dear departed ancestors. Not everybody knows this, mind.' His eyebrows rose and fell for emphasis.

She stood up stiffly and shivered. Wrapping her cardigan tighter she trudged back over the field towards the car. What a bizarre old bloke. She had never heard of that nonsense before. Glancing behind her towards the stones she saw the old man and the dog had disappeared.

She slumped down into the driver's seat and sat with her eyes closed for a few minutes, feeling drained. Maybe there was something in what the old farm fellow said. How would anybody know? And how would he know, anyway?

She opened the map app on her phone to see where she was. She really was south, further south than the border of England. The large body of water was the mouth of the River Cree.

Dark clouds were gathering and she had nearly two hours to drive home. On the road she struggled to keep her eyes open. Finally she reached the coast again where road signs urged 'Haste ye back'.

Having not eaten all day, she stopped at an old pub for dinner and to refresh herself. As usual, heads turned when she ordered a meal and a drink. She was becoming used to the way her accent attracted attention wherever she went.

She overheard a group of men at the bar talking about the eclipse. 'No, ye will not see nothin' from here, the moon will be too low over the horizon. You'd need to go down south, up high on them hills near where them stanes are, and look towards the sou' east, then you might see somethin'. Except for them dark clouds.'

After finishing her chargrilled chicken burger and chips she made her way down a path to a sea wall to look for the eclipse but the pub bloke was right — it was so cloudy it was impossible to see anything. The eclipse was a fizzer.

But the place he described sounded like the standing stones she had just come from. Maybe the farmer had been trying to shoo her away deliberately so he and his spooky old mates could come out and dance naked around the stones, chanting at the blood moon. Had she really even seen the old guy and his dog, or had she dreamt it?

The sharp salty air and pungent smell of seaweed reminded her of the cottage in Staffin. She breathed in and stared out at the dark night. She missed Ross deeply.

Chapter 43

It was nearly midnight when she arrived home. She yawned and opened a bottle of red wine. After a brief search on her laptop she found the National Records online. She registered on the website, paid £7.50 to access the records, and searched for deaths in 1991.

She found what she was looking for: Simon Dee's death certificate at age twenty weeks, signed by his mother, Isla Dee. Nurse McFeeter was right. The cause of his death was documented as asphyxiation.

She downloaded the image of the certificate and stared at it for some time, reading it over and over. How unbearably sad. He would have been alive today, if it hadn't been for her. Nurse McFeeter said she had been holding her teddy down on his face. Whatever had happened that night, she had repressed it, far out of reach of her memory. Her head ached, and her eyes were red and raw from crying. She went to bed with her friend, the sleeping tablet.

✦ ✦ ✦ ✦

'Anton, what's that banging?' She reached her hand out under the doona. The bed was empty. She opened her eyes with difficulty. Where was she? Oh, Scotland, of course. *Anton?* Where did that come from?

There was banging, however. On her front door. Something was not right. She wrapped her dressing gown around herself and padded to the door, glancing in the mirror as she passed. Shit, what if it's Ross?

'Who is it?'

'It's Harish, Morgan, ma'am.'

Harish. Thank God it wasn't Ross.

She opened the door to Harish without his turban. He bowed.

'Hello Morgan, ma'am. I did promise I would bring you some curry. And I'm thinking you liked the butter chicken,' he said, holding up a bulging plastic takeaway bag.

'Thank you, Harish, that's so thoughtful. Come in, please. I'll have it later for dinner.'

'It's six-thirty, nearly dinner time.'

'Eh? six-thirty? It can't be.' She glanced out the window at the afternoon drizzle. That's what was wrong — she'd slept all day.

'Everything is all right, Morgan, ma'am?'

'Yes, thank you. I just didn't realise I'd slept so long.'

'A good day to sleep … not very nice weather.' Harish put the curry on the kitchen bench. His eyes travelled to the empty bottle of Cabernet beside the packet of sleeping pills.

254

Then he spotted the past life regression therapy brochure she had left on the bench. He picked it up. 'Are you interested in this kind of thing?'

'I'm not sure. A librarian at the Carnegie Library gave it to me. He seemed to think I would benefit from having a session. God knows what gave him that idea. What do you think about it … is it something you believe in? Sorry, I'm making assumptions. I guess I assumed you're a Hindu. Are you?'

'Yes, you're quite right. Hindu, yes, in essence. That is to say, I don't adhere strictly to all the teachings — it is complex.'

'And do you believe we have more than one life?' she asked.

'Of course. I have no doubt we have all had many lives and will continue to have more lives. Instead of lives, maybe I should say *experiences* in a physical body. Is this what you believe also?'

'To be honest, Harish, I really don't know. I have no religious background. I don't even know what religion I was born. But poking around with past lives sounds like Ouija board stuff to me; I would be afraid it might leave you vulnerable to all sorts of evil spirits to take control. I'm not totally against the idea — I guess it seems possible, just a bit … sinister.'

'Maybe that is what you are meant to think,' he said. 'I believe all religions are different vehicles to exactly the same thing — sharing the same kernel of truth but made more obscure over thousands of years by people who have added rules and conditions, enforced by threats and fears. I think the truth is probably much more simple, beautiful and accessible to everyone. I don't think you have anything to fear by exploring your past, if it is there for the knowing. Would you visit this past life regression person do you think?'

'Probably not. I'm curious I suppose, but I have enough trouble staying in control of this life. Anyway, would you like to share this lovely curry you've brought? For dinner, or breakfast in my case.'

'Thank you, but I won't. I eat enough curry already. Tonight I am having fish and chips.'

He refused payment for the meal. He bowed and went back downstairs, leaving her to enjoy her curry and contemplate the meaning of life, and whether hers, in fact, had any.

There was no point changing out of her pyjamas. She sat and watched the rain drizzling down the windowpane. She could see half a dozen small birds on a tree outside flitting from branch to branch, shaking their wet wings. She had no idea what kind of birds they were. Finches and robins probably.

If she could just talk to Ross, only to hear his voice. It had been two days since he had phoned but it seemed much longer than that. She toyed with her phone. Should she ring him? What would she say? She didn't want to tell him about her visit to Nurse McFeeter, or that she had been responsible for her own baby brother's death. Or that she had found out where her parents had died, or about her bewildering drive to the standing stones, or that she couldn't sleep without him. She could just ask how he is, though.

Ringing. Her heart beat faster. 'Thank you for calling Ross McFarsund. I'm sorry, I'm not available right now. Please leave your message after the tone.'

Voicemail. This was the first time she had heard his recorded message. 'Hello bonnie lad. I thought I would just see how you're getting on, what you're doing. I miss you heaps. Can't wait to see you again. Call me sometime, if you're not too busy … Bye.'

She had to stop herself from saying 'love you'. She tapped off her phone and stared out at the rain again. She sighed and stood up to clear away the curry containers. She hadn't even bothered to dish the meal onto a plate.

She put the empty wine bottle in the recycling bin, then picked up the box of sleeping tablets. Only two left. She opened her laptop, logged on to the website and ordered three more boxes. They were horrendously expensive but she liked them. She liked how, not only did they give you a sound sleep, they also flooded your body with a comforting, warm euphoria.

Chapter 44

She waited until an appropriate hour to Skype Don and Lou. She told them she had explored sites in Ayr and the south of Scotland but she didn't mention her visit to Nurse McFeeter.

'How are things going in Oz?' she asked.

'We're fine, trucking along,' Lou said. 'Don is doing really well, aren't you dear?'

'Yes, I feel pretty good, for a nonagenarian. We are missing you though — we think about you all the time.'

'And we're glad you've met a new fella and you're happy there, dear,' Lou said. 'We noticed Anton has a new girl living in the house.'

Morgan was silent for a second. He hadn't wasted any time finding a substitute. 'Are you sure it's a girl?'

'Oh, yes, she's a girl all right,' Lou said. 'Someone tall and blonde.'

She knew who that was. Good on you, Leeann. In like Flynn. She had been meaning to email Leeann to catch up but now she decided she wouldn't. Good luck dealing with his 'feminine side'.

A phone was ringing. She blinked her eyes open. Phone … where's the phone? She was pleased to hear Kirsty's loud, cheerful voice.

'Helloo! How're ye doin'? Tell me all about your trip. Hasn't the time flown! What's been happening?'

Where to begin? 'Plenty,' she said. 'But how are *you* going up in Edinburgh?'

'Oh, Morgan, you'll no' believe it. Callum and I are engaged. We've set a date to get married next May. I'm so excited! I cannot wait.'

'Kirsty, that's fantastic. Congratulations! I'm so happy for you both. That is lovely, lovely news.'

'I know, I can't believe it. I got such a surprise. You'll like Callum — he's a real sweetie. We're going out tomorrow to look in jewellers' shops for a ring.'

'I bet your mum is excited.'

'Is she ever — she's over the moon. I only told her today and she's started to make plans already. And how are you and the gorgeous Ross going? How was your trip away?'

'It was fabulous. I loved Skye. We stayed in a lovely secluded cottage, away from the tourists. And I met my aunt Minnie. I wished we could have travelled for longer, though. Ross had to get back for work at the hospital, and I haven't seen him for nearly three weeks.'

'Oh, aye, he's in Edinburgh, I remember. I keep forgetting to ask Callum if he knows him. Had a bit on my mind, ha ha.'

She smiled. Kirsty was so bubbly and full of life, a major chord against Morgan's minor chord.

'Well, I'd better get on … so much to do!' Kirsty said. 'I'll see you before I start the course — we'll have a good catch up then.'

She phoned Ross again but heard the same voicemail message. She tried not to sound as desperate as the last time. 'Hi Ross, nothing important, I just wanted to say hi and see how you are. Anyway, I hope everything is good, talk soon. See ya.'

She took her bike from the downstairs locker and rode the short distance to the shore, just to do something physical, and feel the invigorating cool breeze on her face. She sat on the concrete wall overlooking the windy shore, breathing in the salty sea air, made saltier by her own tears. She stared out to sea, watching the colours change, until the sun was low in the sky.

When she returned home, she watched television until late. Then she yawned and shuffled over to the kitchen bench where she'd left her packet of sleeping pills.

✦ ✦ ✦ ✦

Two days later, her phone rang. That *must* be Ross. She looked at the caller identification — Kirsty again. Her heart sank momentarily.

'Hi Kirsty. How you doing?'

'I'm okay, thanks.' Kirsty cleared her throat. 'Can you talk?'

'Of course.' She settled down on the couch. 'What's up?'

'How are you?' Kirsty asked.

'I'm fine. I was thinking about going for another bike ride but it's raining again. What's happening?'

'Um. I need to tell you something.'

'Okay.'

'We went into town yesterday to look for a ring.'

'Oh, wow, that's great. Did you find one?'

'Yes we did. It's lovely. But when we were walking to the jewellers, I saw Ross.'

'You did? Did you speak to him?'

'No, we didn't. He was in his car, that Jaguar, in a car park. But, Morgan, he was with a woman, a very young woman. And they were being, well, more than friendly. They were pashing. He was all over her.'

Her stomach lurched. 'Shit, Kirsty, are you sure? I mean, are you sure it was him?'

'Oh, aye, no doubt at all. No mistaking that car. He didn't see me, but I pointed him out to Callum as well.'

'Jesus.'

'But that's not all. I really didn't want to tell you this, but you need to know.'

'What? Know what? Tell me.'

'Callum had never heard of Ross, but he mentioned his name to a doctor pal, who said Ross *is* a surgeon but he's a cosmetic surgeon. He only does breast enlargements — implants. At least he did. He's not allowed to practise right now because he had an affair with a patient so he's being investigated by the NHS board.'

'What? Really? He told me he was busy at the hospital.'

'Aye, I know. But also … it gets worse. He's married with two children. They live in Edinburgh. Callum's pal said he thought there's some nasty divorce court case going on at the moment. The girl in the car wouldn't have been his wife. I mean, she was younger than me.'

'That can't be true. Fuck, that's awful.'

'I'm so sorry, Morgan, I didn't want to tell you. I feel sick about it.'

She was shaking, her hands ice-cold. 'No, I'm glad you did. Thank you for telling me. I guess that explains a few things.'

'What are you going to do?'

'I don't know if I should phone him again. Every time I do, I get his voicemail. I wouldn't know what to say to him if I did get through. I'll have to think about it. What a prick.'

'Will you be okay?'

'Sure, Kirsty, thank you.'

Her stomach had been ripped out. Stupid, stupid. No wonder she couldn't find any information about him on the internet. How could she have been such an idiot? How could she think a man like Ross would be interested in a drip like her? She had just been a novelty to him — an Antipodean novelty. Betrayed again, by another arsehole. She leant her head on her arm and sobbed.

Chapter 45

She opened her fridge: an apple, a bottle of Sauvignon blanc and half a litre of milk. Two frozen meals remained in the freezer. Although her eyes were sore and swollen, she wearily forced herself to drive to the local Sainsbury's to stock up on groceries. She also stopped at a florist to buy a silk flower wreath. Then, to save herself the bother of cooking, she decided to drive to Harish's restaurant and order a takeaway.

On the way she couldn't resist making a slight detour past Ross's town house on the seafront. It was locked up and looked neglected. She knew how it felt.

She turned the car off and stared at the house. Glancing around she saw the street was empty; only a few dog-walkers strolled on the esplanade. Should she try to get into the house? What would she look for? Some evidence of his life, photos perhaps. A tempting thought. If anyone questioned her, she could say she was meant to be meeting him here.

She locked her car and ambled up the driveway to the back

of the house, trying not to look suspicious. The property was fenced; no neighbours overlooked the garden. She tried the back door. Locked. But she remembered he had once mentioned a loose window, so she tried pulling on all the window frames. The second bedroom window, at the far end, did stick out more than the others. She wiggled her fingers under the frame until she could get a grip. Then she tugged firmly and it creaked open.

Blood pounded in her head. This was breaking and entering. But so far, so good; no one had appeared. She looked around for something to stand on and spied the wheelie bin. She turned it on its side and levered herself in through the window, panting with the effort.

It was odd being in the locked-up house without him. Standing in the garden was one thing, but she wouldn't be able to explain actually breaking in. She'd have to be quick. She could always say she had left something inside she needed urgently. Like her heart.

Starting in the main bedroom, she searched through drawers and cupboards. At the back of the bottom drawer of the tallboy she found a stash of loose photographs and sat on the floor to go through them. There were pictures of Ross in various locations; lochs and mountains in the background. She also found pictures of eight different girls, some close together with him. The location in these ones she definitely did recognise — it was the cottage at Staffin.

Kirsty was right. He was a serial philanderer. She sat studying each one over and over, tears streaming down her face. Why was she torturing herself? She just had to know. And now she knew.

There were no family photos of his wife and children. Of course, there wouldn't be. This was his little hideaway from his family. She searched further in the tallboy drawer and found a set of keys labelled 'Staffin'.

So he either owned the cottage on Skye or he rented it frequently. She guessed he probably owned it. It was where he took all his girlfriends.

She picked up one photo of an attractive girl taken in the garden of a different cottage. In the background she recognised the town of Portree. She realised he probably visited at least one regular lady friend on the island, including the distillery guide, that Jacinta moll, no doubt. And while he had been with her.

She wiped her eyes and stood up from the floor. She returned the photos and the keys where she had found them and leant against the tallboy. She looked at the bed, the king-size bed, where they had made love many times. And also, she assumed, where he had done the same with numerous other girls.

She walked through to the kitchen, opened the pantry door and took out a sealed two-kilogram bag of sugar. With a knife she poked a small hole in the bag and poured a trail of sugar from the back doorstep through to the bedroom.

Then she pulled back the bedcovers and tipped most of the rest of the bag into the bed, leaving just a small amount in the bag. To make sure ants could find their way into the bed she smeared honey on the bed legs and into the bed, then sprinkled the rest of the sugar onto the honey.

In two weeks, he and whatever hapless paramour had

currently taken his fancy, should be greeted with a lovely infestation of ants. Sugary, sweet revenge.

✦   ✦   ✦   ✦

The restaurant had only just opened and there were no other customers yet. A beturbaned Harish greeted her. 'Hello, Morgan, ma'am, nice to see you. I could have brought you some food, you know.'

'I know — it was kind of you to bring me the butter chicken. It was so delicious, I thought I would order it again. Not exactly adventurous.'

'But it is very popular. I will put the order through pronto.' He tapped a few keys on the console. Then he looked at her and frowned. 'You are looking a little tired, Morgan. Are you well?'

'To be honest, not great. I've just found out my boyfriend is a massive liar, and a prick.'

'Oh dear. A liar and a prick. Not a good combination.'

'Indeed. He told me he was single but he's married with two children.'

'I am sorry to hear that. If you ever want someone to talk to, you know where I live.'

'Thank you, Harish. Actually, you probably know him. He's our landlord.'

'Oh *him*. Yes, I've met him quite a few times. I did think he was a bit of a ... what would you say ... a dandy.'

She laughed. 'Yes, that is a good description.'

'I have lived in my flat for two years,' he said. 'And in that time, there were three girls before you living in your flat. Did you know that? I could not help thinking he keeps that flat specifically to rent to girls, and then he takes them out. You are the nicest, I might add. I do not suppose that makes you feel any better, however.'

'I did think the rent was cheap. What a scumbag.'

'I hope that doesn't mean you will be moving out of the building.'

'Good point. No, I've got a lease contract for six months and I paid the rent in advance. Probably a dumb thing to do, in hindsight.'

'Ah, yes, the hindsight. Well, remember, if you ever want a shoulder to cry on, don't hesitate. I have two of them. And here is your butter chicken. Enjoy.'

'Thank you, Harish, I most definitely will.'

After dinner and a glass of Sauvignon, she tried phoning Ross again. This time he answered. 'Hello, bonnie lass.'

Her heart lurched. The sound of his voice made her pause and draw breath. 'You've got a nerve.'

Silence. 'Oh, aye?'

Her voice wavered, 'You told me a whole pack of lies.'

'Like what?'

'Like you are single and you don't have any children. You even said you don't want children. And yet you have two of them.'

'How would you know that?'

'Someone who knows you told my cousin's fiancé. Anyway, that's not important. What is important is you lied to me and used me.' She was crying now. She had been determined not to.

'We had a good time, though, didn't we? Nothing lasts forever. I never said it was a forever thing. Just a wee bit of fun, a bit of fantasy. Let's just leave it at that shall we?'

She had nothing more to say. She was gutted by his offhand, dismissive manner. But it was true, he'd made no promises. She had read too much into the relationship. She ended the call without saying goodbye.

Despite two pills and another glass of wine she slept restlessly. She dreamt of a wolf chasing Little Red Riding Hood who was carrying a baby and running through a forest. The forest opened out to a circle of standing stones in a clearing. In the centre stood Ross wearing a *Nirvana* album t-shirt from 1991, with the picture of the baby swimming underwater. Except the title of the album was *Nevermine*.

Chapter 46

She set up her laptop on the dining table and flicked through her photos — the ones from her childhood, her mother and father, many of Ross and their trip to Skye, the little cottage at Staffin. One of Kirsty outside Ali and Iain's house. What a great girl Kirsty was, and how lucky. She had a lovely fiancé and a lovely life to look forward to. She was going to be a teacher. She had it all together, and she was only twenty-four.

Stewart had shown her where the bridge crossed the river Ayr on the B742 road. She opened her maps app and worked out how to get there.

She took out the cairngorm pendant and slipped it over her head. She put on all the other jewellery from the shortbread tin too, even the brooches, and went downstairs to her car. The wreath of flowers still lay on the back seat.

She drove through the industrial area past the showroom where she had bought the car, then six or so miles further inland to the riverbend, where the road became a narrow lane with thick hedge growing on both sides. It was a picturesque area but she wondered what her parents had been doing out there.

The road bent at a ninety-degree angle immediately after a single lane bridge crossed over the river. She drove over the bridge but there was nowhere to stop until she reached a series of holiday cottages. Here, she turned the car around and approached the bridge again from the opposite direction. There wasn't much room but she pulled over and walked with the wreath to the bridge.

Dense, dark green foliage reached down to touch the water on one bank of the deep river. On the other bank she saw an open farm gate and a walking trail leading down to a gravel beach — probably good for fishing. In fact she could detect a whiff of dead fish, mingled with the smell of decaying vegetation.

A newer metal guardrail spanned the bridge; the original low stone wall was visible at the ends. It spoiled the look of the bridge but the old stone parapet would have been much too low and crumbling, definitely unsafe. She wondered why people would bother to spray graffiti on the bridge, out here in the middle of nowhere.

She tied the wreath with string to a metal strut on the guard rail and stood still for a moment. The place had a palpable atmosphere. She shivered as she gazed down into the swiftly flowing river. The water was so dark, the colour of sarsaparilla. This is where it happened, then. This is where her parents ended their lives.

She walked slowly back to her car, pausing to look back at

the bridge. She clearly understood how her parents' car could have hit the low stone railing at high speed and flipped upside down into the river. What she couldn't understand was why.

Sitting in her car, she instinctively rested her hand over her cairngorm pendant and felt a vibration emanating from it. Her mother must have been wearing this when she died, seeing she never went anywhere without it. She held the stone and gazed intently at the bridge. A warm buzzing began in her head, then a frisson enveloped her whole body. She closed her eyes, and she was there.

✦　✦　✦　✦

It was icy-cold, and dark. The car sped along the narrow, twisting road.

'Jack, please slow down, darling. Can we pull over and talk about it?'

'No, we fucking can't. We're getting her back from your brother tonight — *now*. That kid's going away — somewhere far away, the further the better. And that's final.'

'But she's only four years old. She's our little daughter and I miss her. Darling, she couldn't possibly have known what she was doing.'

'That's crap, and you know it. She knew perfectly well what she was doing. She's got an evil streak. I don't care how old she is, she's weird, some kind of changeling.'

'That's ridiculous, superstitious rubbish. She's just really sensitive. She has a sixth sense — probably takes after me. Please slow down, you're sliding all over the road. Can't you let me drive? You drank a lot of whisky at that party. I knew we shouldn't have gone. It was too soon. Too many well-meaning people wanting to talk about Simon. Just stop and let me drive. Please, Jack, *stop!*'

'*No!* Stop telling me what to do. She's my child too, and I'll beat the living daylights out of her when I get my hands on her. We're going straight to Jane and Malcolm's tonight. She's mollycoddled her for too long, bloody drug-addled battered pluck.'

'It's not Jane's fault, darling, it's the medication. Anyway, it's late, they won't be up.'

He snorted. 'Don't care. And if she's so sensitive how come she deliberately murdered my son. She did it on purpose, little bitch. She was smiling when she did it, wasn't she, you said. I'm going to give her such a thrashing. I'll —'

'She didn't do it maliciously. Of course she didn't, honestly. She's so young. Jack, slow down, *please*. Mind that old bloke!' Isla started to pull on the handbrake.

'No, fuck off. My car, I'll drive how I like. Don't you fucking touch the handbrake, you bitch.'

He lashed out with his left hand and smashed her in the face. Blood spattered onto her evening dress. The car swerved from side to side on the icy road as it approached the sharp turn onto the bridge.

Through her tears, she leant over to pull on the steering wheel to bring the car to the side of the road, but he punched her hard in the head. He pressed the accelerator further as the bridge approached. At the last second, she grabbed the wheel and pushed it the other way, away from her, with all her strength. Instead of turning onto the bridge the car slammed straight into the low stone wall with an almighty crash. It flipped over and tumbled upside down into the icy water of the river below.

✦ ✦ ✦ ✦

Morgan opened her eyes. He hadn't wanted her. She wasn't wanted then and she wasn't wanted now. The accident had been her fault. Her fault, again. Everything — her fault. An insistent voice in her head told her what to do. *You have only ever caused misery and sorrow. People have died because of you. Your brother, both your parents. Let it all end. Nobody will care. It will be a relief. End it all now.* The voice became louder. *End it.*

She opened her handbag and took out her box of tablets. Never leave home without them. She gulped down three and sat, with eyes closed, waiting for the euphoria to kick in. When she opened her eyes, everything looked hazy and unreal, shrouded in mist. She felt strangely dissociated from her body; a pleasant, blissful feeling.

She pressed down the electric window. Cool air rushed in. She opened all the windows then she fastened her seatbelt, started the car and drove slowly towards the bridge.

Once over the bridge, she turned in through the open farm gate and drove over the walking path towards the gravel beach. The little car's tyres skidded on the pebbles. She accelerated, urged on by the voice in her head. *You have caused pain and suffering. A burden to everybody. Nobody wants you. People have died. All your fault. End it all. Let it be over. Let it go. You will be free. End it all.* The voice became louder, impelling her to drive forward, straight into the swift flowing sarsaparilla water.

The car floated for a few seconds, then the engine cut out and it tilted forwards. Water gushed in through the open windows. After the initial shock of the cold water her body went numb. She felt nothing. The car was sinking but she was held in place by her seatbelt, water rapidly swirling around her. In less than a minute the car was completely submerged. All was silent underwater.

The car sank deeper. She felt the pressure of the volume of water above her, and let the seatbelt restrain her, like arms encircling her, arms that actually wanted to hold her. The last thing she saw was the mileage on the odometer: 105974. She had driven only 974 miles. It had seemed like so much more. She choked on a lungful of water and her body convulsed, an involuntary reaction. Then she lost consciousness and let herself drift blissfully away.

She floated above her body, looking down at where the car had sunk into the gurgling black water. Funny how the headlights are still on under all that water. An overwhelming sense of peace enveloped her as she began to drift upwards, drawn through a tunnel towards a bright, beautiful white light. *Let there be light.*

She *was* light, surrounded by a warm, soft mist, being drawn onwards. Sheer ecstasy. She was free, weightless, unencumbered by a body. She could hear music — a low tone, and a relaxing vibration like gentle wind chimes. A figure emerged from a group of amorphous people and approached her; it looked like a male but she couldn't be sure. His arms were outstretched towards her. This, at last, felt like home. Surrounded by love, she was being welcomed home.

But, no, she wasn't. The figure, shrouded in blue light, held up his hands. She recognised the figure now, it was Don. He was saying something to her: 'No, no, it is not your time, it is not meant to be. Turn around — you must go back.'

'But I want to be here. Am I am not wanted here either?'

'You are very wanted, and loved, but first you need to love and respect yourself. Open your mind to possibilities, listen to your intuition, and do not waste this beautiful life you have chosen. You are not finished here, there is something important you need to learn. You have much more to live for. But you need to go back. You will be guided and given the energy to do this.'

Suddenly she felt heavy, and cold. She unclicked her seat belt and groped for the open window. With both hands she pulled herself out of the window and kicked herself free of the car towards the surface.

She gasped for air but her lungs were full of water, and she choked. Somehow, with a superhuman effort, she swam to the gravel bank of the river and collapsed. She coughed and vomited a copious amount of warm water, and passed out, exhausted, on the rough beach.

Chapter 47

Someone was patting her hand. 'Morgan? Morgan, can you hear me?' She opened her eyes and looked around. Everything was white. Was she in heaven? She had something plastic covering her nose and mouth, a drip in her arm, and a sore throat. A doctor was hovering over her. Not heaven. He lifted the oxygen mask off her mouth.

'Ah, you're awake. That's good. How are you feeling?'

'Okay.' Just a bit bewildered.

'Good. I'm Doctor Liebenheim. You're an extremely lucky girl, Morgan. Mr and Mrs Reid were out walking their dog and found you lying on the bank of the Ayr River. It seems you drove your car straight into the river. How did you happen to do that? Was it an accident?'

'No.'

'I see. Well, I don't know how you managed to get out, but you're lucky to be alive.'

Was she?

'Your family are on their way to visit you. Emergency

Services have retrieved your handbag from the car. I'm afraid everything's been damaged, but we found your ID. We also found these …' Doctor Liebenheim held up the soggy packet of sleeping pills.

'Have you been taking these?'

Genius, this guy. 'Yes.'

'Where did you get them from, may I ask?'

'Darknet.'

Doctor Liebenheim tutted. 'Right. Well, Morgan, these are powerful, and highly addictive. Did you know they're stronger than heroin? And they can cause hallucinations and psychotic episodes. Which is what I suspect you might have experienced. Now, we can prescribe you some other medication so you can get off these things, and we're going to give you all the help you need. I don't want you to take any more of these. Okay?'

'Okay. I need to talk to Don.'

'Who is Don, one of your family?'

'Yes, in Australia.'

'Right, well that can wait for a wee while. Just now, I want you to rest and get strong. It seems you were underwater for possibly six minutes so we need to monitor you closely to make sure there is no brain damage. A nurse will come in shortly with some food, and I'll be back in to see you tomorrow.'

A young nurse came in wheeling a trolley. 'Here we are,' she sang, 'some dinner for you.' She looked at Morgan. 'You've been here before.'

Oh for fuck's sake.

'Yes, I recognise you. Didn't you bring those lovely flowers for Nurse McFeeter?'

She looked up at the nurse. 'Yes, that's right. How is she?'

'Oh, she made a quick recovery. I think your flowers cheered her up no end. She's gone back home now. I'm quite pleased, to be honest — she made me nervous. I always felt like everything I did was being scrutinised.'

Morgan smiled at her and began on her grilled fish dinner, a slow process with her throat so raw. She knew what she had experienced was not a hallucination — it was absolutely real. She had seen and spoken to Don. She had left her body and travelled to another realm, a beautiful one.

Ali and Iain, bearing flowers, appeared in the doorway. They kissed her and found chairs to sit on.

'Morgan, love, what happened?' Ali asked. 'We're told you drove your wee car into the Ayr. Was it an accident?'

'No, it really wasn't. I did it deliberately.'

Ali and Iain exchanged glances. 'But why?' Ali said. 'Why did you try to commit suicide? What's wrong? Is there anything we can do?'

Tears rose to her eyes. 'I'm sorry, I really am. Everything just got the better of me. Ross turned out to be married, and I realised many things that happened in the past were my fault. I know how my parents died — they were arguing about me. People died because of me.'

'Oh, dear, you can't possibly know that. None of it was your fault. What on earth made you think that? I knew it was a bad idea to go raking up the past. The past is gone — over and done with. And none of it was your fault.'

Ali stood up and bent over to hug Morgan in the bed. 'You poor wee thing. We should have taken better care of you.' She spied the soggy packet of pills on the bedside table. 'You're not taking these things, are you?'

'Sleeping tablets. I was. Not anymore. They're giving me some other tablets to take instead.'

'Dear, these are what your aunt Janie was taking for severe cancer pain. They are definitely not sleeping tablets. They're opioids, very strong ones. People have died from taking them, you know. Who on earth prescribed these?'

'No one. I got them from the darknet.'

'Hell's bells. Don't get any more, for goodness sake. You're in safe hands now. They're good here. And when you leave the hospital, I want you to come and stay with us for a wee while. You look like you need feeding up, and you're all peely-wally. We'll look after you properly.'

'Thank you, Ali, that's kind of you. I'll think about it.'

'Do you want to talk about what was upsetting you? You need to get it off your chest.'

'Not yet. One day.'

'Aye, okay. Well, I'm only too happy to sit down with you whenever you're ready.'

Iain spoke for the first time. 'And your poor wee car underwater. But don't worry, the Emergency Services will be winching it out first thing in the morning. It will probably be all right once it dries out.

'You know,' he said, 'it was a few years ago now, but they pulled a German World War Two tank out of a lake in Russia, or Estonia maybe. It had been underwater for about sixty years. Incredibly, there was no rust, and they were able to get it started. It was a diesel, mind. It just shows you though — good cars those German cars. Or maybe it was Russian, not sure now.'

'Thank you, Iain. Yes, poor little car, I hope it goes again.'

Visiting hours were nearly over. Ali and Iain stood up to go. 'Kirsty and Callum will be coming down to visit you tomorrow,' Ali said. 'Is there anything you need us to get you?'

'Actually, yes, if Kirsty could get my laptop.' She rummaged through her waterlogged handbag for her keys. 'This is ruined, I'll need a new one.'

Suddenly she realised her keys were all on the one keyring in the car's ignition. No one would be able to get into the flat until the car was retrieved.

She held up her phone, also waterlogged. 'And this is cactus too. No, thank you, nothing I need,' she said. 'Don't worry about the laptop. Thank you for coming to see me. I'm sorry for being a burden and causing so much trouble.'

'Och, not at all. It's no bother, pet. We just hope you rest up and feel better soon.'

After Ali and Iain left, she resumed thinking. Something had happened to her, and it wasn't necessarily caused by the drugs.

Where was her jewellery? She opened the bedside drawers and was relieved to find someone had put it all away safely.

She yawned deeply. She watched the digital clock on the wall. It was just after eleven pm. She kept watching until the numbers clicked over to 11:11. Her time. A line of standing stones; Roman soldiers on guard; or two identical parallel channels — an open portal, reaching up to the otherworld, open only for a minute, waiting for your choice. And the day she was born. To a father who didn't want her.

Chapter 48

Morgan's austere hospital room overlooked a car park, but at least she had the room to herself. She noticed the packet of tablets had been removed during the night. A pity. She would have liked one, soggy though they were. She shivered. Her muscles ached. The pills the nurse doled out were feeble; they didn't have the same euphoric effect.

Why was she still alive? She had fully intended to end her life. The memories of witnessing her parents' accident, and Ross's callous dismissal of her came flooding back.

What a disaster. Things were exactly the same as they were before, only worse. Because now she had also caused everybody a lot of hassle and anxiety. Ali and Iain were kind, but goodness knows what they really thought. Probably that she had arrived and disrupted their lives, creating problems they didn't need. And they weren't even related to her.

Something Don had told her during her near-death experience came into her mind: she had more to learn, more to live for, and she'd be given the energy to do it. Only right now she had no energy, she couldn't think of anything to live for, and she felt like an unwanted failure.

Was it arrogant to feel she should be wanted? If nobody wants her then … so what? There must be millions of people who just get on with their lives, whose self-esteem didn't depend on validation from other people. She sighed. She wasn't one of them.

Doctor Liebenheim arrived early, after breakfast. Apart from feeling weak and stiff, she was keen to leave the hospital.

'Not today, Morgan, sorry. We'd like to keep you here for at least one more day, for observation, and to run some tests. Also, I'd like to suggest something to you. We have the privilege of having access to a highly skilled clinical psychologist, Doctor Philip Vaughn-Williams. He has had notable success in assisting with attempted suicide cases.'

That's what she was now? An attempted suicide case? Doing well, Morgan.

'Now, he has made himself available to come and talk to you later this morning. How does that sound?'

'Yes, that sounds fine. And then can I go home?'

'Well, probably … maybe tomorrow, but let's just see what Philip thinks first. You might find some of his methods a little unusual but just keep an open mind. I think you will like him.'

Keep an open mind. That's what Don had said — 'open your mind to possibilities'.

'Okay, thank you.'

She searched everywhere in the room but couldn't find her clothes. She couldn't leave even if she tried.

At morning teatime she heard a knock on the open door. The cup rattled in the saucer as she put her tea down on the bedside cabinet.

'Hello, Morgan, I'm Doctor Vaughn-Williams.' He entered the room and offered her his hand. 'Please, just call me Philip. May I have a seat?'

'Of course.' She turned off the television with the remote.

Philip looked to be in his fifties with thinning brown hair, turning grey, a short stubbly grey beard, brown eyes, and a kind face with eyebrows that slanted upwards over his nose, giving him the appearance of an inquisitive Labrador. He wore a casual, loose white top; it wasn't a shirt. He had a slightly different accent. Not Scottish, maybe Welsh.

'Now, Morgan, what a lovely name. How are you doing here today?'

'I'm doing okay, thank you.'

'That's good. Well, I'm here to see if we can work through a few things. I'm a clinical psychologist and therapist, as Doctor Liebenheim would have mentioned, and we might start by having a little chat.

'Doctor Liebenheim tells me you're lucky to be alive. How you made it out of that car underwater with lungs full of water is something of a miracle. He actually used the word "remarkable". You must have a robust constitution. Would you like to tell me what led you to being there? Start at the beginning and take your time. We have all the time in the world.'

He had such a calming presence that, for the first time, she felt here was someone she could relax with and talk to honestly. She told him everything. She expected him to explain that the opioids she'd been taking had caused delusions. She said, 'These visions were as real for me as sitting here talking to you. It wasn't my imagination or a hallucination. Everything crowded into my head until it all became too much, and voices urged me to be done with it, and end it all.'

She was surprised to see Philip nodding, his eyes shining. 'May I see the pendant?'

Not what she expected. 'Yes, all the jewellery is in the drawer here,' she said, handing him the pendant.

'It's a beautiful piece.' He held it up to the light.

Shit don't do that, she thought.

'So do you know what this is then, Morgan?'

'Yes, my mother's keek stane she used with clients in her clairvoyant practice.'

'I know who you are,' he said.

'You do?' *If he tells me I've been here before I'll scream.*

'Oh, yes. My friend Stewart from the library gave me your number. I was hoping one day you would call me. He saw signs in you that could indicate a troubled past. To explain … as well as being a regular psychologist, I'm also a hypnotherapist and past life regression specialist. And from what you've told me, I believe you would benefit enormously if you'd be willing to explore a past life.

'You see, often problems in our present life can be traced back to an event or trauma, something in the past. And I'm not just talking about our childhood memories in this life, I'm talking about a previous lifetime. This is where we can really try to get to the source of the problem.

'By re-experiencing the unresolved influence we can release the memory, let it go and erase it, and then we can stop repeating the same damaging patterns. It is a very liberating process. I, myself have helped more than a thousand patients to live more fulfilled lives once they let go of the past. So what do you think, Morgan? Are you willing to confront whatever in the past has been causing trouble in this life?'

'Okay, I suppose so,' she said. 'I always feel there's a part of my memory I can't access, and I feel guilty that things have happened which are my fault. And anyway, I'm sure that's what happened to me spontaneously when I looked through my mother's keek stane. I've never been game enough to do it again.'

'That's grand. I'm sure you will find this an uplifting experience. Let's see where it takes us.'

'Sure. So, Stewart contacted you, did he? You said he gave you my number.'

'Yes, he knew your mother. We all did. He's a druid by the way, and a highly enlightened soul.'

'Wow, a druid, is he? So they still exist then?'

'Absolutely. You might be surprised at just how many of us there are.'

'Oh, right. But modern-day druids are not the same as the ancient druids, are they? I thought they never wrote anything down, so all their old knowledge would be lost over time, surely.'

'Ah, but therein lies the wisdom of it. You see, exactly

because there were no written texts to be misinterpreted, mistranslated, and argued about, means the philosophy is always evolving, relevant to the current society. It never gets bogged down in dogma. And one of the key teachings is reincarnation. Which is what we are going to explore with you today.'

'And the doctor knows this is what you do?'

'Yes, he certainly does. Doctor Liebenheim is a progressive man. He has seen the undeniable success we have had healing the present by addressing the past. I wish more practitioners were as open minded. But I don't usually treat clients at the hospital — I have my own clinic.'

'Now, how this works is I will guide you to a state of deep relaxation, just like in meditation. You will be the channel, not me. I only guide the process. You will be in control at all times. You can stop at any time, and you can move to a different lifetime if you choose. It can take between one and three hours so I will just pop out and make sure the staff know we are not to be disturbed.'

Philip left the room and she took the opportunity to use the bathroom and get comfortably settled back on the bed.

He returned carrying a small voice recorder. 'Because we are exploring past lives,' he said, 'you will inevitably experience your own death. But this is nothing to be afraid of. It is in the past. It has already happened. You will feel no pain — you will just be observing, and reporting. Remember you can move anywhere you want to at any time. Are you comfortable with that?'

'Yes, I think so. Sounds intriguing.'

'Okay, now I'll just start this recorder and I'll give you a copy so you can listen to your session later. What I will do is guide you back to your early childhood. In your case, even this may help you address problems you are experiencing. Then we will progress back further into your mother's womb and from there back to the time before you were born.'

'Wow, okay.'

'So are you ready to begin?'

Philip had a warm, soothing voice, and before long she entered a pleasant, deep state of relaxation. He took her back through her life, younger and younger until she reached age three. 'Go to the incident that is significant to you. Where are you now, Morgan?'

'Bedroom. Simon's and my bedroom. I am in my bed. He starts whimpering and crying. Nobody comes to pick him up, for a long time. I think he is unhappy. I want to stop him being sad.

'I have a good idea. I think he would like to cuddle my teddy, to help him sleep. I get out of bed and climb onto a chair. I lean into his cot and I put teddy on him. After a while he stops crying. I am pleased. I have made him happy.

'Mummy comes into the room. I smile at her; I think she will be pleased with me. She runs over to the cot and throws teddy off Simon. She is not pleased. She shouts at me. I don't understand. She says he is not breathing. I don't know what that means. I don't know why she is cross with me.

'Daddy is not home so Mummy takes Simon and me in the car. She is crying and driving fast. I have done something wrong; something is my fault. A lady in a red cape grabs

Simon and runs away with him. I don't see him again. Daddy hits me, very hard. Then I am at Janie's.'

'Morgan, what do you think happened here?' Philip said.

'I see I was too little to understand if you stop breathing you die. I wasn't trying to kill him at all.'

'You do not have to feel guilty about this anymore,' Philip said. 'It was not your fault. Release the guilt from your memory. Let it go now, you are free of that burden.'

'Now, Morgan,' he continued, 'travel back to the time you were in your mother's womb. How are you feeling?'

'Happy … excited. I'm ready for this life. I can feel my mother's love for me. She wants me and is looking forward to being a mother.'

'That's great,' Philip said. 'You're doing really well. Now go back even earlier, to the time before you were born. Take a moment and go to the life which has had the most impact on your life today … where are you now?'

Chapter 49

84 AD

I'm in the south of Scotland but it wasn't called Scotland then. The Romans have invaded and are trying to take over our land and rule us. I live in a settlement of family and friends. We don't have towns, as such.

'Rhu, have you done with that grain yet?'

That's my mother. She's wanting the oatmeal for the bannock bread. I've been grinding it for hours … well it seems like hours.

'Yes, Mama, just coming.' I gather all the meal into a basket lined with cloth, dust off my hands, and take it into the hut.

'Good girl,' she says, stroking my hair. I have thick blonde hair which is unusual around here. I have blue eyes, and I've lived seventeen summers.

Mama is kind and loving to us. She has lived thirty-seven summers. She looks old because she has worked hard all her life.

'Have you seen Conal?' she asks me.

'No, sorry, Mama. I saw him walking down the path to the shore earlier.'

'Hmph,' Mama says. 'If you see him, tell him I need him to collect more wood.'

'Yes, Mama.'

We live in a lovely area, on the coast. The land belongs to us and all the neighbouring families together because our people have always lived here. There is plenty to eat. My father is good at catching fish, and we gather shellfish.

Conal, my brother, has lived two summers more than I have. He is lazy and likes to escape down to the shore, but he's not gathering food for us. He's just playing on the sand.

We have our own goat for milk, a sheep for wool and some chickens. We grow oats and some spelt. There is always a lot of work to do. Every few days we share and swap food with the neighbouring families. Nearby live our relatives — uncles, aunts, cousins, and many friends. We get together often to sing and tell stories and laugh. We celebrate a lot of special days with feasting and ceremonies.

A wise man, a druid named Arion, lives in our area and travels around visiting every family. He mostly likes to teach us and hold discussions and celebrations in the oak woods because it is secret, quiet and safe, but for the really important days — mid-winter and beginning of summer — we all gather at the ancient sacred stones where he conducts rituals. There are old tombs here, the tombs of our ancestors who were buried thousands of summers ago. We worship our gods here and give offerings, of food, and things we have made.

When Arion visits, he teaches us about the stars, numbers and measurements, tells us poems and stories, and makes sure everybody is happy, and getting along with one another. If we have a problem we want to talk about, we can visit him in his home on the hill.

Sometimes when he visits, he brings his son Bryden. He's always eager to talk to me and tries to help. He's polite and respectful but he is too skinny, he has a big nose, big teeth and red hair. I don't find him handsome. I've seen him looking at me and I know I sometimes attract attention from men.

We love it when Arion visits but he has to come to us wearing ordinary clothes. Only inside his timber and clay hut, and for special ceremonies will he wear his coloured cloak, his small sickle made of gold and his torc with the bull heads. But he always wears his gold triskele hidden on a leather string under his tunic. It is dangerous to be a druid ever since the invasion.

Arion told us that some summers before I was born the invaders, who are called Romans, massacred many druids on the sacred island of Mona. Not all the druids were on the island though. Some were here further north and over the sea to the west. It was lucky he was not on the island when this atrocity occurred.

Arion has warned us the invaders are dangerous soldiers. They wear metal armour and carry metal shields for defence and they will kill or take people as slaves. We must be sure to keep together and be home by dark.

We asked Arion why are they here and what do they want?

He said they want to conquer all the people in the world, and our best protection is to keep hidden.

He said the Romans are here to stay and one day we may be ruled by them and have to live with them. We said we would fight them off. He said it was important we understand what they are saying so he has been teaching all the young people in our clan another language called Latin. He said the Romans also make marks on thin leather and each Roman could understand what it means.

I have a secret. Once, when I am walking with the dog over to the north and east, I come across a man bathing in the river. I am frightened, but also fascinated. He has dark golden-coloured skin and short dark hair. He isn't one of us — we all have long hair.

He has strong muscles in his arms and legs. After he bathes, he dresses in a tunic and leather sandals. The dog suddenly barks and I am too slow to stop her. The man looks up and sees me. I start to run but he calls out to me and I stop to turn around. He catches up to me and smiles. He says hello, but it is in Latin. He holds out his hand to me and seems friendly.

He is a beautiful man, tall and strong, handsome, with dark brown eyes, almost black, and long, thick eyelashes. He takes my hand and asks me to sit down with him on the grass. He introduces himself as Marcus Petronius Marcellus.

'Three names? We have only one name, and I am Rhu,' I say.

He cannot believe I speak some Latin. He asks me how I know Latin and I say, 'I am just very clever.' This seems to please him and he laughs. He tells me he is twenty-two years old and he is a soldier with the Roman army but he is not from the place called Rome. He comes from a country village somewhere to the south of Rome. Many of the men come from different places all over the world and they get paid to be a soldier for twenty-five years.

He takes me to the top of a hill to look down on his camp without being seen. I keep my hand on the dog so she won't bark. I see a fort in a clearing, protected by wooden walls. There are leather tents and some grand looking wooden structures.

I see men in the metal armour Arion described. I am frightened, but the man with three names tells me not to be afraid. I see that not all the men wear armour. Some are wearing the same kind of ordinary tunics and leather sandals as the man who is holding my hand. The ones in armour seem to be guarding the rest of the settlement. I can also see a group of huts outside the enclosure, not unlike our own huts.

He tells me he is a fast runner and because of this he is a scout. His job is to return to the camp each day and report.

'I will not report you though,' he says. 'You don't look too dangerous.'

He asks me to come back and meet with him again, and he will teach me more Latin.

'I might. Marcus Petronius Marcellus,' I say.

He laughs again. 'You can call me Marcellus, or just Marcus if you like.'

I cannot stop thinking about him.

✦ ✦ ✦ ✦

My brother Conal's job is to tend the animals and to cut and bring wood and peat. Father is teaching him how to fish. He likes being around the animals but I know he doesn't always treat them well. I have seen him breaking the wings of pigeons and laughing at their attempts to fly. I run, crying, to Mama and she tells him not to be cruel. But later I see him doing it again.

After I have ground the grain with the quern and washed the clothes in the stream, I sneak away to meet Marcus. I leave the dog behind. He is there by the river again, waiting for me. I take him some bannock bread Mama baked this morning.

He is pleased to see me. I give him the bread and he gives me a bracelet of black beads. He says it is jet. It is the most beautiful thing I have ever seen. He puts the beads around my wrist. I have to be sure to take them off before I go home.

He has brought a new drink for me to try. He carries it in a leather flask with a wooden stopper. I take a sip. It is sharp and fruity. I am amazed, I have never tasted anything like it, only father's mead, when he lets us. Before long we are both giggling.

He tells me the Romans have brought many wonderful things with them. He tells me Romans live in grand houses and have fine tableware and clothing. He takes a small sharp metal stick and a leaf. He scratches into the leaf the drawing of a large stone house with many rooms. He calls it a 'villa'. He says one day he would like to have a son and a grand house. It all sounds so marvellous; I wonder why we couldn't have these things too.

I'm feeling sleepy. Marcus puts his arm around me and

kisses me. It is the first time I have been kissed like that. I like it and I let him do it. Then he starts to feel my body. My breasts are full and I can tell he likes them. He feels me all over the top of my shift. He tells me I am beautiful. I tell him he is handsome.

Then he feels me under my shift, his brown hand feels rough on my soft skin, but it is exciting, and I let him do it. He slides his hand down to my private part. I know what he wants to do. He takes my hand and puts it onto his private part. I can't believe what I'm feeling, it feels like there is a bone in it. He wriggles on top of me and I gasp. It hurts, but only for a moment. He kisses me and makes soft moaning noises. I enjoy what he's doing to me. He puts my arms over my head and pins them to the ground with his big hands and I love it. We are both wet with sweat, and afterwards we laugh and drink more wine.

I bathe in the river and kiss him goodbye. He holds my hand for a long time, like he doesn't want to let me go. I hurry home, slightly unsteady, pulling twigs out of my hair as I go. I'm careful to take the beautiful bracelet off. I will have to hide it somewhere.

'Where have you been, Rhu? I need you to milk the goat and collect the eggs.'

'Sorry, Mama, I was out walking and forgot how late it was getting.'

Conal looks at me and makes his eyes narrow. Sometimes I think he is a strange boy.

I meet Marcus secretly again and again. It is so much fun to sneak away and see him without anyone knowing. He is teaching me many more Latin words. We enjoy each other's bodies, and I think I am getting better at it. Afterwards we lie in the soft grass and caress each other, and I never want to leave to come home.

One day, two full moons later, Arion sends a message for me to visit him in his hut. I get a sick, churning feeling in my belly. Am I in trouble? I come to his hut bringing bread and honey as a gift. He is wearing his coloured cloak around his shoulders but he is not wearing his sickle. My hands shake as I give the basket to him. He is a wonderful teacher but can also be formidable.

'Thank you, Rhu. Please sit down.'

I sit on a low timber bench, fold my hands in my lap and look down at the earth floor. He asks me how my mother, father and brother are keeping. I reply that we are all very well, thank you.

'I've asked you to come and see me because I am aware you are of the age, and it is time you married.'

I look up. I was not expecting that.

'Now, as you know, my son, Bryden, is a fine young man, studying to be a druid. He is bright and he will make a fine leader one day, and a fine father. He is keen to get to know you better, and, if you agree, he is willing to marry you.' Arion smiles at me, as if he thinks this news will please me.

I am horrified. I stare at him without speaking.

'I can see this is a surprise to you. That is natural. All I ask is you give it consideration, for say, one moon. Discuss it with your mother and father. If you agree to this union, and I hope you do, there are things you will need to know about.'

In my head I think, *I already know about 'things'*. I stand up and Arion says a blessing over me, gives me two rowan twigs tied into a small cross for protection and a cloth bag full of acorns.

I walk home dragging my feet. I give the acorns to Mama. I do not want to talk to anyone.

We are having pigeon stew for supper. Father found the dead pigeons with broken wings and he made Conal pluck all the feathers off them as punishment. I make bannock bread from the grain I ground. I still don't speak to anyone.

Mama asks me what is wrong.

'Arion wants me to marry that buffoon Bryden,' I say.

'That is very rude, Rhu,' Mama says. 'He is a nice boy. He would take care of you. I think it's a good idea.'

I say a swear word in Latin. It means 'bum hole'.

'Rhu is not a virgin. He will know,' Conal says.

'Conal, don't be so nasty, and don't talk such nonsense,' Mama says. 'Do something useful — go and fetch some water.'

Conal bumps into me as he walks past. He curls his lip up into a sneer and whispers, 'Roman fucker'.

Chapter 50

I meet Marcus every day I can. We always make love. He gives me a present — a coin made of silver, with a raised picture of a skinny eagle on one side and a head on the back. He says it is a picture of Domitian, the emperor of Rome. He says the coin is valuable and I can use it to buy things. It is what he earns in one day for being a soldier. I say it is pretty but there is nowhere I can buy things. I'm not even sure what it means. But I am happy to have the gift.

I tell him I am depressed because I am expected to marry a boy. I am careful not to tell him we have druids living among us. I secretly hope he will offer to marry me. I could live a good life and have wonderful things. But all he says is, 'I sincerely hope you won't marry the boy. I will miss seeing you.' We hear twigs breaking nearby and we quickly kiss and say goodbye in case someone sees us together.

The month is nearly up and I will have to tell Arion what I have decided about Bryden. I return home and I see Arion at our hut. People are milling around, gathering things and putting them into barrows and onto horses.

'What is happening?'

'Quickly, Rhu,' Mama says, 'collect everything you can and load it on the horse. We have no time to waste.'

'Why, though?'

Father gets impatient and says, 'Because we tell you to.'

'Arion has seen a Roman camp over the hill,' Mama says. 'It is much too close to us. We need to travel in the safety of darkness towards the west, following the coast. We can cross the sea if we need to. We must get far away from the Romans. We do not want to become slaves. One day we may come back when it is safe. Now, quickly.'

Conal is gathering the chickens into baskets. I bring all the clothing and linen from the hut and load it into a wooden barrow. I don't hurry. I don't want to go. I will not see Marcus again. Bryden comes over and smiles at me with his big teeth.

'Can I help you with that, Rhu?' he asks.

'No thank you. I can manage,' I say, and turn away, busying myself with the packing.

We start trudging our way along the coast towards the west, with all our relatives, friends and animals. We do not get far because a river blocks our way. We must travel north to find where the river is narrowest so we can cross.

As darkness falls, we make a camp for the night. We are lucky the moon is bright so we can see what we are doing. We set up animal skin tents and try to sleep wrapped in blankets. The small children are crying. It is cold, and not much fun. I cannot sleep. I hear Bryden snoring in Arion's tent. I cannot possibly marry that. I think of Marcus — his fit, muscular warm body. If only I could see him one more time.

Besides, he needs to know something. I wasn't sure before but now I am. He needs to know I have a child growing in my belly. He will definitely want to know about that. It might be the son he said he wished for. He will rescue me from smarmy Bryden and protect me, and we can live a fine life.

Quietly, I climb out from the blanket. I wrap my rabbit fur cloak around me and pull on my leather boots. The night air is crisp and with the moonshine I can see perfectly well. I know where to go. It is easy to find my way back to our settlement, and then to the clearing by the east river near the Roman camp. If Marcus is not there, I will have to wait until he arrives in the early morning. I feel certain he will want to hear my good news.

I have almost reached the clearing when I hear leaves crackling behind me. I turn around and I'm shocked to see Conal. 'What are you doing here?' I whisper. 'It's dangerous. You need to go back.'

'More to the point,' Conal says, 'what are *you* doing here? Roman in the gloamin'.' He laughs at his own stupid joke.

'Be quiet, idiot!'

We hear bushes rustling. Is it Marcus? I can't see anything.

'You have to go back, Conal. I mean it. I need to have a pee.'

I go behind a large rock and squat down. I hear a scuffle and a yelp. Is it Marcus? I look out from the rock and I see two soldiers gripping Conal by the arms. I panic and hide back behind the rock. My heart is thumping so hard it hurts. He is struggling but the soldiers are much stronger. They start dragging him away. He squeals and shouts.

What I hear next makes my blood run cold. He yells out, 'Let me go — sister — girl — behind rock,' in Latin. The soldiers stop dragging him and talk between themselves. One holds Conal and the other comes after me. Why would you do that Conal? Why tell them where I am hiding?

The big soldier easily finds me behind the rock and drags me up by the arm. 'No, no,' I cry. 'I know Marcus. I'm his friend.' I have no power against the soldier.

He drags me over to Conal and the other soldier. 'Marcus … Marcellus?'

'Yes, he will tell you. We are not dangerous. Please let us go.'

The soldiers laugh. 'Speaks Latin.'

They are wearing tunics and leather armour, not the full metal. But they both wear round metal helmets and have swords. They talk and laugh to each other, too fast for me to understand. They drag us roughly towards their camp but they don't take us in through the wooden gates.

I am terrified, but I know if I can see Marcus he can explain and make them let us go. The two soldiers talk rapidly as if they are deciding what to do with us. They tie us to a tree with coarse rope that feels like plaited horsehair. Conal is whimpering.

One of the soldiers disappears towards the fort, leaving the other one to guard us. I can see he is looking at me in a way I don't like.

'We have to escape,' Conal says. 'I have a knife in my boot. I can cut the rope.'

'And then what? Run back to our family and lead the

Romans right to them? You don't think, Conal. The best thing would be to wait until I can see Marcus. He will set us free. And why did you tell the soldiers where I was hiding?'

'I thought they might let me go and take you instead.'

Conal disappoints me. 'Well now they've got both of us.'

He starts whimpering again. The soldier watches us but he can't understand what we are saying. The sky becomes lighter; the night is ending. Our family will soon realise we are missing. I wish Marcus will come to rescue us quickly.

Before long, four more soldiers arrive with the one who left previously. These soldiers are also wearing just the leather armour and round helmets. Marcus is not among them. I become anxious. The six soldiers talk a lot and laugh. I can't understand them.

Two of them untie Conal and me. I rub my hands and arms. They ache from having been pulled backwards around the tree. Instead of taking us to the fort, the soldiers roughly drag and push us in the other direction, towards the ancient standing stones. I don't understand this, and I am very frightened.

When we reach the circle of standing stones, one soldier climbs a tree as if he is a lookout. Two other soldiers hold me by the arms while two more tie Conal to a stone facing me. He is crying and shouting and kicking out but he is no match for the soldiers.

They don't tie me up. They pull off my rabbit cloak and push me onto the ground. One of them takes my hands, one of them holds my legs, and they lift up my shift. I scream and cry and try to twist away from them but I cannot get free.

The more I struggle, the more they hurt my wrists and ankles. The soldiers laugh and begin taking off their leather armour.

'Where is Marcus?' I shout. 'I want to see Marcus.'

One of the soldiers says, 'You are stupid. He is with his girlfriend in the village outside the fort.'

Chapter 51

The soldiers jostle around, staring down at me. I plead with all of the gods, 'If Conal and I are spared, I promise I will marry Bryden.'

Another soldier grabs one of my legs so now there are two of them holding down my legs. I scream and cry out but there is nothing I can do. I hear Conal screaming and yelling but he is tied to a standing stone. He cannot help me.

'No, no, stop!' I shout, but the two soldiers pull my legs apart and another soldier roughly shoves his way into me, while the others watch, excited, awaiting their turn. It is not like with Marcus who is gentle and loving — this is a brute who forces and hurts me. He breathes his hot stinky breath in my face. I feel like I am losing consciousness and I go limp. It hurts less that way.

Suddenly there is a deafening crash of thunder, a yelp, and a heavy thump. I hear shouts and scuffling. The smelly soldier jumps off me. I open my eyes and cover myself up. The sky is dark grey, the colour of mud, and lightning splits the clouds with a blinding violence I have never seen before.

The air feels charged, making the hairs on my arms stand on end. I can smell approaching rain, but also something stronger, an acrid burning smell. The soldier who was keeping watch in a tree has been struck by lightning on his metal helmet. I think he is dead.

Six more soldiers arrive, these ones in full armour and on horseback. The new soldiers dismount and question the others. Orders are shouted in amongst general commotion and yelling.

The dead soldier is thrown over a horse. Another soldier unties Conal but binds his hands together in front of him instead; the other end of the rope he attaches to a horse. I hear the soldier say, 'slave'. Conal screams and the soldier ties a cloth over his mouth.

Two soldiers roughly lift me to my feet. They drag me to a tall stone and tie me to it, my arms drawn behind me painfully again. Rain begins to fall. Through a blurry haze I see Marcus, in full metal uniform. He doesn't look like a scout now. He looks like an officer who gives orders. I call to him, 'Marcus, it's me, Rhu.'

He marches over to me and looks at me as if he is inspecting me. He says, 'male parta male dilabuntur.' Easy come, easy go. He turns away.

'No, Marcus, please!' I am crying. 'I have your child inside me.' He stops momentarily. I think he will turn around. But he doesn't. He walks over to speak briefly to another soldier also wearing metal armour. I hear him say, 'Kill her … head on spike'. I scream. The soldier nods, draws his sword, and comes over to me.

The storm is raging now, torrential rain and hail pelts down. Leaves, sticks and branches are being blown around in a furious gale. I see Marcus mount his horse and turn it away towards the path. The soldier in front of me raises his glinting sword and holds it to my throat.

I look into his blue eyes. They are breathtaking, the colour of the sea on a sunny day. He doesn't look anything like a Roman. He turns his head to one side and shouts loudly over his shoulder, 'Let this be an example to your pathetic people — the Roman army will conquer all.' I scream as loudly as I can.

Marcus disappears down the path on his horse. The soldier clangs his sword hard on the stone near my shoulder. It is a deafening sound, making my ear hurt. Then he cuts me once on the neck with the incredibly sharp blade. It makes just a small gash, but it is large enough to draw blood. I gasp. Bright blood flows down all over my shift, mixing with the rain.

He looks at me directly in the eyes. 'Close your eyes and be quiet,' he says. I am surprised at this but I do as he says. After a moment I half open my eyes and see all the soldiers hastily making their way back down the path leading to their fort, dragging Conal with them. I can hardly see through the deluge. The soldier in front of me turns away and follows them, leaving me crying and shaking, tied to the stone.

I hear a bird call. It is the secret bird call Arion has taught us to use if we are in danger. Through my blurry eyes I see

Arion creeping towards me with Bryden, weeping, behind him. Arion quickly saws through the rope binding my hands. He cradles me in his arms. He too, is weeping.

He says, 'Rhu, oh, Rhu, you poor darling. It is all right; we are here now.'

The rain begins to ease. I know it was Arion who summoned the lightning and storm. He makes a wad of clay and mixes it with herbs he carries with him. He holds this to my neck and applies pressure for a few minutes. He gives me nectar to drink from a flask. I feel weak but gradually I start to revive.

'The Romans have taken Conal,' I say.

'I know,' Arion says. 'There is nothing we can do about that. But you are safe.'

Bryden collects my rabbit cloak from the ground; it is heavy with mud. The weather clears and we begin our slow journey towards our clan still making their way to the coast. When we reach them, Mama is overjoyed to see me. But I cry because Conal has been taken.

She thinks I followed Conal to the Roman fort, and Arion does not tell her otherwise, although I know he knows it wasn't like that at all. I feel ashamed to have put my whole tribe in danger. Eventually we reach the coast and establish a new settlement. We hope the Romans will never come this far west.

I have a meeting with Arion. I tell him I am prepared to marry Bryden. He is pleased and we organise the union as soon as possible.

I have grown to love Bryden. He is a good husband; steady,

considerate, and a good worker. I have had two more children — two boys — with Bryden as well as Marcus's child.

Everybody thinks the dark-skinned child is the result of the rape, but Arion knows she is not. He has never divulged this to anyone, and I am grateful to him. When she was born people wanted me to take her into the forest and leave her there because she is a Roman. I could not do that. I love her, and Bryden treats her like his own daughter. I have given her my jet bracelet to play with. I never want to wear it.

I am also grateful to the Roman soldier who pretended to kill me. I have often wondered about him and why he let me live. And I will never forget his blue eyes.

We never do move back to our settlement on the south coast. We make our home here on the west coast and re-establish our crops and animals. It is beautiful looking out to the big sea. It's often windy, but we like it here.

I miss Conal. I do not know what became of him but I imagine he would have made an extraordinarily bad slave. It was my fault he was taken and I have never forgiven myself for this, and for endangering my whole clan.

I am old now, older than Mama was when she died. My father and my beloved husband, Bryden, are also dead. And Arion died long ago. Now it is my time to pass over.

My children are gathered around me. We have a new druid in our clan, Lochan, and he says a powerful prayer over me, asking for the blessing, safe guidance and passage of my soul. I do not feel I deserve to be blessed. I have carried such a lot of guilt for so many years.

'You are loved, and will always be loved,' Lochan says. 'Go

peacefully to your spirit home. It is not the end but a new beginning for you. You will never die; we will all meet again. Everything is as it should be. All is well.'

I am cold but suddenly I feel warm as I float up above my body. I look down to see my three children kneeling by my body. I want to tell them it is all right. I am in no pain; I am feeling peaceful. They cannot hear me.

Chapter 52

After a few moments, and while she was still in the hypnotic state, Philip asked, 'Morgan, do you recognise any of the people in this past life as people you know today?'

'Yes, many of the people are familiar to me — Arion is the same soul as Don, Marcus is the same soul as Ross, Conal is the same soul as Anton, and, oh my God … Bryden is the same soul as Evan Paterson. My dark-skinned daughter with Marcus was my mother in this life. But Mama is my aunt Janie, and oh … Kirsty was one of my children. That's incredible. They're all people I know who shared another life with me. Now I see.'

'Was Simon there?'

'Yes, he was the other one of my darling sons. And oh … he's here now. He says, he is happy. He says he's glad I finally listened. He's been trying to tell me to not feel guilty about anything. I see I have been carrying guilt with me for a long time.'

'Morgan, now you can let go of all this guilt. It is over. Forgive yourself, delete the guilt, and know you are valued and loved. You can stop repeating this pattern of choosing people who betray and hurt you. You can move on with your life, take control, free from the encumbrance of the past. Start anew. Whenever you feel ready, you can slowly awaken and return. Take your time, come back only when you feel you want to.'

She felt herself returning to her body and waking up.

'How do you feel?' Philip said.

'Amazing. That was just extraordinary. It was a clear memory. It's like I'm still punishing myself for something that happened long ago, like I don't learn. I keep falling into the same trap of choosing destructive relationships.'

'Exactly. Our soul progresses through each lifetime, learning each time, except sometimes traumatic soul memories are persistent and stay with us until we can release them. It is a continuous flow of birth, life, death, and rebirth.'

'And I nearly threw it all away.'

'Suicide is never the answer; it just wastes time,' he said. 'It means you would have to deal with the problem again in another lifetime until you can work through the issues. Your father's soul, for instance, definitely has some long-standing issues to address. Your parents in your current lifetime would have chosen each other for a reason.'

'You mentioned Don,' he said. 'Is he someone significant to you?'

'Yes Don Erskine. My godfather. I lived with them in Australia.'

'Don *Erskine*? Is he Scottish, from around here?'

'Yes, why?'

'He was a member of our group, with Stewart and your mother. In fact he *started* the group, long before I joined, way back in 1974 or 1975.'

'Really? What a coincidence.'

'I am perfectly sure it is no coincidence. What we think of as coincidences are often actually soul choices made prior to this current life. Our soul energy, or consciousness, is connected to all our previous incarnated lives, and to all other souls.'

'So, when people say they've met their soulmate,' she said, 'they really mean they've met one of many?'

'Yes, we are each in a group of souls we continually reincarnate with. In different lifetimes they may appear as your husband, or child, mother or a friend, not always as a romantic partner.'

'And if the people I know had regressions would they experience the same memories as me?'

'If they regressed to the same time, yes, they absolutely would. These are genuine memories, not fantasies.'

'What about my mother's keek stane, does that have any special power? When I first touched it, I felt an energy, and then I had that vision of the Roman fort.'

'The keek stane is something to focus your attention, like a crystal ball, a scrying stone, or even a candle flame. It has no actual power of its own. The power is in the person using it. The cairngorm is quartz crystal, though, and that is well known for having electrical transference properties, which is why it's used in microchips — silicon chips. Any time you want to visit another life you could just do what you did before — gaze into it.'

'So I have had other lives as well?'

'Oh, hundreds. Every life is important for growth and further enlightenment of our soul. And you are guided along the way. There's a lot of wisdom in the saying "go with the flow" but it doesn't mean to blindly follow the crowd. It means to listen to your intuition.

'And if you ever hear voices in your head goading you, know they are not from the spirit world — they emanate from yourself. Just ignore them, treat them like background noise, birds chirping in the trees. So, Morgan, how are you feeling now?'

'Like I have a lot to think about,' she said. 'For one thing, I can see how I'm continually drawn to physically attractive liars.'

'Exactly. Your tendency to repeatedly choose partners who hurt and betray you is not coincidence but a pattern, which can recur until something changes. You'll feel a burden has been lifted off you, and you'll probably have loads more questions.' Philip opened his bag and drew out a book.

'If you'd like more proof and validation of what we've done today, I'll leave this book with you. The author is a highly respected American regression specialist and psychiatrist, and I think you'll get a lot out of it. Having said that though, call me any time if you want to chat, or have another regression session.'

He smiled and handed her the book, and the recording on a USB stick. 'I usually play golf on Wednesdays, but I made an exception today, seeing it was you. We all thought highly of your mother, you know. She was immensely talented. I wouldn't be at all surprised if you followed in her footsteps. Don't be afraid to keep an open mind and explore your own potential.

'Oh, and when you listen to the recording, you might be surprised to hear yourself as a young child — you spoke with a Scottish accent.'

Philip held out his warm hand to hold hers. A perceptible current travelled through his hand to her. After he left, she lay back on her pillows and contemplated the eternal flow of energy, from one person to another, from one lifetime to another. She could see her life in perspective for the first time.

She thought of Don. He would understand completely. It was no coincidence she had grown up with him and Lou. They'd been together in a previous life, when he had been a druid. She wondered if he knew. She couldn't wait to tell him.

She lifted the jet bracelet out of the bedside drawer. She hadn't given it much thought before. Now she examined it closely. It was chunky with interlocking links, worn smooth with age. In the light she could see faint markings on the inside, a series of barely detectible vertical lines.

She recognised this bracelet as the one Marcus had given her, and which she had dismissively given to her daughter. Somehow, miraculously, it must have been kept in that family, passed down through the generations. The blood throbbed in her temples. It was nearly two thousand years old and probably priceless. She replaced it in the drawer.

Then she held the cairngorm pendant and thought back to the mysterious episode in which she had witnessed her parents' accident. No wonder she had repressed any psychic ability she may have once had — her father had tried to beat it out of her.

And her poor mother. She had chosen to end both their lives rather than allow him to hurt her child anymore. In his rage it was entirely possible he would have killed Morgan. She was sure she felt a vibration coming from the stone and her mind became unusually lucid. She sent a telepathic message to her mother: *Thank you,* and *I'm sorry.* She dabbed her eyes with a tissue.

A nurse came in with lunch on a trolley.

'Do you know where my clothes are?' Morgan asked.

'Oh, aye, they'll be in the laundry. You'll get them back in a wee while.'

'Will that be today? I must get to my laptop today.'

The nurse looked at her chart. 'You're scheduled to go home tomorrow. Doctor wants to keep you in under observation for tonight. Is there someone who can get your laptop for you?'

'Yes, maybe my cousin will be visiting.'

'Oh, okay then. Let me know if you want me to call someone for you.'

She ate her lunch which was surprisingly good for hospital food. She had a sudden alarming thought: who is paying for all this?

Chapter 53

At two o'clock, when visiting hours began, Kirsty bounced into the room carrying a duffel bag, followed by Callum.

'Look at you, you poor wee thing! What have you done to yourself?' Kirsty looked smart wearing a denim shirt dress, her dark hair cut in a bob. 'This is Callum. My betrothed.'

Callum extended a pale hand to her, smiling with eyes so dark she couldn't discern his pupils. His hair and eyebrows were almost black to match. He was handsome, although he would possibly benefit from a good dose of sun. He spoke in a professional manner, befitting the doctor he was about to become.

'Pleased to meet you, Morgan. Kirsty never stops talking about you. I'm sorry to see you laid up here, though. Are you being looked after well?'

'And pleased to meet you Callum. Yes, they're great, thank you, very attentive. But I'm keen to be going home.'

'I'll see what I can find out,' he said. 'Look, we passed a

wee coffee shop downstairs and we're craving a coffee. Would you like one?'

'Love one please. Just a flat … er … cappuccino please.'

'Okay, one flat cappuccino coming up.'

Kirsty giggled. Once Callum left the room she said, 'Oh, Morgan, I'm so sorry. It's my fault. I shouldn't have told you about Ross over the phone. I just thought you should know straight away. I'm so stupid, I'm really sorry.'

'Kirsty, no. It was absolutely not your fault in any way. There were so many other things I hadn't told you about before. And I was taking drugs to sleep which were apparently opioids. The whole thing was a clusterfuck, and nothing was your fault. Do not think that — ever.'

'Is it no' something you can tell me about?'

'Of course I will. Remember how we found out from Bella my father was violent towards my mother and me? Well, he hated and blamed me for my baby brother's death. He'd been drinking and was on his way to get me from Mal and Janie's so he could beat the living daylights out of me but my mother shoved the wheel and they skidded off the bridge and were killed. Knowing that, on top of taking the opioids, made me feel guilty and worthless. There was other weird stuff, too, visions, and voices in my head.'

'Jesus, Morgan. How would you even know that? It's not possible. Finding out about Ross wouldn't have helped either.'

She was right but Morgan was never going to tell her that. Kirsty leant over her on the bed and gave her a long hug. 'Are you getting treatment? Have you talked it out with anyone?'

'Oh, yes, I had the most fascinating experience. A

hypnotherapist regressed me to a past life … in Roman times … and I was able to see where the source of my problem began. We were able to release the memory and let it go.'

Silence from Kirsty. 'Okay.'

She sensed Kirsty was considering if she had sustained brain damage. 'I know it sounds like I'm delusional, but I'm not. It was a very liberating process.'

'Well, if it helped that's great. Tell you what, though, I've brought you some stuff.' Kirsty held up the duffel bag. 'I'll leave this with you too. Ma said your phone was cactus, so we've got you a new one. But you will have a different phone number. And here's a handbag for you — it's one I don't want so you can keep it.' She pulled out a denim handbag covered with sequins.

'The good news is they've hauled up your car. It's drying out at the place you bought it. So we got your flat keys off Jimmy, the car bloke. Here they are. Then we went round to your flat and got you a nightie, some toiletry things, a bit of makeup, and your laptop and charger. We've been everywhere man! Oh, I brought you some sneakers too, I thought your shoes were also probably cactus.'

'Bless you, Kirsty, you're an angel! Exactly what I need. Thank you so much.'

'Och, no bother at all.'

'How did you know what "cactus" meant anyway?'

'We didn't. Ma and I found it on that tea towel you gave her.'

Callum returned with the coffees. 'Sorry, they didn't have what you wanted so I just got you a flat white. I hope that's okay.'

She smiled. 'That's perfect, Callum, thank you. Kirsty's been showing me the things you've brought. This is all so thoughtful of you. I really appreciate it.'

'It's no bother,' he said. 'And I asked if you can go home today, but they really want to keep you in overnight, just to be sure.'

'Probably a good idea,' Kirsty said, nodding. 'Call me when you're ready and we'll come and collect you. I've put my number in your new phone. We'll take you back to Ma's. She's made up your room for you.'

'We've got another busy day tomorrow. First thing we're taking Iain to get fitted for hearing aids. Finally! It took Callum's persuasive bedside manner to talk him into it — he got tired of all the shouting.'

The neighbours would be pleased.

After Kirsty and Callum left, a nurse came in to clear away the lunch tray.

'Would it be possible to have the name and address of the people who called emergency services after my ... accident?' Morgan asked. 'I would like to thank them.'

'I don't see why not. I'll ask at the admin for you.'

She lay back on her pillows. She hadn't been completely honest with Kirsty. She had not been able to admit she had actually been responsible for Simon's death and her mother had taken the blame. It was a grief she would always have to bear privately.

She was eager to Skype Don and Lou, but it would be midnight in Australia — too late. She opened her laptop and saw five missed Skypes from them, the last one only half an hour ago. Her stomach twisted. She immediately logged on to call them. Lou answered in a wavering voice.

'Oh, Morgan, I'm so glad you've called, dear. I've got some terrible news. Don has died. I tried to tell you earlier but I couldn't reach you.'

Her blood ran cold. She choked back tears, 'Oh my God, no. When? What happened? I'm so sorry, Lou, I should have been there for you. Are you all right?'

'Yes, my friend Trish from next door has been marvellous. She heard the ambulance early this morning and raced over in her dressing gown to help. We followed the ambulance to the hospital but he was already gone.'

'I can't believe it, my wonderful Don. Was it sudden? I mean he was fine, wasn't he?'

'Yes, he was doing really well. He had to take some pills for his heart, but they were working and he was perfectly fine. He woke me up about one o'clock this morning, yelling, "Go back, you must go back." Something like that. I think he was delirious.

'And then he grabbed my arm and looked at me, but he wasn't seeing me — his eyes were faraway, and wild, like he wasn't really here. At first, I thought he was saying "Lou" but it wasn't that. He was saying, "Roo. Look after my roo." It was so strange. He's never had a roo. We don't even have a dog. And that was the last thing he said.'

Morgan couldn't control her tears any longer. When she finally managed to speak, she said, 'I'm sorry I wasn't there for you, Lou. I'll come back.'

'I would love to see you, dear, but it's too far away. You don't have to come all that way.'

'But we will have a funeral for him.'

'Yes, we'll have to think about that, organising a funeral. There is much to do and I'm just so tired. I've been tired all day but now I can't sleep.' Lou wiped her puffy eyes.

'I'm sending you a hug, Lou, a virtual hug. I will definitely come back as soon as I can get a flight.'

'Well, if you really are, love, we'll try to book the funeral for late next week, maybe Friday, so you'll have time to get here. I can't wait to see you.'

'Okay, I'll be there. I'll let you know when. You look after yourself. I'll see you soon. Love you.'

She closed her laptop and lay back on her bed. Poor Lou would be lost without Don. Morgan would be lost without him. He had always been there for her. She never got to tell him about her past life with him, the one person who would have understood. She never got to say goodbye. Now it was too late. She closed her eyes and shook her head. She should have been there for them.

She sat up. There was something else — another feeling, a realisation. Don had died twenty-three hours ago. Twenty-three hours ago, she was underwater, being told by Don to go back into her body.

She needed to think. She tried to remember back to when she had left her body. The memory was hazy but she knew she had encountered Don as a spirit. He had told her she had to go back. She knew that much — the same words he had said to Lou. And 'look after my Rhu' were his last words. He had been thinking about her, as Rhu, when he died. Her arms were covered in goosebumps.

An almost unbearable thought occurred to her: what if he had died *because* of her? At his exact moment of death he was telling her she had to go back. Was that an uncanny coincidence or had it taken all his earthly and spiritual energy to send her back into her body and give her the strength to swim out of the car?

Philip had said there were no coincidences. If Don had saved her it had been his choice. Her life was important to him. She wouldn't waste it again.

She lay back, closed her eyes, and tried to ignore the birds chirping in the trees.

Chapter 54

Doctor Liebenheim appeared in her doorway after breakfast. 'How's the patient this morning?'

'A bit *imp*atient actually. Will I be able to leave soon?'

'Oh, yes, I think so. Your tests show favourable results. How did you like Dr Vaughn-Williams yesterday? Did you find the session interesting?'

'Yes, I really did, most enlightening, thank you. I know what you meant when you said his methods were unusual. He told me he appreciated that you allowed him to see me here in the hospital.'

'Well, normally patients consult him in his own rooms but we made an exception. And, yes, not all my colleagues see merit in alternative treatments. But you can't refute his success in helping troubled patients. I've known him since our student days. He was always a bit of a hippie — we used to call him Kombi because of his initials.'

She smiled at the image of Philip and Doctor Liebenheim hanging out together as uni students.

'You can have someone take you home whenever you're ready,' Dr Liebenheim continued. 'I'll give you a legitimate prescription, to help you get off those opioids and something to help you sleep. You might experience withdrawals, shaking, chills maybe. Try to work through it. Come back in two days for a check-up. If you're struggling, come back sooner. Don't self-medicate, okay?'

A nurse brought in her clothes and some forms on a clipboard to sign. 'Is there something I need to pay?' Morgan asked.

'Oh, no. Medical treatment is free in Scotland for residents. It's a very good service. You'll just need to pay for your prescription repeat when you take it to a pharmacy.'

Kirsty and Callum arrived half an hour later. He carried her duffel bag as they navigated through the corridors of the hospital. Kirsty looked at her closely. 'Are you feeling any better?'

'Yes and no. Lou told me that Don — you know, my godfather in Australia — died on Tuesday night. Early Wednesday morning there. So I've been a bit weepy.'

'Oh, Morgan, I'm so sorry. You were very close to him, weren't you? I thought you looked a little peaky.'

Suddenly, Kirsty stopped walking. 'Does this mean you'll have to go back to Australia for his funeral?'

'Yes, I've promised Lou I'll be there as soon as I can.'

'Shit. I mean, shit that you've had such a lot to deal with, and now you've got a funeral as well. It's not been easy for you, has it? You will be coming back though, won't you? I mean you have to. I want you to be my maid of honour at our wedding.'

'Yes, of course I will,' she said. 'Scotland is my home now. A million feral camels couldn't keep me away. Look, do you mind if I just nip into the florist on the way out and order a bouquet for the people who called emergency services?'

'Of course not. Do you know where it is?'

'Yep. I know my way around. I've been here before.'

She ordered a flower box and thank you note to be delivered to the Reids at the address the nurse had given her.

Callum drove back to Ali and Iain's. 'Nice car, Callum,' Morgan said.

'Thanks, aye, late model Honda Civic. I chose it because it's good and reliable, and I thought it would be suitably doctor-ish.'

'Callum has to drive back to Edinburgh tomorrow,' Kirsty said. 'We're going to have a full house at Ma's tonight.'

'I know your mum has kindly made up a room for me already,' Morgan said, 'but would you and Callum like to stay in my flat tonight so you can have a bit of privacy before Callum has to go back?'

Kirsty and Callum exchanged looks. 'Okay … that would be fabulous. It's a deal. Thanks.'

'No, thank *you* — for coming down all this way for me and getting the things I needed. You've got no idea how much I appreciate it. Just change the sheets, okay?'

Kirsty and Callum stayed until after dinner, then Morgan handed her flat keys to Kirsty. She had much to think about and organise but Ali was keen to chat. She sensed she was anxious about her mental state.

'I'm fine now, Ali, I really am. The doctor has given me

proper medication so I can get off those opioids. I had no idea what they really were. I've been warned to expect some withdrawal symptoms, but I can cope. The first thing I need to do is book a flight to arrive in Brisbane on time for Don's funeral. Can I get a flight from Prestwick?'

'Oh, no, they don't go that far,' Iain said, fiddling with his new hearing aid. 'Nowadays they mainly do military operations, and passenger flights only to Spain and Italy, I believe. You'll have to go to Glasgow for a long flight like that.'

'That's a shame. It would have been convenient.'

'Aye, and I'm not sure how long they'll be able to operate at all, more's the pity. Although it's handy for when the United States' President wants to play golf.'

Upstairs, in the tiny, cosy room Ali had prepared for her, she gazed out the window towards the sea at the last remnants of the orange sunset. She swallowed a prescription capsule and sleeping tablet Dr Liebenheim had given her. She rubbed her heavy, achy arms. Her skin prickled. She was going to have to find the strength to get through this.

She actually did have another box of the opioids in a drawer in her flat but she wouldn't touch them. She would throw them out. Even though they were expensive. She had told Ali she had no idea what they were. But she had ordered them. She knew exactly what they were. She could get through this.

Kirsty returned the next morning, looking teary after having said goodbye to Callum. She held the keys out to Morgan. 'Thanks for the flat. It's actually quite pleasant, isn't it? Quiet and cosy. We liked it.'

'Why don't you use it while I'm gone? You might as well. I've paid the rent until the end of October so it would be wasted otherwise. You can have your own space for studying. And also, the car, if you want it, once it's dried out and checked mechanically. Iain's friend Jimmy can give you the keys in about a week.'

'Oh, brilliant, yes, I'd like that. Thank you.' She counted up. 'About eleven weeks for the flat. I can look around for another one for you after that. Do you have any idea when you'll be coming back? No, I don't suppose you've thought about that yet. But you wouldn't be wanting to come back to a Scottish winter, would you?'

'I'll have to see how Lou is, but you're right. Good point. I'll probably stay there over Christmas and New Year. It will be our first without Don. And, yes, I will need a new flat. I don't want Ross as my landlord.'

'No, indeed not. If he comes sniffing around me with flooers I'll tell him to stick them up his fanny-magnet. Hey, I did see that wee brochure in your kitchen about past life regression. Is that what the hypnotherapist did with you?'

'Yes, that's him, same guy — Philip. He's lovely. If you're curious you can book an appointment with him. You can find out about your past lives and who your soulmates are.'

'Thanks, but it's probably not for me. I already know who my soulmate is, anyway.'

Morgan smiled at her. So did she.

Chapter 55

She booked a flight for Sunday night, two days later. She wouldn't be going back to the hospital for her check-up. It had been a condition of her release that she stay with Ali for two nights but she was returning to her own flat for the final night so she could pack.

'I'll take you round by the car yard where they're working on your car,' Iain said. 'Jimmy's making sure it's all serviced and good to go back on the road. It will cost a few hundred pounds but I will pay that for you as a present. I know you're skint. By the way, I told him the car's handbrake had been off and it slipped into the river accidentally.'

He was right. The cost of the car retrieval had cleaned out her finances; her 'incident' had not been covered by insurance.

'Aye, these are a good car, no mistake,' Jimmy said. 'It will run okay but it will never be quite the same. The seats will take a wee while longer to dry out. They might always be a bit pongy, mind, but hopefully not. I'd like to keep it here maybe another week. You were lucky the water wasn't salt. That would have been a different story.'

Iain paid Jimmy, then he dropped her off at her flat. 'Are you sure you'll be all right on your own the night, pet?'

'Absolutely, I've got loads to do, packing and stuff. Thank you, Iain, — very much. I can't thank you enough. I'll see you tomorrow.'

She looked around her little flat. She had become fond of it, despite it actually being owned by Ross.

She opened her laptop and saw an email from Bella. Dear Morgan and Kirsty, I cannot tell you how much Evan and I appreciate the gift of tickets to Jamaica. We are here now, and the flight and everything went without a hitch.

I have some news. My sister Hannah has insisted we live here. We can stay with her for a wee while until we can get our own house. I think it is the right place for us. It is lovely and warm, hot in fact, but there is always a cooling breeze. And it is so beautiful and tropical. Evan loves it. I am sending you a few photos of us both in front of my sister's house.

I have asked a solicitor to put our old house on the market. Well that is all for now. And again, thank you both so much. We would not have been able to do this without you. We will stay in touch. With love, your friends Bella and Evan.

Evan Paterson. Whom she now knew shared the same

soul as her once husband, Bryden, nearly two thousand years ago. Evan, who could do nothing for himself in this physical life, was actually innately connected to her in his spiritual life. How many other people was she connected to? Maybe thousands, maybe people she met every day.

She rubbed her prickly arms. She replied to Bella, congratulating them and wishing them all the best, then forwarded it to Kirsty. It was too early in Australia to Skype Lou so she sent her the flight details and arrival time in an email.

She flipped through all the photos she had transferred from her old phone. She paused over the photos of Ross. Should she call him and tell him she had to return to Australia? Would he even care? Probably she should let him know out of courtesy, as a tenant.

And she should give him her new number. He wouldn't be able to contact her otherwise. She had never given him the opportunity to explain. What if she had it all wrong and he was divorcing his wife? Had she been too impatient? If she could just hear his voice one more time.

She took a breath and touched his number.

A girlish female voice answered, 'Doctor McFarsund's phone,' then giggled. 'Helloo?' the voice sang.

She ended the call.

It pained her to remember the fun and intimate times they had shared, but they were, like he'd said, just a bit of fantasy. He had lied to her easily, without hesitation or remorse. A believable actor, playing a role. Something he would, undoubtedly, continue to do with other women. She shook her head. The ability of people to lie to each other so convincingly was alarming.

She had lied though. She had lied to Ali about the opioids. The box was in a drawer in the bathroom. She massaged her arms. Would one hurt? Just one to feel that magic silver warmth one more time. To help her sleep.

She went into the bathroom and opened the bottom drawer. Not there. She opened all the drawers and the mirrored cabinet doors above the basin. Had she left them in the kitchen? She searched every drawer and cupboard in the flat. Someone had removed them. You bitch, Kirsty. You *bitch*.

She took her prescription medication and prepared for bed, her last night in the flat, with a sadness especially acute since her reason for leaving was Don's funeral. He had been more of a father to her than her biological father ever had. The thought she would never see him again was unbearable. She now knew she would one day, but it wasn't the same as seeing him in *this* life.

Through her tears she smiled. Kirsty had remade the bed with fresh sheets, as instructed.

✦ ✦ ✦ ✦

She blinked her eyes open and lay awake for some minutes. This was the last time she would sleep in this comfy, warm bed. Warm only because of the electric blanket she had bought. She must remember to tell Kirsty to take it when the lease runs out.

There was something else though. Something different. It

dawned on her — no dreams. Since she'd had the regression session her sleep had been peaceful and dreamless. It couldn't be a coincidence; she had been plagued by disturbing dreams her whole life.

After breakfast she packed all her belongings. She had more clothes than when she'd arrived but she managed to squash everything into her one bulging suitcase. Except the coffee machine, which she left for Kirsty.

She went downstairs to call on Harish. It was the first time she had been in his flat. She could see it wasn't as modern or as well-appointed as her own honey trap.

He bowed and beamed a smile at her. 'So long since I was seeing you, Morgan, ma'am, have you been well?'

'Not bad, thank you Harish, but I have to leave for Australia tonight for a funeral. Kirsty will stay in the flat sometimes now until the lease ends in October.'

'I am sorry to hear about the funeral, and I'm sorry I will not be seeing you again at your flat, but you always know where you can find me.'

'And, guess what?' she said. 'I had a past-life regression session. I found out I lived a life in Roman times here in Scotland, and people I know lived with me then too. Things make a lot more sense to me now.'

Harish grinned. 'Ah, so you don't think it is all Ouija board stuff anymore? I am pleased to hear that. I think it is better to know than to not know.'

✦ ✦ ✦ ✦

Kirsty arrived in Iain's Land Cruiser to take her to the airport.

'Did you throw out my tablets from the bathroom?' Morgan asked.

'Eh? Tablets? God, no,' Kirsty said. 'I certainly wouldn't touch anybody else's stuff. Callum might have though, if he thought they were no good for you. Do you want me to phone and ask him?'

'No, never mind. Good riddance if he did.'

They called round to collect Ali and Iain. Once inside the house, Kirsty became excited. 'I've got a surprise for you. Wait here.' She returned with a dog-eared envelope. 'Look what I found.' She tipped out nine colour photographs.

'Oh, Kirsty! This is brilliant. Where did you find these?' They were photos of her as a small child, her mother, and Simon.

'I was looking for something else and I found this envelope flattened inside one of Pa's old books. Ma didn't even know it was there.'

Three of the photos showed Morgan, as a child, holding Simon as a tiny baby. She saw how carefully she held the baby, how she smiled and looked on him with love, and she knew that, even as an infant, she would never have hurt that little boy intentionally.

At the airport, Kirsty gave Morgan a book of Burns' bawdy poetry. 'Here's something to keep you amused on the plane. This is what I was looking for when I found those photos. I was going to keep it for your birthday but now you won't be here.'

Morgan leafed through the book:

His pintle was o' largest size,
Indeed it was a banger,
He socht a prize between my thies
Till it became a hanger.

She snorted. 'That's priceless, Kirsty. Thank you. What a scream. Scotland's national poet. I will really enjoy reading this.'

'Do you know where to go now, pet?' Iain said.

'Yes, I'll find the business class lounge and they'll call the flight from there.'

'Business class, that's a bit posh.'

'I know, isn't it? The flights were a gift from Don and Lou. I really wasn't expecting to have to use this return one so soon.'

'You take care of yourself now,' Ali said. 'Give our love to Lou, and just call us whenever you want us to collect you again. We've loved having you stay. The time has passed too quickly.'

Ali and Kirsty, with misty eyes, hugged her goodbye, and Iain's bear hug squashed the air out of her lungs.

At eight-fifty pm she snuggled into her wide seat. She gazed down to her last view of Scotland, bathed in the evening sunlight. She watched, mesmerised, as the River Clyde, myriad green fields, the distinctive coastline and just a glimpse of the Ayr River gradually receded from her vision.

Chapter 56

Brisbane, early morning. She queued to have her passport checked. The security officer compared her with her passport photo for some time, then handed it back.

'Welcome home,' he said.

She looked at him, surprised. She was about to shake her head, but instead she smiled, took the passport and said, 'Thank you.' The airport was full of Australians. No one took any notice of her or tried to listen furtively to her accent.

Outside, although she squinted in the bright daylight, the temperature was much the same as Scotland. She had forgotten how pleasant a Brisbane winter could be. A chauffeur-driven white limousine arrived. Another advantage of a business class ticket.

After confirming Lou's address with the driver, they travelled over the Gateway Bridge and away from the airport, past vegetation, not emerald green, more like fifty shades of olive. Brisbane city, illuminated with the morning sun, sprawled towards the mountain range in the west. Everything was familiar but she was seeing the place as a visitor, as if for the first time.

They arrived at Lou's modest brick bungalow, the house she had grown up in. She took her wallet from her handbag but then remembered she didn't have to tip the driver; it was not expected. She tipped him anyway.

Lou was waiting for her at the door, and they fell into each other's arms. 'Darling, you're all skin and bone,' she said. 'I'll put the kettle on. You'll be tired and hungry from the long trip.'

Tired she was, but hungry she certainly wasn't. The food on the plane had been sensational and plentiful. She wheeled her suitcase to her old room which was always ready for her. Over tea, she gave Lou the gifts she had bought at the airport: shortbread, whisky fruit cake and a woollen tartan throw rug with red and green colours.

'It's called Erskine modern tartan,' she said. 'It's to remember Don. Not that we could possibly forget him.'

'It's beautiful. Just what I need on these chilly mornings.'

Lou unwrapped the rug and draped it over her knees. She looked so sad. 'Don and I spent forty wonderful years together,' she said. 'I can't come to terms with him not being here. I can't believe it has all come to an end. It's just so final.'

Morgan put her arm around her. She regretted she hadn't been there at the end for Don, and that she hadn't had the chance to say goodbye. But she strongly felt his presence in the room.

'I feel he's here all the time,' Lou said. 'That's why I'm having trouble believing he's gone.'

'Yes, I feel he's here with us now, looking out for you. I know he is. He'll be wanting us to remember all the happy times.'

And how could she come to terms with having been told by Don to go back to her body at the exact same time he himself died. She would never, ever tell Lou that.

She yawned. 'Gee, I really am tired. I might go and lie down for a bit. Is there anything we need to do to get ready for Don's funeral?'

'The funeral company has been wonderful,' Lou said. 'They've taken care of everything, even organised the wake at the reception area in the crematorium gardens. There isn't anything we need to do unless you want to say a few words at the service. I really don't think I'll be able to.'

'I'll put something together to say.' She stood up.

Lou noticed her pendant. 'That's pretty, dear. Where did you get that?'

'It was Isla's. It's a kee … cairngorm. My uncle Mal gave all her jewellery to my father's sister — my aunt Minnie, and she passed it on to me. I'll show you the rest of it later. I have dozens of photos to show you too. Another day.'

She went into her room to lie down, but first she checked her emails. She saw one from Kirsty.

Gidday mate. I hope you had a good flight. I just had to tell you the news. Callum heard that Ross's court case was decided on Friday and he has been struck off the medical register because of impropriety. That means he can no longer practise as a doctor.

He had affairs with his patients — loads of them apparently. It seems he was using his position as a tit doctor to meet girls. Yuk. Serves him right for being a root rat, I mean fair suck of the sav, right?

Iain has been told by his doctor to go easy on the whisky, and Ma is enforcing it. She's got him on Ribena, ha ha! She said she wasn't prepared to lose another husband.

I hope you get through the funeral okay, let me know how you're getting on. Love always, Kirsty xx.

Ross. What a piece of work. She thought back to the words Philip had said — her tendency to choose partners who betray her was a pattern. But had she chosen him, or had he chosen her? It sounded like he chose lots of women; no point in feeling special.

Still, she had loved him. It would be a while before she stopped having feelings for him. She would take her own advice. She would remember the happy times, and one day she would forget him completely.

The day of Don's funeral arrived. She'd had nothing suitably funereal to wear so she borrowed Lou's car to shop for a skirt and jacket, dark blue to go with her antique jewellery and her tartan scarf. This she proudly wore, and no one had any idea what clan tartan it was.

He had been highly respected. People spilled out of the crematorium chapel doors. She recognised some neighbours and his past students, and some of Lou's family, but many others were unknown to her.

Reading out a short poem at the lectern was one of the hardest things she'd ever done, especially since Don was standing in the back of the chapel smiling and waving at her. Instinctively she turned to look at the coffin. It was sealed, covered in a white linen cloth and dressed in an elaborate flower display. No one else had noticed anything. The funeral company staff hadn't moved or changed their professionally compassionate expressions.

It would be inappropriate to wave back so she smiled and nodded at him, hoping the gesture didn't look out of place for the poem she was reading.

The moving service concluded with his favourite music. She managed to keep her tears in check until everybody filed out of the chapel to the tune of *Going Home* played by a lone piper: no matter where in the world you die, you will return to Scotland, your birth country. Lou had chosen the song for him specially.

Once outside the chapel, Don disappeared, but with a shock, Morgan saw Anton standing with a tall blonde woman. Leeann. Her heart sank. When the woman turned around, she saw it wasn't Leeann but someone unfamiliar.

Leeann was there though. She came over and offered her condolences. She introduced her male friend who had thinning hair and wore glasses. Greek god he was not.

'This is Gavin,' Leeann said. 'He's a professor at my Uni, and we'll be moving in together shortly.'

'How nice of you to come,' she said, taking his hand. She noticed a small, subtle trident embroidered on his shirt — the Maserati logo. She grinned at Leeann. 'And it's so lovely to see you, Leeann. For one horrible moment I thought you were with Anton. I don't know why I thought that was horrible, I just did.'

'Oh, God no. Not after what he did to you. He's not really my type, anyway, not mature enough. You look fabulous, by the way. I love your hair, beautiful copper colour. You should wear it that way all the time.'

She hugged her friend. She was strangely grateful Leeann hadn't taken the easy advantage to slide into her place. Plus she knew how Anton treated women.

'What do you think of Anton's lady friend?' Leeann asked.

Anton was ignoring his companion to flirt with two other girls. Some things never change. No sign of Shannon. That, at least, was a blessing. She studied Anton's new girlfriend. Tall and blonde, fit, and immaculately dressed. Perfect. In fact, too perfect.

Morgan looked at Leeann and raised her eyebrows. Leeann grinned and said, 'She has a deep voice.'

They moved away when Anton caught sight of Morgan and came over to kiss her on the cheek. 'You look great,' he said. 'You've lost weight. You look really Scottish; did you know that? Your skin is super pale.' He noticed her pendant and the jet bracelet. 'Nice bling. Love the tartan scarf. If you're not doing anything after this why don't you come around to the house and we'll all have a drink or two and catch up.'

She realised anew how attractive he was. No wonder girls fell for him. And boys for that matter. He had flair, charisma, and a flawless olive complexion. She couldn't believe she had failed to recognise his sexuality before; it was obvious to her now. Sorry, mate, not in this lifetime.

'Thanks but I've got things to do. I have to look after Lou.'

'Sure. By the way, Mum was furious with you for letting her moth-eaten parrot out of its cage. She was going to get another one as a replacement but I talked her out of it. They're going to be travelling a lot, now they've caught the cruising bug. Anyway, I thought it would be cruel to keep a bird like that in a cage.'

She smiled at him. He wasn't all bad. He was what he was, and she couldn't hate him for that. Her leaving had been a liberation for him too.

'Thank you for coming to Don's funeral,' she said.

'Of course I'd come. He was your father.'

'So what have you been up to?' she asked.

'Well, something pretty exciting, actually. Douglas and I are planning on starting a new business venture — a big indoor go-kart racing track. And he's got this great idea for a sideline business. It'll make a ton of money.'

'Do you mean Douglas McTwat?'

'Yeah, but that's not his real name.'

'No. Really? Let me guess — you're planning to grow dope on the side. Literally.'

Anton narrowed his eyes at her. 'How would you know that?'

'I told you I was psychic.' The sooner she and Anton got divorced, the better.

She stood alone in the doorway of the chapel for a moment, looking at the curtains behind which Don's coffin had silently disappeared. Over at a table covered by a white linen tablecloth she wrote in the guest book, 'You were with me. You were always with me and always will be. We will meet again. Thank you for everything.'

She moved away from the crowd hovering around the sandwiches to be by herself. She sat on a timber bench under a gum tree, overlooking a stream. Behind her a slight breeze stirred fresh, eucalyptus scented air. She breathed deeply. This could be nowhere else but Australia.

A magpie landed close to her feet and tilted its head to one side, watching her. Then she saw it had yellow eyes. Not a magpie, but a currawong. Magnificent. It stared at her, then soared up to perch on a branch of the gum tree. She closed her eyes and lifted her face to feel the warmth of the afternoon sun. A shadow passed in front of her.

'Hi there, I'm Tom. I'm so sorry about Don. He was an extraordinary man.'

She looked up, shading her eyes from the sun. 'Hi, Tom is it?'

'Yes, Tomas MacLeod. Tom. I'm Lou's cousin. Actually some kind of second cousin, I think. I flew over this morning from New Zealand. South Island. We have a sheep farm there.'

He was tall, and with the sun behind him his hair appeared to have a reddish aura. He held out his hand. She suddenly realised something — how Scottish that accent sounds. He shifted slightly, shielding her vision from the glare. Smiling, she took his warm hand and a frisson tingled through her body. She could see his eyes now. They were a striking blue, the colour of the sea on a sunny day.

About the Author

Alaine M Neilson is passionate about history, art, theatre, the sea, and our place in the Universe. She has a background in education and design, and degrees in Literature, Visual Communications and Writing. *Are You Sure You Want to Know?* is her debut novel.

Born in Scotland, where she spent her early years, Alaine grew up in Australia and now lives on a bush property in South East Queensland with her husband and a family of wallabies.